REA

ACPL ITEM

Fiction
Steinke
The fires

DISCARDED

3 1833 0369

P9-EEC-841

6-7-99

ALLEN COUNTY PUBLIC LIBRARY
FORT WAYNE, INDIANA 46802

You may return this book to any agency or branch
of the Allen County Public Library

DEMCO

THE
FIRES

THE

▲ ▲ ▲ ▲ ▲

FIRES

RENÉ
STEINKE

WILLIAM MORROW AND COMPANY, INC.

NEW YORK

Allen County Public Library
900 Webster Street
PO Box 2270
Fort Wayne, IN 46801-2270

This is a work of fiction. Names, characters, places, and incidents either are the product of the author's imagination or are used fictitiously. Any resemblance to actual events, locales, organizations, or persons, living or dead, is entirely coincidental and beyond the intent of either the author or the publisher.

*The epigraph on page ix from Theodore Roethke's "The Shape of the Fire" copyright ©
1947 is reprinted by permission of the Bantam Doubleday Dell Publishing Group, Inc.*

Copyright © 1999 by René Steinke

All rights reserved. No part of this book may be reproduced or utilized in any form or by any means, electronic or mechanical, including photocopying, recording, or by any information storage or retrieval system, without permission in writing from the Publisher. Inquiries should be addressed to Permissions Department, William Morrow and Company, Inc., 1350 Avenue of the Americas, New York, N.Y. 10019.

It is the policy of William Morrow and Company, Inc., and its imprints and affiliates, recognizing the importance of preserving what has been written, to print the books we publish on acid-free paper, and we exert our best efforts to that end.

Library of Congress Cataloging-in-Publication Data

Steinke, René
    The fires / René Steinke. — 1st ed.
      p. cm.
    ISBN 0-688-16150-2
    I. Title.
    PS3569.T37926F5   1999   98-36203
    813'.54—dc21   CIP

Printed in the United States of America

First Edition

1 2 3 4 5 6 7 8 9 10

BOOK DESIGN BY ANN GOLD

www.williammorrow.com

FOR CRAIG MARKS

ACKNOWLEDGMENTS

I would like to thank my editor, Betty Kelly, and my agent, Simon Green.

For their help and encouragement at various stages of the writing of this book, I'd also like to thank Peter and Kelly Steinke, Ellen Hunnicutt, Thomas Bontly, Joanne Tangorra, Richard Maxwell, Stephanie Paulsell, Rita Signorelli-Pappas, Stacy Malin, Tina Epstein, Darcey Steinke, Kim France, Charles Aaron, Ann Powers, Maria Antifonario, and Dan Green.

These flowers are all fangs. Comfort me, fury.
—Theodore Roethke

THE
FIRES

I

Smoke has as many different scents as skin. Part of the pleasure is not knowing what it will be—sulfurous or closer to incense or airier and sweet as I imagine the smell of clouds. Nothing relieves me so much as burning something old, watching it flicker and disappear into air. Dresses dance as they go, lifted as if by some music. A photograph flaps like a wing or a hand waving. Perfumes hiss, then shatter, papers curl, plaster jewels curdle. Once I tried to burn an old toy—a mechanical duck. When I'd found it at the bottom of a drawer, it reminded me of the groggy sunrise Easter service and the hunt for eggs in the graveyard. After I set the match to its tail, it started walking pitifully on its metal legs, and it knocked around the room singeing the walls and linoleum until it burned down to its metal frame and folded with a crackle and small battery explosion. It is less dangerous to burn things than to save them.

▲   ▲   ▲

I'd poured myself six thimble shots of bourbon and walked the edges of the bedroom touching the walls and windowsills, hoping to work the starry twitches from my legs so they'd lie still. If I let go, I'd fall off the night that was galloping fast. Every time I got into bed, I heard an intruder finagling the catch on the window or slowly climbing the basement stairs. My heart raced. My eyelids fluttered. I jolted up, walked to the kitchen, ears stinging at the silence, and poured another shot.

The train had gone by three times, rattling into the air. Porter was the kind of Indiana town where the whistle sounded cheerful, not plaintive, but then the wheels chewed ravenously on the tracks.

I listened for the man until he turned phantom again—the trees, the wind. *Ridiculous to be twenty-two, a year past adulthood, and still afraid of stray noises.* I went into the kitchen and sat down at the table, turned on the clock radio, and fiddled with the ridged knob until I heard the song about lightning and the crashing sea of love, just at the point when the guitar strummed in waves. My bare feet pressed on the cool, grainy floor; my nightgown bunched up around my knees.

I traced a panicky finger over the constellation of glitter in the Formica—two nights of not sleeping, with nothing to do for long, bare hours except worry over the crucial thing it seemed I needed to remember and couldn't: that blankness revolved in my head like a siren.

Twirling the salt shaker in my fingertips, I groggily felt that if I acted asleep, sleep might come. Sprinkling a little salt in my palm, I dabbed a few grains into the corners of my eyes before I closed them and put my head down on the table. But when I tried to breathe slowly and think of nothing, I began to crave potato pancakes and apples.

Over the stove hung the cast-iron skillet my father had used to make them, crisp and salty in a way my mother and I had never mastered. After he died, the drinking started—secretly at first, from sticky bottles next to the flour in the pantry cabinet, and for the same reason I often couldn't sleep now: an old sensation that I was falling, or about to fall, from some roof or ledge or stairs.

Bourbon gave me the courage to loosen my grip. It wasn't that I wouldn't fall anymore, but the fall would be pleasant, and it wouldn't matter so much when I did.

I was about to drift off when I heard a scratch, a mouse or something, in the pantry. I got up to open the door and turn on the light. The colored boxes and gleaming cans glared back at me. I knew I was hanging on too tightly, but this time couldn't make myself let go.

The landlord had asked me to leave my apartment on Birch Street, and I was staying at my mother's until I could move into one of the rooms at the Linden Hotel, where I worked. There the insomniacs made anxious trips to the ice machine after midnight, and by morning they were already showered and dressed as if there were some purpose to their being awake so early. When they came down to the lobby to check out, their faces swollen and pale, a lostness about them, I'd keep my voice quiet and slow as I gave them directions or simply thanked them and said good-bye. I knew they'd sleepwalk through the day, just as I often did, wincing at light and hoping not to stumble, all along hearing that murmur: *If you couldn't sleep last night, you might not get to sleep later, or ever.*

I went back to the metal chair and sat staring out the window at the grass, my stomach hollow from all the bourbon. I got up and opened the refrigerator, peered into the cold light. In the lingering smell of leftover cherry pie lay a quart of milk, a hunk of molded bread, a dozen eggs. I grabbed the egg carton and shut the door.

I was going to scramble them, but immediately lost my appetite and just lay them on the table in front of me. I thought of all the people I knew sleeping then, their heads nestled in dreams like those eggs in their cups. I visited each bed, examined the sleeping face, the mouth pressed closed or slightly open, the deep slow breaths or snores, the sprawl or curl of limbs. I wanted to know how they let go so easily, how they managed to spiral so bravely into sleep, unafraid of all they had forgotten.

The dark sky was bluing. Taking the first egg from its bed, I palmed it in my hand, shook it just slightly, and felt the weight of the yolk wiggling in its sack. In the gentle press of my fingers, the shell felt brittle and fragile. I tossed it at the window, and it smacked against the blue-black surface, a toy sun. I threw another one at the glass. It cracked and splashed yellow, then dripped sleepily.

▲   ▲   ▲

It happened later that same August. I was cold at the funeral, and I kept touching the book of matches in my skirt pocket, the plain black cover and the twenty red heads, lined up and full-cheeked like a choir. Flicking my thumbnail at the thin cardboard, I looked up over the casket at the empty cross of pale wood.

When my grandmother had called that Monday night, sobbing so I barely understood her murmur over the phone that my grandfather had died in his sleep, I pretended she was telling the truth. But when my mother and I got there, what really happened was clear from the empty glass vial, the tipped-over china cup on the nightstand, the pinch of white powder blurring the delicate flowers on the saucer's rim. His small head was turned to the black window, his mouth blue and slack, his eyes serene but plastic, the folds in his cheeks frowning. He had been formal and guarded in a way that made him inscrutable, but now his face lacked wariness, his eyes and mouth vulnerable in a way I hadn't seen before.

His left arm was flung across the pillow, a scrap of envelope crumpled in his fist. I was afraid to touch his skin, but coaxed the paper out from the tension in his fingers and saw that he'd scrawled a few lines in pencil, then tried to erase them. Kneeling down to hold the paper in the lamplight, I stared through that fog of smudged marks, but could only make out three words where the pencil had indented the paper: "NOT YOUR" and near the ripped corner, "LOVE."

I looked up on the nightstand and watched the round clock's hands tick past frilled numbers. I counted. Behind me, I heard something small fall on the bureau and my mother softly weeping. I wanted to console her, to weep myself, but instead counted the seconds, my heart that clock, impatient and achingly brass. When I turned around to my mother and grandmother, I felt the ticking dryness in my eyes, a metallic bitterness in my throat.

I quickly turned back to him. Even not blinking from my stare, the tears wouldn't come. I was a clock trapped behind a flat, oval face, ticking and ticking—what was wrong with me?

My mother, my grandmother Marietta, and I rode in the hearse at the front of the procession, a dozen cars with twittering yellow flags that said FUNERAL. My limbs were shaky, as if my leg might kick the seat, my arm fling out at the driver's head, but I held still, afraid of what might happen if I moved. "It was a good service, wasn't it?" my mother said, her voice phlegmy. I'd learned to read her by the angle of her face, her gestures, and the changing shape of her eyes, rather than by what she said. When I watched her this way, she held me at a distance, but she still held me.

She kept smoothing the dress in her lap as if this motion soothed her, her thin mouth strained into a smile. She was worried I might see how much his death terrified her.

My grandmother's shoulders curled in around her body. As usual, she looked more vivid than my mother, wearing her best dress, nude stockings, and precise red lips so that no one could say she'd let herself go—but there was something mournful in the way she'd made herself up so brightly.

We passed the old community theater, an elaborate, stone building with a lion at the greened copper crest near the roof, which, as a girl, I'd used to ask questions: *How many puppies will the neighbor's dog have? When will my mother be happy? What did you see on the street last night?* "Are you okay, Ella?" Marietta asked me. A handkerchief edged with embroidered roses was gathered in the manicured, freckled hand she placed on my knee.

"Sure," I said, rubbing my eyes, knowing how afraid she and my mother were that I'd start to cry. My forced-back tears made a sparkly, prismed shield.

My mother's hands were clenched. The fingernails bitten down to the quick and the torn red cuticles resembled my grandfather's hands, which were huge, out of proportion, even, to his six-foot frame. But my mother's hands were small—rough white knuckles and fragile fingers with swollen joints—the hands of a woman who worried too much. I knew she just wanted to get this over with, to go back to our routines. That was how she managed, structuring each day like a house she couldn't leave.

"It's warm in here," I said, folding my palms together in my lap. There was a marbled amulet of skin around my left wrist, and though I'd grown used to hiding it, I didn't now. Its ugliness even pleased me. I stared at the rivulets of pink and white, the strange curvy lunge the scar took toward my thumb.

The driver stopped short at a red light, and the coffin rattled in its straps. It was easier to fathom his death now that they'd closed the coffin and put away the portrait of him in middle age that had been propped on the lid. It had been the undertaker's idea to do that, "an old Midwestern tradition," he'd said, but it hadn't been comforting to see his young face battle with the dead one. I'd noticed my mother looked only at the coffin, but had kept her eyes on the collar of his shirt, the pointed tips and the knot of the tie.

We drove past the Paradise Lounge, its neon palm tree sign flashing pink and green. It was a place where I could dodge my reflection in the bottles against the bar's mirror, or disappear in the shadowy tables pushed up against the wall, but people who knew me wouldn't have believed I ever went there.

"I didn't see Mrs. Schone, did you?" My mother didn't really care whether or not this friend of my grandmother's had come— she was only afraid of what else one of us might say.

"In the back," I said.

She nodded, her face gray as cement. I wanted to take her hand, but she'd clenched them tightly in her lap on the opposite side and leaned away from me, against the door.

We drove through the graveyard entrance past a white set of praying hands, taller than a man. I thought about pulling the flask of schnapps from my pocket and drinking from it—a small motion, really, just the lift of the fingers, a firm twist—but even a motion this small seemed impossible.

We wound along the narrow gravel road, past stone angels and small, bent trees, and a little farther on we stopped in front of the fenced family plot. We got out of the hearse, and slowly walked to the grave site.

Car doors slammed. A man said, "You never know, do you? In his sleep? Was it a stroke?"

"Something like that."

My blouse pinched under the arms, and from the strain of holding tears back, my nose was running. There was a rustle of dress clothes behind me as people whispered about how kind my grandfather had been, how he'd lived a full life, how much he'd loved his roses, how they'd seen him, healthy, only the day before he died. I knew then that his death didn't belong to him, that our lie had covered his final escape. We didn't even discuss it, we'd learned so well to keep the surface of life unwrinkled and clean, like a well-made bed.

"Dear friends, we are gathered here to remember a man who fought the good fight." Pastor Beck was standing in front of us, next to the perfect rectangular grave, his white robe blowing dramatically in the breeze. I stood behind Marietta and my mother and looked down at their narrow ankles, their heels sunk into the soil. Pastor Beck bent to gather some dirt, and when he stood up again, dropped it from his fingers over the grave. "Ashes to ashes, dust to dust." They'd told themselves he hadn't meant to vanish, but someday we would have to admit he meant to leave us. My mother's shoulders began to shake, her fingers grasping at air.

I couldn't listen to most of the homily, but stood separate from it all, as if I were looking on through a screen door—just a thin wire mesh, but I didn't have anything sharp enough to break through it.

Marietta leaned forward, her eyes watery. My mother glowered at one of the poles holding up the tarp above us, as Pastor Beck went on, "For all of us, but especially for Marietta, for Catherine, Hanna, Ella." Cars shushed from the highway. No one had seen Hanna, my mother's older sister, for several years, and her name had been set apart from all the others for so long it had a holy sound that hurt my chest.

As the men lowered the coffin on ropes into the ground and one by one we tossed carnations into the grave, I thought, *She doesn't even know this is happening.* I wiped the sweat from my forehead and stared at a tin vase of silk flowers that had tipped over in the grass.

Afterward we went to the graveyard pavilion for coffee and a potluck supper. The smell of tomato sauce and cream of mushroom soup was so thick in the air, something swiveled in my stomach. My best friend Jo was in the corner talking to her fiancé, but no matter how much I wanted to go over to her and say *Thank God you're here. I can't stand it. Let's go,* the space between us seemed too loud and crowded to cross. I leaned toward my mother, whispered in her ear that I didn't feel well, and took a step back. She turned to me, stumbling over her shoe. I knew how badly she wanted to keep her composure for these people, but her grief made her clumsy.

Marietta was distracted, accepting compliments from a group of elderly women on her new black dress. "I didn't have one," she said in a high, prim voice. "I like colors." *She doesn't want anyone to blame her,* I thought.

I slipped out the screen door, hoping not to see anyone. It was dusk by then, and the graveyard looked magnetic and still as I wandered the spindled paths, fingering the torn envelope in my pocket, not exactly telling myself where I was going, but I knew. My mother would worry when she noticed I'd left the pavilion, and though it pained me to think of her searching the room, asking people if they'd seen me, I was used to her worry, and there usually wasn't any way to avoid it.

I turned onto the highway and walked on the gravel shoulder. Seven years before, at my father's funeral, I'd also watched myself walk among people and my mouth form words, all the while floating above like a torn-up cloud. They hadn't been able to find an organist to replace him, and the service had been silent. So many tepid voices and gingerly handshakes—as if death made people move in slow motion, disturbingly out of tempo in a way that would have annoyed him.

I walked past the popcorn warehouse and a field of munching cows. By this time the sun had blurred behind the trees, and my head was spinning. I'd gone as far as the paint-tester site and in my pocket felt the flask, the envelope, and the fold of the matchbook.

It was a field of shingles, propped up on legs, as if paint samples grew and could be harvested. The company must have figured if a housepaint lasted two winters in Indiana, then it would be durable enough to last two years anywhere in the country. In the dusk, the gray and green boards looked muted, the whites and yellows more intense.

Drinking from the flask, I walked down a row of white shingles, each a slight variation with a different name: *Granite, Shell, Bone*. I stopped in front of one near the end. Where the paint had worn away, the plank showed strands of dull gray wood. Not durable enough. I stood there and looked out at the dozens of shingles on wooden legs like chairbacks in an empty theater, whites, yellows, greens, browns. I straightened up, took a deep breath, and in a steady, clear voice, said, "He poisoned himself."

Pulling the flask from my pocket, I unscrewed the cap and took a mouthful of schnapps. A sharp sensation cut along my teeth. I didn't particularly like it, but that was part of its appeal, along with the numbness I first felt along the bridge of my nose.

I was getting pleasantly drunk and didn't look at my hand pull the matchbook from my pocket, feel along the cover to pluck one out, hold the two sides together as I pulled the head against the sandpaper strip until it snapped and flared. At the funeral I'd felt all those eyes expecting me to come apart, the truth about what happened pulled from my skin like straw out of a stuffed animal. But I'd kept our secret crinkled next to the flask in my skirt pocket.

With the heat pulsing in my fingertips, I carefully set the match on the flat rotten edge of the gray-white shingle and stood close enough to protect the little paw burning at my waist. It was thin at first. I was afraid it would go out. I cupped my hands around it, and my palms lit up, pale and wrinkled, as the flame swelled toward them. When I pulled away, it leaped along the top of the board.

The yellow flames muscled and flinched. The wood blackened. I wished I could have asked him what it felt like to drink arsenic, if it was tasteless or somehow sweet, if it numbed you slowly like alcohol, finger by finger, or if it suddenly stopped your heart like a bullet. I felt a press behind my eyes then, not because I couldn't ask but because—despite the habitual affection between us—if he'd lived, I wouldn't have had the courage. I could count on one hand the things he and I could talk about.

When the first Buddhist set himself on fire in Cambodia, my grandfather, rustling his newspaper, had said, "It's a sad thing, isn't it, how they believe burning themselves alive is a good religion." I tossed the envelope with his scrawled marks into the flame, watched it crumple and wither in the blue center. I didn't think we'd ever know what he'd meant to write, and the thought of how much we'd misunderstood him, how little he'd let us see, put a soreness in my throat I couldn't swallow.

The fire hurried higher in the air. He'd usually kept his hands fisted, whether leaning back in a chair or walking into the next room, and he'd often stood at the kitchen sink, ferociously scrubbing them ten or twenty times a day, sometimes until they bled. One hand viciously grabbed the other, slid away, and the other, released, did the same, the water coming out so hard from the faucet that it splattered up in the sink and we all had to raise our voices to cover up the clamor.

The yellow light circled around me in the gathering darkness. The flames jabbed at the air and chewed through the board, fell off the legs and rolled in the dirt. I stepped back, crossed my arms on my chest, and rubbed the lumps of my shoulder bones, my face prickling in the heat.

It was usually the only relief, this hot, upside-down waterfall and its salty light. It ebbed first beneath my eyelids and then under my tongue, soaked through my muscles and veins and gently wore at them until I lost strength in my legs and could barely stand.

Under my blouse, I touched the silky part of my stomach, then moved my hand under my damp breast to the braided scar, a core of old pain to hang on to. The wind quickened and shrieked. The fire bent over and flicked sparks into the dry weeds.

▲ ▲ ▲

When I walked back to town, I went to Jo's apartment, thinking I would tell her, but when I got there, and we were sitting among her girlhood pink-and-gold bedroom set, the canopy bed shifting above us, I couldn't. She had been exercising, and a calm, pious female voice on the tape recorder kept giving instructions and counting. Jo tried to comfort me, but I couldn't hear her. It kept pricking at my skull: *He killed himself. He killed himself.*

I left Jo's and went back to the hotel and changed. The dress was red and fit so tightly you could see the tilt of my hipbones in the sheen of the silk. Glass beads cuffed the sleeves and ringed the hem in black circles, and a rhinestone hung on the catch to the zipper in back. I'd found it that summer at a yard sale, crumpled under a set of chipped dishes.

At eleven that night I went to the Paradise Lounge to get drunk so that maybe I could sleep. It was so late I hadn't planned on meeting anyone, but this Billy sat down on the stool next to me. He was from Appleton, Wisconsin, and said he worked for an insurance company, though with his wide purple mouth and honey-colored skin, he looked awkward and too young in a suit. When he ordered his drink, he turned to me and asked if I knew any good places to eat. He stared at my breasts and then at my eyes. He took out a little notebook and wrote down what I said, pushing out his puffy bottom lip and squinting at his pen. Somehow, the diner on Willow Street led to our talking about basketball. He told me about his high-school team and then about his sister, who was fat and a good card player—but pensively, as if he were eighty years old and these things were already lost to him. In his hunched shoulders, I recognized a choked sadness that reminded me of my grandfather.

To change the subject I said I wanted to go to Paris and asked if he knew any French. "La Porte—that's a French name, isn't it?" He pushed his glass to the edge of the bar. Even as it shunned strangers, Indiana hoarded exotic names—La Porte, Valparaiso, Vincennes—as if it could contain all the world and obliterate the need to travel.

"Doorway to the Midwest," said the bartender, pouring.

"No. You? Polly whatever?" He turned back with a new drink and a little bounce. His lips were shiny with booze, and I could tell he was nervous. It made it easier.

"A little," I said, laughing. I glanced down at his fingers wrapped around the glass and saw his thumb cock back.

"Say something." Gulping his drink, he leaned toward me. He had nice hazel eyes.

"*Est-ce que la douche est chaude?*" I said.

He stirred the ice in his glass with his finger. "Say something else."

"I could say anything, and you wouldn't know the difference."

"I know." He nodded. "Say anything. It sounds nice."

"*Voulez-vous aller à la plage?*" I said. "*Comment allez-vous?*" I could only remember the questions from the phrase book. Tearing his napkin contemplatively into little squares, he said, with the false sincerity of a drunk, "I have a feeling you'll go there sometime." He leaned in close to me and spoke softly, "A pretty girl like you probably has a boyfriend, right?" Sometimes I thought it was funny how little they knew about what they thought they saw. They noticed long brown hair and a heart-shaped face, or wide-set eyes and breasts and hips. Even as they were appraising me, they couldn't see the horsehead scar or the one like a prickly boat, or the red cup with teeth hidden inside that dress.

"Not at the moment," I said, smiling. I had only these ones I met at the Paradise, but my mother never asked about boyfriends, partly, I thought, because she considered dating frivolous, and partly because she didn't want me to get my hopes up for nothing.

A few stools down, a lit match hung in the dimness between some man's fingertips—this radiant, trembling tear. The fragment of what I suddenly wanted: to walk over and take it from him, set it to the bar's old wood, and watch it go.

Billy glanced over his shoulder. "What's wrong?"

Cupping his hand, the man lowered the tip of his cigarette, sucked, and then, as if it were filthy, swabbed the match at the air. "Nothing."

I rubbed the taut seam at my hip. I had a system. When I'd counted seven bourbons he'd drunk and heard him slur the word *happier,* and when, after an effort to touch my arm he stumbled from the barstool, I asked him if he wanted to go somewhere.

We went to his room in the Dunes Hills motel off the highway, and he rushed in before me as if there was something he didn't want me to see. The air didn't smell anonymous as it did at the Linden Hotel, but particular, like someone's old hat. There was a television with tin foil wadded around the ends of the antenna, a thick beige curtain for a bathroom door.

After I heard him flush, I sat on the lumpy bed, watching the light spill out of the lamp. I felt all over its grimy base, but couldn't find the switch, my hand stiffened from nervousness.

He slid back the curtain and stood smiling lopsidedly. He'd

unknotted his tie and unbuttoned the top of his shirt so you could see the T-shirt beneath it. "I like that dress," he said, and I felt my breath catch.

It was the dream of the dresses that lured them. I'd strip in the dark and wait to see if they'd notice the scars—the marbled ruddy skin next to my navel or the pink chains swirled over my shoulders—if they'd pull back, murmuring penitently about a girlfriend or a wife, or if they'd draw in closer, curious.

He sat down next to me, rubbed his finger over a gather of fabric at my elbow. He circled my wrist with his fingers. "You're so small. How old are you?"

"Twenty-two." I shrugged, wondering if he'd seen them. "Not corn-fed. Were you?"

"Me? I hate corn." He put his hand on my shoulder and eased me back, the mattress yielding like warm mud. Stretching out his body next to me, he leaned up on his elbow, pulling one eye aslant. He was tall, his shoulders wide.

He put his hands on my face, murmured "All right," and kissed me. My mouth and eyes were hot. "I don't usually do this," he said, pulling back. "But you're so sweet." He ran his hand over the curve of my waist, the sink of my belly. One stocking slipped low on my thigh.

I glanced at the shoehorn scooping up air on the nightstand, the black toiletries bag half unzipped, a lonely black comb in the opening. His hand wriggled under my bra strap to my breast, and I felt his breath, noxious with bourbon, on my cheek. His other hand pushed at the stocking at the top of my leg, and our teeth clacked together as he groped at the nape of my neck, grabbed the rhinestone, and slowly dragged down the zipper. In my knees and fingertips a current sputtered, almost an itch. He couldn't have known how I was turning to porcelain, perfect and hard, just as his finger poked roughly inside of me.

When I opened my eyes and pulled away, black stubble crept across his upper lip. His eyes were closed, his mouth slightly open. "What's wrong?"

I reached back for my zipper. "Nothing." Staring into the paneling on the wall, I guiltily tried to decide how I'd come to this spot again on the very night of my grandfather's funeral, and the film of dust I saw made me ashamed. "Stupid," I murmured. When Billy sat up straight and moved closer, his elbow bumped the lampshade, and the light spit over us. He ran his finger up and down my spine.

I stood up, pulled my dress down from where it had gathered high on my thighs. Walking backward slowly, I said, "I've got to go." I unlatched the screen door, leaned my shoulder into it. When it screeched shut and I looked back, he was standing behind it, a grimy shadow. Already I'd forgotten his face. "You don't really want to leave," he pleaded.

I walked onto the shoulder of the highway, the dark sky jeering down. I'd fooled him but hadn't been able to fool myself—sometimes I could slip out of my body as if it had never belonged to me in the first place and fly through the top of my head, lose the scars to air.

As soon as I got inside my room at the Linden, I took off the dress and, in my stockings and bra, lit up the hot plate, the electric burner singing. The orange heat spiraled around and fitfully pulsed. I held up the shoulders of the dress so it mimicked the shape of a woman, let the hem dangle above the coiled light.

II

I spent the next few days with Jo, trying to distract myself from my grandfather's death and how we'd had to lie. Jo was the only person I knew who could tell when I was lying. She'd point the sharp planes of her face at me, her chin or cheekbones, and say, with her pale gray eyes and white skin so translucent a blue vein thorned up from one brow, "That's not it." But she couldn't see this one.

We went to the movies, played records in her room, walked around the college campus. One day we went to Herstein's department store, where we could spend hours in the bluish light and air-conditioning, wandering among the racks, altering the clothes in our minds so they'd better imitate ones we'd seen in fashion magazines.

At the first glass counter, I tried on a pair of white leather gloves with buttons at the wrists, and Jo slipped on a pair of black satin ones that reached to her elbows. "You're supposed to wear these for evening?" she said, wiggling her fingers. "You'd think they'd make you drop your champagne glass—they're so slippery, and you can't feel anything."

Pursing her lips, the plump saleswoman bent down to pull out more pairs: dull brown mittens and driving gloves. "These are practical for fall," she said, setting down a shallow drawer of them. But we were interested in the opposite of warmth and usefulness: whatever small gem of glamour we could find.

We thanked her and wandered over to Cosmetics, where Mrs. Gordon, her blond hair teased and sprayed, perked up from her stool. She was lonely and didn't care if she sold anything, as long as she had visitors. Years before, her only daughter had been at a party when she leaned too far back from a windowsill where she was sitting, fell two stories, and died.

"Ella," she said in a throaty voice that squeaked in the middle of long *a*'s and *e*'s. "Let's do your eyes today."

Jo and I exchanged glances—the last time she'd "done" me, I'd walked out of the store looking sunburned. But I was willing to be distracted by anything. "All right." I sat down on a high stool with a purple velvet cushion, and Mrs. Gordon went to work, sliding over a tray of shadows lined up in the graduated pattern of a keyboard.

"Okay, close," she said, brushing some powder over my eyelids. I concentrated on not fluttering my lashes, so I wouldn't unsteady her hand. "I saw in the paper last week about your grandfather. I'm sorry. Was it a heart attack?"

"Yes," I said, hating how easily the lie slipped out, wanting to talk about shoes, stockings, anything else.

"You never know when you might lose someone. The older I get, the more I learn—you've got to savor every day. Open." Her face was close to mine. I looked at her white, even skin, exquisite powdered wrinkles barely visible at the corners of her mouth. But what if you couldn't savor even one day? What if all the days choked you?

"Look up."

I gazed at the fan twirling on the ceiling and the pattern of ovals rippling around it.

She pulled out a tiny brush and ran it along the rims of my eyelashes. "I never knew either of my grandfathers. You were lucky that way, being so close to him. . . ." She let her voice trail off in her concentration on my face, her little finger smudging my eyelid. Sweeping the brush in another color, she said, "This is going to be stunning." Somehow, I didn't think she saw a contradiction between makeup and grief. "And when we're done, we'll do you," she said, winking back at Jo.

Jo frowned and shook her head. "I look like a clown in makeup." Her pale, bare face seemed to vex Mrs. Gordon, as if Jo were petulantly refusing her ability to charm, like a too-thin girl who wouldn't eat.

They were both studying me intently, and I felt my jaw clench.

"Look down," Mrs. Gordon said, brushing on mascara. "You look like Ava Gardner."

When she'd finished, Mrs. Gordon placed two soft fingers under my chin and, staring at my eyes, gently lifted my face. Could she see it there, behind her handiwork, how much I couldn't say? Her mouth was two straight pink lines. She shook her head and smiled, handing me the mirror. "To be young."

I mostly looked *awake*, I thought, with a fairy-dust frost under the arch of each brow. I thanked Mrs. Gordon and told her I'd buy the eye shadow. She went around the counter to put it in a bag for me.

"Someday you should let her," I said to Jo. "Just to see."

We went up the staircase in back, which wound beside a gilded banister with floral flourishes as if for a lady's grand entrance, but the red carpet had brown stains and bald patches.

Upstairs, Jo and I circled the racks, pulled out the clothes we

liked, and draped them over our arms. The saleswoman, a girl
with a sharp nose whom we'd hated in high school, gossiped on
the phone at the register and left us alone. My mother had always
sewn practical clothes for me, so at Herstein's I was drawn to
velvets and satins, even if they looked cheap, and sophisticated
cuts, even if they didn't fit me.

Jo and I didn't share a dressing room as we tried on clothes. I
pushed aside the green curtain and came out to study the shiny
red dress on my figure. Jo had put on a black turtleneck and black
skirt and with her hands on her hips squinted at herself in the
mirror. Her muscular legs curved out under the hem. "I was
thinking Audrey Hepburn." She widened her eyes and made a
teacup flourish with her small hand. She frowned. "Too somber."

She looked at my red dress and made a flatulent sound between
her lips. "You can't wear that."

"Why not?" I was teasing her, partly choosing the gaudy dress
just to see what she would say. It had a low neckline shaped like
the top of a heart, and the bottom hem pressed together my knees.

She smiled with her mouth closed and quickly shook her head.
"It's too tight on you."

We both broke out laughing as I slid aside the curtain. In Herstein's dressing room, I knew Jo would tell me exactly what she
saw, good or bad, and among all the white lit mirrors, and the
lingering smells of hair spray and perfume, for once, we wanted
the same things.

I zipped up the next dress, a silk as dark as blue can be before
it's called black, with a slim skirt and a boat neck, sleeves fitted
with cuffs at the elbows. The silk felt airy and cool against my
skin, and fit me exactly.

When I went out and stood before the mirror, I couldn't believe
how different I looked: like a woman who had spent her childhood in Hong Kong, her college years at Vassar, a woman who

wouldn't flinch at ordering eel because she actually liked it. I turned to look at the back. The zipper was invisible. A woman who kept it a mystery how she got into her clothes.

Jo pushed aside the curtain, muttering, "Couldn't even button it." She tossed her head back. "That's gorgeous."

The color made my eyes darker and cast a warm tone on my face, the snaky sheen of the silk echoing curves of shine in my long hair. When I let myself think of falling in love, the man was always taller than I was, with slender hands, and now I added to the fantasy that dress. Looking at my reflection, I wanted to kiss him in the rain.

"How much is it?" said Jo, touching the sleeve.

I pulled the price tag out of the neck and looked down. It was more than three of my paychecks. "Too much."

"Why don't we split the money my dad gave me?" She fumbled in her change purse. She'd told me that he'd called in sick to work three days the week before, and I knew how much they needed whatever he'd given her.

"That's all right," I said, casting one last look at the three-sided mirror. The sad part about going to Herstein's was that it made you wish so hard you were someone else, some untouchable woman trailed by admirers and luck.

I went back into the dressing room, undid the zipper, and when the sleeves and bodice fell away in the harsh light, the scars lashed up at me. Closing my eyes, I quickly changed back into my skirt and sweater.

As I came out, I slid the blue silk onto the hanger and said, "It's just a dress."

Jo slowly nodded. "It's too bad." Going back downstairs to the first floor, we tried on charm bracelets and pearls, sprayed perfumes on our wrists and arms, and went out again to the street, to that gray Indiana light.

When I was a girl and Hanna would still visit, her presence was like an X-ray machine, suddenly exposing the skeleton and muscle of my surroundings: the worn keys of my father's practice organ, our mended furniture, the fat-cheeked Hummels frenetic on the shelf, the sinking corner of flecked linoleum. "*You could leave,*" she told me, but I didn't believe her then.

When I'd first seen the picture of her in the family photograph tucked into their Bible, my grandfather had pointed to her and said in a cottony voice, "That's your mother's older sister. She doesn't live here anymore," and though the knot of his face frightened me, I wanted to meet her.

Except for their round noses, he and Hanna hadn't looked alike. She'd inherited Marietta's Cupid's-bow lips and wide-set green eyes, and my mother had her father's blunt mouth and small dark eyes, the skin on her cheeks roughened and pocked from blemishes. Except for the round noses, they wouldn't have looked like sisters.

Whenever I asked my mother why Hanna hardly ever came back to Porter, she stiffened her shoulders, stared at a spot in the middle of my forehead, and said there were a few things in the world she would never understand, or else, "She'll visit in a couple of years after she settles some things." She looked so pained and tense at the very mention of her sister that I learned not to ask her, because I did whatever I could to prevent her mouth from folding at the corners like that.

"That's your mother's business," my father always said when I asked him about Hanna.

She appeared changed each of the few times she did come back, like an actress in different films. Now and then I'd see her hurried writing on an envelope tucked behind the penny bowl, and when my mother left the room, I'd read as much of the letter inside as I could, the lines running off the page and crowding into shrunken script at the bottom. I'd hear my mother whisper into the phone late at night and know it had to be her, far away, at the other end of a long, long line.

A couple of weeks after the funeral, I drove over the bridge near Gary, heading for Chicago to look for her. Silhouettes of factories stood against the sky, pumping smoke in an urgent rhythm, the clouds a fantastic pink color. I snapped on the radio, glancing at Hanna's souvenirs on the dashboard, the toy arrows' turquoise feathers fluttering, the chalky white spots on the carved wooden deer. I'd brought them along with the letter I'd found— for luck. The green sign said CHICAGO, 20 MILES.

Even in her late forties, though her skin was wrinkled, Hanna had the round features of a girl and high fickle eyebrows, as if she'd in some sense never grown away from the teenager she had been when she left. The last time she'd come to our house she said to me, "I haven't seen you since you got bosoms" and embarrassed me, though I quickly forgave her for it. She often said the wrong thing, but it wasn't malicious, just misplaced. Simply standing in the doorway that day in her man's shirt and worn-out white shoes, she unnerved me because I couldn't tell what she might say or do next. She said she was on her way to the dunes, but it was cold and the lake would be wild and mossy, the sand still iced. Her legs and head were bare, and she wore huge sunglasses with purple lenses. She didn't belong to Porter, this place that valued belonging so much.

At the edge of Chicago, I turned down a busy road and stopped at a gas station with a phone booth next to the pumps. Someone had spray-painted the outside of the glass black. I went inside and pulled the hinged door shut, feeling as if that small, confined space would give me more control over what happened. If I could find Hanna, I would tell her what I hadn't been able to tell Jo, and then she would help me get away, maybe let me live with her for a while until I understood better what was needed. The edges of the pages in the phone book were tattered, and the page I opened to was ripped in half. I flipped through the *c*'s to Cornell and found (with the middle initial T.) his name, checked the address against the one on the letter I'd found in my mother's attic next to the souvenirs in the box with Hanna's name on it. It was the same. I stood there for a few minutes, listening to the traffic outside, the friendly bell that rang each time a car pulled up to the gas pump.

Chicago wasn't far from us, exquisite hotels and towering buildings with windy shadows, a lake flecked with ice or nightmarishly murky, a city like the Monopoly game, where anything, bad or good, could happen to you.

Cornell lived on the South Side in one of a long row of old brick apartment buildings with wrought-iron gates and chipped lion statues on pedestals, tracery and stained glass in some of the windows. I opened the heavy front door and went inside the foyer, where another door was propped open with a cinder block. I started up the dim, uneasy staircase, past peeling wallpaper with a thick stripe and hand-shaped leaves falling through the bars. I didn't know how he and Hanna had parted, if at the mention of her name he'd invite me in or spit in my face.

Knocking on his door, I heard jazz music turned down and padding footsteps. When I saw his puzzled eyes over the chain catch in the door, I knew he didn't recognize me, and there wasn't any reason he should have. He'd come to our house eight years before in a torn coat, and I'd imagined Hanna still holding a scrap of its wool in her hand, that she was the reason for his dazed expression when he'd said her name and it exploded and lingered above our heads like a mushroom cloud. Now that I was here, I saw how wrong I might be.

He opened the door wider. The skin around his eyes had wadded and yellowed. He stooped around his folded arms. "Yes?"

"Cornell?"

"Do I know you?" I pushed my hands into my skirt pockets, fiddled with their silky lining. His lips were full and kind, posed to burst into laughter, even if he wasn't joking. "Remember Hanna Kestler?" It took all of my mouth to say her name.

He leaned his hip against the doorframe, jutted his chin into the air. "But who are you?"

"Her niece. A long time ago you came to our house?"

After he'd left, my mother had warned me not to mention it to my grandparents, who didn't know about him. "But he's her husband," I'd said to myself. I'd pictured her with him riding somewhere in his blue car, his papers between them on the white vinyl seat, the windows down, Hanna humming, and the wind ruffling her short red hair. He would look at her, relieved, and tell her how unhelpful my mother had been. Hanna would be sad, but she would laugh lightly anyway. "But Ella," he would say, "she wanted me to find you." It was crazy, but that was why I expected him to remember me.

He looked into the empty space in the hallway, drew his lips back between his teeth as if he wanted to hide them while he thought for a moment. My heart pounded, and my head felt light. Then he opened the door. "Come on in." He led me into a small room with a radiator, a green couch, a cluttered bookshelf, a large chair, and a pair of brown socks on the dusty floor that embarrassed me.

"Sit down," he said. "You're the one she likes, right?" He sat in the green leather easy chair, browning on the arms and cracked in places as if it had been baking.

"She wrote to me sometimes," I said, leaning back on the

couch. I mean—" I folded my arms across my chest. "She didn't visit much."

He gazed at the pocked wood floor momentarily. "She only writes when she's sad," he said. "But you're the one over there in Porter?" He pointed with his thumb as if it were only down the street.

I nodded.

"So, Hanna sent you?" He leaned over on the chair arm, smiling expectantly. He had been looking for her, too. She took hold of people that way, even if they wanted to forget her and hadn't seen her in a long time.

"No," I said.

His smile vanished. I wanted it back; I wanted him to be happy just to see her blood relative. "I thought you could help me find her."

He shook his head impatiently. "I haven't seen our Hanna in years."

"Actually," I said hurriedly, "I'm surprised I found you." The letter I'd come across with Hanna's souvenirs in the attic was fifteen years old, and here he was, in the same apartment he'd lived in then.

He took off his wire-rimmed glasses and began to shine them on his shirt. "Her last letter was from Cincinnati. I don't know where she went after that. Never heard back from her."

He put his glasses on again. "It could be a good sign, though. She used to only write when she was miserable. It was because of my songs—she wanted the literary consolation."

He picked up from the floor a couple of scraps of paper with scrawled writing and pushed them into his shirt pocket. "Want something to drink? I have some bourbon."

I was flattered that he wanted me to stay and thought maybe

if I talked to him long enough, he might tell me something I didn't already know. "Sure, a little would be nice."

He went out of the room and came back with two emptied jelly jars, still frosted with the fragments of labels, and placed them in front of me on the coffee table before he poured.

"I don't usually get a chance to talk about Hanna," he said, tipping the bottle and filling each glass. He handed me the fuller one. "That's supposed to be her," he said, settling back in his chair, as he gestured with his glass at a painting on a blue-pink taffy-swirled background, a woman with large, round eyes, a little rosebud nose, something of Hanna's smile. "One of those street painters on Michigan Avenue did it. Funny, my girlfriends always think it's just something I found to put on the wall. Doesn't look like a real person, does it?"

I took a sip of whiskey, felt the ridged lip of the jar. "Not really." The face in the picture looked empty and perfect, but Hanna's face was always moving, hard to catch, eyes lifted here, mouth turned there, and at the next word they would switch, eyes down, mouth twisted, all very quickly, as if she had more nerves and muscles in her face than most people.

"What did she tell you about me? I'm worried," he said, lighting a cigarette. He shook the match rhythmically like a tiny drumstick.

"In a letter once she told me you played the piano."

"That's all she said?"

I wished I could have thought of a convincing lie then, something to spare his feelings, because I saw how he needed to feel important to her, how he wanted her to feel the loss of him. "And I knew you were married."

"We weren't married," he said quickly, putting his finger behind his glasses to rub his eye. "That was a lie she told the family, because—I don't know—either she wanted to test them or get back at them." He moved his leg and accidentally kicked over a pile of books, but left them sprawled there on the floor. "I'm Jewish, you know."

I didn't, but nodded. I'd never met a Jew before—there weren't any I knew of in Porter.

He emptied his glass, got up and went into the other room, came back with another bottle, and put it on the coffee table between us. Pouring whiskey into his jar, he said, "Not fond of outsiders, are they?"

"No," I said, ignoring an impulse to apologize. "I guess that's why she stayed away."

He nodded. "Yeah, she had to." He filled his glass to the rim this time. "I think she told me you were smart, that true?"

I took a drink, shrugged. "I read a lot."

"So what, they finally felt guilty, huh?" He was pushing me to make an excuse, to defend them, and I didn't want to. I'd put my grandfather's death in a big black box in my head marked DON'T and I didn't even want to admit that I had a mother and grandmother just then, or to have to think how absurd it was that we'd each invented a different death for him—aneurism, virus, stroke—because to correlate our lies would mean flatly looking at his death, and none of us could do that.

He narrowed his eyes, crossed his legs and arms in a hoarding gesture. "Well," I said, slumping so my elbows hit my knees. "But they'd like to see her. And my grandfather died. She needs to know that."

"Yes, she does. I'm sorry," he said, gulping his drink. A couple of minutes later, he said, "But they don't want to make peace. They want to invade her like a country. If she'd stayed with them any longer, she'd be in the loony bin now. At least she's not there. We can be grateful for that, can't we?"

I looked at the white plastic radio the shape of a grapefruit perched on the bookshelf and wished I could turn it on to look for my new favorite song. I didn't want him to know how little I knew. I was afraid he'd be less likely to trust me, or might even ask me to leave, and I began to think, superstitiously, that just talking about Hanna would help, that somehow she'd hear us.

I asked him about his job at a printer's, about his neighborhood, his family in New Jersey. Then, abruptly, he asked if I thought Hanna was happy. It was a question that made me think of stiff half-circle smiles and tight patent-leather shoes I once wore.

"I read somewhere that the secret is to have good health and a short memory," I said. "She seems to have both."

"You think so?" he said, wincing as if the vulnerability in his face were painful or had somehow clouded his vision. "Once I threw a party for her—her birthday—I went out and got her blue cheese, some nice bread, a case of wine, chocolate cake. I invited all these people, and they didn't have to, but they brought gifts. People danced. I remember there were lily petals all over the floor, from people jostling against the flowers. She had on a pretty long dress, she was smiling and laughing, and everyone was having a good time when near the end, she sat down in a corner on the floor and burst into tears. Just sat there crying into her lap. I couldn't get her to say what it was. No one could."

A flick of memory brushed past me, just a moth wing: *tree bark and branches like a girl's arms.* "You think you know why now?"

He nodded too certainly. "She was melancholy. Too much of a party knocked her off balance, scared her." I remembered my father once said that she needed more than she could imagine anyone giving her.

I told Cornell about the time we were eating dinner at my grandparents' house when she suddenly appeared in the dim dining room, more like a wish than a person. As if she'd been expecting her but forgot, my grandmother Marietta set a place and filled a plate, my mother talked breezily about Hanna's skirt, with its gold-coin buttons, and my father squinted at her and kept wiping his eyes. When I hugged her, she whispered, "Don't believe what they say about me." My grandfather looked down at his turkey and went on eating. She sat down and said, "I can't stay long," smoothing a napkin in her lap and glancing at him nervously.

Before the pie was cut, she bent over to say to me, "He can't keep this up forever, can he?" Her dark hair, its natural color, was braided tightly and twisted over her ears, and her nails were dirty with blue paint. She looked tired but smiled with her lips closed, so the dimples curled in her full cheeks, and she patted me on the knee under the table as if to signal she was okay. I was just a girl, but she always acted as if we'd taken a long car trip together and shared a hundred meals, as if we'd seen things others would be envious of and so we had to keep them secret. As much as I liked this, I always knew she could just as easily invent another thing that would please her even more.

Hanna kept trying to catch my grandfather's eye, but he went on ignoring her. Whenever she spoke, he turned his head slightly to the wall. While my mother and I collected the dirty plates, he said, "We don't have meals like this often enough," and I wished he'd meant it. While my parents asked Hanna about her life in Chicago, he played with crumbs of piecrust. I was furious. *Ask her anything*, I thought. *At least look at her face*. I couldn't think of what on earth she could have done to him to make him act this way.

"It's already seven o'clock, goodness," she finally said, breathlessly checking her watch. In my hand she pressed a ten-dollar bill and one of those rain caps in a pink case that the banks give away, kissed me on the cheek, and left, waving at everyone else as she ran out the door to catch the train.

"That sounds familiar," Cornell said, looking somewhere to the left of me. We each sipped at our drinks and put our glasses down on the table. My parents had often sat like this after dinner with their beers, even after they'd run out of things to say to one another. I didn't want to leave. Outside, a car door slammed, children were squealing, and an ice-cream truck idled, its miniature music sounding rushed and nervous.

He told me about his life with Hanna, the dresses she bought at secondhand stores and the Polish restaurant where they ate every night and knew all the waiters, how she'd made friends with the old Chinese woman upstairs and had taken care of a seminary student's children. It was an ordinary, pleasant life, and I understood why she'd had to leave it—she'd wanted to feel as if she'd chosen it or earned it, not as if she'd been destined to meet Cornell, the first person she happened to befriend when she ran away to Chicago. That was cheap chance, and there had been plenty of that for her in Porter. The breeze through the open window smelled of exhaust. I felt sorry for Cornell, because it seemed he *had* chosen her.

"I had a way of bringing her out," he said. "Let me show you how a cheer-up song went."

"All right." He got up and went to the other room, then rolled in an upright piano. He put a chair in front of it and sat down. When he looked hesitantly at his hands and wiggled his fingers, I was embarrassed for him and wanted to laugh until he hit the keys. It was a short and catchy song about Paris, the tune riding up and down a hill, and after he'd finished, it struck me that both my mother and Hanna had fallen in love with musicians, one a church organist, one a piano player, how music seemed the closest thing to a kind of love that came from a lot of discipline and practice.

"That's nice," I said. "I've always wanted to go there."

"Me, too," he said, his finger pounding a key. He showed me what his brother had brought back for him: an ashtray with a street scene from the Champs Élysées painted on it. "He was in the army," Cornell said. "Hated it." Later, as he smoked and we drank two more glasses of bourbon, he flicked his ashes like gray snow over striped awnings and women in extravagant hats.

It began to get dark outside. I felt the liquor wiggling in my arms and chest. "I wonder if it's true what they say about French-women."

"I don't know." He cocked his head. "But I'd like to see for myself."

"Maybe we'll go there someday," I said. "You look like the stubborn type."

He smiled. "Maybe. Hanna and I always said we'd go. But we made a lot of crazy plans."

"What happened, anyway?" I said, taking another drink. "Why aren't you still together?"

He leaned back and sighed. "Oh, well, she was in love with me, I guess, until she realized we were too much alike, and she said she couldn't tell anymore what was hers and what was mine— she even got our clothes mixed up in the end, the stories about our childhoods." It was a shock that he wanted to tell me so much. "She took it personally if I was unhappy for five minutes, because she thought she should be able to save me from that—even five fucking minutes of it." He swung the leg crossed over his knees as if getting ready to kick something at the ceiling.

"And she left you then?"

"Oh, she ran off, with someone else I think, I still don't know for sure. She left a note that said she felt like she was disappear-ing—what was it? that the 'we' was about to murder the 'you' and 'me'—didn't make sense." He stared at the smoke stringing up from his cigarette. Outside, a car horn blared.

In my imagination I'd woven a life for her that made sense, and he was tugging at all the loose ends, unraveling it. But with the liquor running in my limbs, it wasn't an unpleasant unraveling, like the slow breakup of a chord my father sometimes played just before the real beginning of a hymn.

"I have to tell you," he said, shaking his head. "She's the loneliest person I ever knew." I thought she just had an independence he couldn't see. "It's like she's walking around with a big hole blown out of her, where most people's hearts are."

"But she never listened to anybody's stupid rules," I said.

His face strained into a longer, hollower shape, and it seemed as if he were looking down at me from a height of several feet. "No," he said hoarsely. "She listens too hard. To everybody. That's her problem. She has to fill up that hole." He leaned forward, so close I felt his hot breath on my neck. "Otherwise she'd come back to me."

The dust particles in the beam of window light between us shimmered. His Hanna had a different face, a different past. I thought if I could part some warm curtain, I could look inside him and find her.

His eyes crinkled. "Well, you can't be a universe to each other for very long. Everything starts to seem really small."

I knew I'd drunk more than I should have when I looked up at the ceiling and the cracks shivered like black lightning. "You still want her to come back, don't you?" I smoothed the folds in the lap of my skirt. I was talking too much, but couldn't help it. "Wouldn't you do almost anything to feel as if she were closer?" I felt light. The room looked blurry from under my lowered eyelashes.

He laughed uncomfortably and rubbed his knees. "I wouldn't do anything. No, the truth is, most of the time I've pretty much forgotten her."

"I don't believe you," I said. It seemed to drag Hanna closer to us.

He swung his finger around the lip of his glass, leaned toward me. Outside, children were laughing. "Oh, well, I'd do something to feel closer to her."

"To pretend," I said, resting my hand on his thin arm.

He edged around the coffee table and moved to sit beside me on the couch, his chest caved in under his narrow shoulders. Our breath was so thick with bourbon, it smelled flammable. "Sometimes when you move your hand that way, under your chin, it reminds me of her," he said.

"Really? No one's ever said that before. Do you think she put her hand there to cover that birthmark?" It was red and could have been mistaken for a love-bite, but she usually kept it hidden with a scarf or thick makeup.

"Yeah, that's right. She was always worried about that—especially if she didn't know people. You have one of those too?" He pulled my hand away from my chin and stroked my neck. "Nope."

When he kissed me, his tongue was soft and insistent, like a thumb dipped in honey. As I felt him stroke my collarbone, I imagined what it must have been like to be her, with her smooth complexion and dimples. The walls started to spin in a pleasant, carousel way as he inched his hand under my blouse, inclined it so it held the edge of my breast. His other hand went under my skirt, slowly rubbing my leg. "What's this?" he said, his finger catching at a ridge of scars. I flinched, but he pushed me back on the couch and turned out the light so I relaxed a little. For a while at least it must have been good, to have someone that in love with you, someone who paid enough attention to think they knew you. His hand swept up my thigh, pulled down my stockings and underwear. Everything seemed fuzzy, rose-colored and gentle. He kissed the thin skin on the inside of my thigh, and his tongue butterflied upward. It was a moment before I knew what he was doing and thought to myself, *Sit up,* but didn't. The room was cool and dark, except for the quivering pink light of his tongue. He flipped back my skirt and rubbed the sides of my legs. I was woozy but opened my eyes just slightly, and then a car's headlights passed through the window and lit the red, withered skin on my thighs. He must have seen it too, felt something feathered, coarser. I drew back and pulled down my skirt.

"What's the matter?" I pulled on my stockings and shoes but didn't bother to find my underwear in the dark. Hanna was far away now, tapping perfume behind her ear or riding in a taxi, having not thought about either of us for some time. I got up, steadied myself on the arm of the couch. "I shouldn't have stayed so long."

He turned on the lamp, looked up at me, surprised, still smiling from one corner of his mouth. "But you did."

"I have to leave." I didn't look at him again but found my purse and ran down the crooked stairs, grabbing the banister at the two crazy turns. I was glad he didn't follow me or call out.

As I drove down the highway in the dark, each set of passing headlights was a pair of eyes widening, lingering on my face, the stare momentarily blinding me until they passed. For a while I'd believed it was Hanna drawing me to him, but now I knew it was just the bourbon. I was ashamed of myself for using it that way again. It never worked unless the person was a stranger, a total stranger.

When I stopped on the side of the road near Gary, the air smelled like synthetic manure, and a few red dots of water-tower lights were stacked beneath the stars. I took a blanket from the backseat, flung it out the window, and lit a match to the pink satin edging. The flame extinguished, so I got out, went to the trunk, and found the gasoline. A semi trundled by. I hurried back into the car and, sitting in the front seat with the door open, soaked one ragged corner in gasoline, lit it up again, and threw it on the gravel beneath me. The pale blanket jumped up like the back of a horse, then crumpled and slithered under the flames. I drove away with the fire seething behind me.

Watching it shrink in my rearview mirror, I knew it wouldn't be enough. I was speeding past the cornfields, worrying what Cornell must have thought of me: *A few drinks and she'd let you do anything. She pretended to be looking for Hanna, but really she was desperate for something else.*

I stopped again on a dirt road between two fields, the breeze in the corn leaves like a faraway tide. I got out and doused some old newspapers with gasoline before I lit them on the ground, but there weren't enough to keep a fire going for very long. Under the cover of the corn, I didn't worry anymore about being seen. I searched my trunk for more flammables and found some cans of spray paint I'd used to touch up the paint job on the car doors. I walked a little way down the road, ignited the tip of each one, and threw it up over the corn tassels, which lit up like tiny crowns, until the cans exploded and the dark sucked in the flare.

The third time I stopped near the Porter exit sign, I didn't even get out of the car. The darkness squeezed at my shoulders. I lit a match to the delicate leg of the wooden deer from Hanna's box. "Damn it, Hanna," I said. "Where are you?" I lay the deer on the seat beside me, looking at its pathetic wide-eyed face and puckered lips like a surprised girl's. I was coughing from the smoke as the seat's white vinyl melted, but it calmed me down to watch the little deer burn out until I snapped on the light to see what was left among the feathery ashes: the blue beads that had been its eyes.

III

▓▓

Then I was back in Porter. The town lay on shifting, stolen ground, somehow dragged to Indiana during the Ice Age, and even if they didn't know why, people were afraid the land their houses stood on would one day be taken back. The streets named after presidents and species of trees marched in a grid around the courthouse until they got as far as the surrounding cornfields, where they could safely forget themselves in dirt. When I dropped out of the local college, my mother was afraid I'd move away, but it was a difficult place to leave. I daydreamed about traveling, but plans to actually go anywhere always faded away like the streets once they reached the edge of town.

The hotel was square, three floors of brick the color of yellowed paper, with four curtained windows on each floor facing Lincoln, the main street. A red-brick path led from the sidewalk to the front door, which was topped by a short, black awning that said LINDEN in sturdy block letters.

Each night at the front desk I counted the change into a small green metal box and put the rest in a zippered bag for the bank. The bills were limp and soft as felt, the coins clammy, and when I finished, my hands felt the pleasant grime of travel and strangers' fingers.

I'd sit with a book, or sometimes just watch the heavy wooden door, anticipating the turn of the knob. Living in Porter had made me good at waiting. I waited for shoes to creak on the wooden floor, then pad onto the flat gold carpet. I waited for the harried voices of people who'd spent too long in a car or a bus, for the smell of cigarettes and soda, for flesh to be reflected in the cheap crystal of the miniature chandelier that had hung there in the lobby since the hotel had opened a hundred years before.

My grandfather had been worried about the germs. "When someone sneezes or scratches or coughs—I don't care who they are—" he said, "take two steps back and look away. No sense exposing yourself." He and my grandmother had stayed at the Linden the night of their wedding. There would have been no cheap paintings or trophy cases in the lobby back then, just the clean white walls and the chandelier's teardropped pieces of glass.

It was Wednesday. The night before at the Paradise Lounge, I'd gotten so drunk with two seed salesmen that I ended up in the ladies' room throwing up pink, sweet, whiskey-sour vomit, and that afternoon I had a bad headache.

Jo came in and sat behind the desk beside me. She pulled out the writing board and said, "You look a little peaked," in that half-British voice of hers that she'd gleaned from old movies.

"I'm fine," I said, putting away the change box in the drawer.

"Sure?" She fixed her eyes on me. "I have some saltines and aspirin in my purse." She took out the adding machine and quickly punched out a tape of the week's profits, her gaze snapping between the ledger and her dancing fingers. Her feet were aligned on the floor, her back straight, her face serious. She took an exacting pleasure in tasks like this. It must have come from so many years playing the viola, practicing scales and counting to the metronome. She sometimes had to bail her drunk father out of jail, after his arrests for disorderly conduct, and when I pictured her talking to the judge, it was this practical face I saw, as if she had to practice and count to make sure her eyes and mouth would work properly for her.

She was unusually quiet today, and I wondered if she'd had a fight with her fiancé, David. I watched the tape snake out from the machine, her fingers tapping, and the mechanical swallow each time she hit the plus sign.

I used to be practical, too. I'd wanted to be a teacher and had finished two semesters and begun the training before I knew I'd made a mistake. Mostly what I ended up teaching the children was how to wait. They were so well behaved. They looked up at me with wide, trusting eyes, crossed their legs and folded their hands prettily, listening for me to tell them what to do. I saw their lives stretched out in those moments of waiting—their little ears tingling, tipped forward—and I thought I'd never be able to teach them anything else, and knew that I had to quit.

Jo punched at the adding machine, pursed her lips, and let the paper ribbon out and curl. She turned to me and slapped her hand down on the blotter. "Why didn't you tell me you'd lost your mind? When did it happen?" I supposed she must have heard through the grapevine about my last night at the Paradise.

I broke open a roll of quarters for the change box. "So I got drunk," I said. "Big deal."

"Stinking drunk." Her eyes flashed furiously. "You know well and good," she said, "that it was stupid to go there by yourself. Why didn't you call me?" She blinked quickly several times as if she couldn't see. "I know you're upset, but you can't . . ."

I stared at the painting of the clown, and the red ball of his nose hurt my eyes.

"And what were you doing with those two men? You know, you're lucky Mark saw you there. He would have taken care of you if you hadn't left." Mark was David's best friend. I barely remembered seeing him now, with his grasshopper eyes and green drippy tie. "How'd you get home anyway?"

"I walked."

"You walked?"

I knew how my drinking like that disgusted her. "Look," I told her, "I was just in a funny mood."

She bit her bottom lip. "You know, if I had your looks, I'd— I wouldn't go wasting them. Why won't you go out with Mark? He's the best thing to hit your pavement in a long time." Jo still thought one of the local boys could rescue me. I pictured the ruddy skin above Mark's collar, his barrel chest and too-broad shoulders.

"I'm not interested," I said. "As soon as things calm down, I'm going to leave anyway. I just have to decide where I want to go."

She gave me a wan smile and sighed. "Not before David and I buy our house, I hope." The color rose in her cheeks.

"You're sure now?" I said. She had been wavering lately about whether or not to marry him.

"I think so," she said, walking over to the glass trophy case on the wall, where little gold men held balls the size of buttons and there were photographs of Mr. Linden as a teenaged basketball player, his impossibly long skinny legs sticking out from his loose shorts like long clappers hanging from bells. "You'd never know this was him," she said. "Hard to believe that penny-pincher was ever this good-looking." She reached down to tuck her heel back into her flat shoe.

"It's the aura of the basketball," I said. "Some kind of orange halo for you, isn't it? How many of them did you date? Seven?"

"Eight," she said, fondling a trophy. "But they were losing. David said they needed me to boost their spirits," she said, laughing.

She went over to the window and flipped the switch for the

neon VACANCY sign. Usually she stayed for a chat, but she was going to meet David later at the Big Wheel Restaurant. "You're in for a slow night, I can tell."

"I'm looking forward to the peace and quiet," I said.

She tilted her head and clicked her tongue sarcastically. "Right."

▲   ▲   ▲

After my father died when I was fifteen, my mother's eyes would tear up whenever I said I was going to Jo's, or leaving for school, and when I came back home, she'd be sitting in a hard-backed chair near the door, mending the same plaid skirt it looked as if she'd just picked up, her eyelids puffy over her small, tense irises.

One Friday night I'd asked permission to go to a party on the lake, and I was looking forward to it because there were going to be boys from out of town there, and one in particular with rangy arms and sandy hair, whom I'd met at the bowling alley the week before. I came into the kitchen, where she stood near the stove. "There's a party at Lake Eliza tonight," I said.

She had her back to me and was stirring something. She turned around, holding the dripping spoon like a scepter. "Whose party?"

"Beth Hanson's."

"Will her parents be there?"

"Yes," I said, though I didn't know, because there was supposed to be a keg.

"Is Jo going?" Her voice wavered.

"Yes."

She nodded, and her eyes faded into the dimness. "I wish you wouldn't," she said, and turned around again, her shoulders hunched over the stove.

I was furious, watching her back, the spoon sadly scraping the bottom of the pot. She'd been like this ever since he'd died, wanting to keep us together in the house, the rooms arranged exactly the same way, the same seven meals on each day of the week, the time when we went to sleep and the time when we woke up the same, as if by keeping the borders of our lives exactly as they had always been, we could also contain my father's death, even tame it.

I left the room and went upstairs to get the cigarettes Jo and I had stolen from her father and went back downstairs and out the back door to sit in the yard. It wasn't dark yet, but the air had an autumnal, heavy stillness.

I hadn't even liked smoking particularly when we'd tried it under the canopy in Jo's room, the smoke trapped beneath the gauzy fabric. And the thought of doing it alone wasn't as appealing as it had first seemed. It wasn't the taste of cigarettes, but seeing how we looked to one another smoking that had been interesting.

The cigarette was in my hand, though, so I lit it and watched my fingers holding it until the white paper shrank back to the brown filter. Somehow I got interested in the way the tobacco disappeared, the wither of the tiny crumpled brown strands, and I lit another match to the end of the cigarette stub. When the flame moved close to my fingertips, I dropped it in the dry grass, and the spark caught. An accident.

When the flame grew to the size of my hand, I stood up to stomp it out, but the fire looked so graspy and unsteady, I wondered what would happen if I let it go. It was only a thin, pallid fire, apologetic and trembling, and after a minute or two the wind blew it mostly out. I ran the sole of my shoe over the black and brittle patch it had made in the grass. It was the first fire I'd set. A hole in the bright green. Even though I wouldn't be going to the party, I felt strangely satisfied, my disappointment burned away and replaced by a small internal radiance. I didn't think much about it, just that it was pleasant.

After the cancer was diagnosed, my father had died so quickly we hadn't had time to fathom it. At first he wouldn't stay in bed, and he insisted on helping with the dishes, played tunes from silent movies on the practice organ, and stayed up watching the late-late show on television, propped up on the Lazy Boy chair with a beer, so it seemed as if he weren't really sick. Finally, he did stay in the guest room, though, his face bony and pallid, the blankets piled so we couldn't see how thin he'd become.

My mother had gone up to bring him breakfast. She came straight to my room afterward, looked at me incredulously and said, "There's blood on his mouth." I think she knew he was dead, but she let me call the ambulance anyway. Maybe she couldn't think of what else to do. Only when the paramedics came and she fell, going up the stairs again, did she cry.

For days the whole house seemed filmed with a foggy light, and once in a while my mother's voice or the smell of shaving lotion would clear the air, and I'd see the lilt of a bowl, the tines of a fork, and they were unbearably sharp and precise.

"What are we supposed to do?" my mother would say whenever she ventured out of her room. Weeks later she began to clean and cook again, but her voice had turned low and scratchy, as if it were coming from a radio not properly tuned, and she began finding ways to keep me with her in the house.

I set more small fires in my room, or in the field behind our backyard. I felt so unlike myself without my father that the fires, held in a bucket or a hole, with water nearby to put them out, didn't seem nearly as drastic as the changes I felt in myself.

It was a few years later, after I'd quit college and it had became harder for me to sleep through the night, that I moved the fires out of their safe containers. These were some of the things I'd burned: the X of the street sign at Oak and Jefferson, an old rag rug someone had hung out on a line, two wigs in the garbage behind Dora's Beauty Salon, a thrown-out tinseled Christmas tree, a rusted washing machine and dryer, a swing set on a playground, a wooden dwarf. I'd come close to getting caught that time. A little girl on a tricycle wheeled up beside me just as I'd lit a match to the sneering lawn dwarf in one of the neighbors' yards. I didn't want her to get burned, so I pushed the tricycle back toward the curb.

"What are you doing?" she asked me.

The dwarf's pointed hat and head were on fire. I told her that he had been so jealous of all the people who could move, all the people who walked by him every day, that his head had exploded.

"Poor dwarf," she said.

Trembling, I took off my jacket and ran over to slap at the flame. It was the middle of the afternoon, and someone should have seen me. The dwarf ended up headless, at least, not sneering, his walking stick still plugged into the too-green grass. I walked the little girl back to her house and let her tell me the story of Cinderella, which she'd memorized and made up a song about.

I hoped I hadn't scared her. When I was a girl, one of the neighbor bullies, Roy, set fire to a pile of twigs in a hole he'd dug up in an empty lot. His older sister screamed that he was a pyromaniac. "It's my lantern," he whined, probably knowing he was going to get into trouble. "When you're camping, you need a lantern." I was watching them from my bicycle on the street and practiced the word. *Pyromaniac. Pyro* sounded like a toy, a plastic thing that shook or spun, but *maniac* scared me—someone's crazy hair pulling their wits out of them like the picture of Medusa I'd seen in *The Golden Book of Greek Mythology*. There was a slow torture in her head that made her mean.

I wasn't unafraid when I set these first fires. I knew they were dangerous. I would tell myself "no more" and quit for six months, but there was something inside me that I had to stop, and it would only get worse and worse the longer I went without touching matches: There were these happily chattering mouths, but their sharp teeth caught at my stomach and heart, and their voices were grating and childlike, and I'd go along with it for a while, but then the futility of the nothingness they said got to me—because what it came down to was a cheerful, nonsensical nothingness that taunted me. When I set fire to something, the mouths and voices trickled away out of the flames, and it was such a relief.

▲   ▲   ▲

On a sunny day, just beginning to get cool again, the leaves yellow and red, I wore a secondhand sheer black dress with long velvet sleeves, much too formal, but with cigarette burns and a brown stain in the bodice, a dress someone must have worn to a party that got out of hand.

It was still too early at the Paradise for the after-work drinkers. "Not many gals care for this place," said the bartender, mixing my whiskey sour in a bullet-shaped metal shaker. I noticed he had a slight lisp, which softened his heavy, stubbled face. Before it seemed he'd watched me sarcastically, and I'd been wary, but now his cracked, razor lips seemed friendlier.

"I like that it's dark in here, even in broad daylight," I said. Against the mirror, the faces on the liquor labels reminded me of cameo brooches, the wine and creme de menthe the exact red and green of stones on Marietta's rings.

"Yeah." He chuckled, a gold tooth glinting as he slid the glass in front of me, floated an orange slice and cherry in the ice. "Don't get many orders for whiskey sours."

"But you make good ones," I said, sipping from the short glass. "Not too sweet."

I'd come to like bar talk, that benevolent, inquiring chatter that didn't ask or answer much, but if you said more than you wanted to, if you got careless, it wouldn't hurt anything either.

He tucked his rag into his pants pocket, folded his arms on the bar, and asked where I worked. "The Linden," I told him.

"Oh." He arched his brows and nodded. "Good job?"

I nodded. "I get tired of seeing all the same faces I went to school with. At work, at least I get to meet new people."

He pulled out his gray rag and swiped it across the circle-stained, shellacked bar. "People are friendly here," he said, and I thought he must have misunderstood me. *Of course they are,* I thought. *They have no choice.* The circles cut into one another, formed tangled chains. I pictured the place Hanna lived, a city, I was certain, a place where it was safe to be rude once in a while.

The door opened, and in the last afternoon light, all I could see was a narrow silhouette walking forward until the door shut behind him and his face cleared out of the shadows. He sat down on the stool next to me and flattened his palms on the bar. "Bourbon, please."

He had a long, handsome face, pale eyes, and curly hair. Right away, I could tell he was from out of town. He put a cigarette between his lips and struck a match. "You smoke?" he said through the corner of his mouth. I stared into the wiggling seed in his fingertips, thinking of the field of yellow it could grow.

"No," I said.

His name was Strom, which reminded me of an old cowboy's guitar. He was a high-school teacher, in town to comfort a brother whose wife had left him, but he drank like one trying to drown his own misery, and I liked him.

We started talking about local legends and characters. I could make Porter sound exotic when I wanted to. I told him about the octogenarian twins who owned a restaurant and a bike shop and spoke a private language somewhere between Spanish and glossolalia, about the wooly mammoth someone had found in the moraine, which the judge ruled had to be split in half between the finder and the landowner, making it practically worthless. The front half was in the natural-history museum in Gary, hung up like stuffed game; the rear end was in somebody's attic.

"*Really*," he said to everything, not smiling, but nodding. I told him about the cursed white house said to be haunted by the mad wife of the mayor who used to live there. "There's a statue of Venus in what used to be the garden. Supposedly she puts rocks in the statue's hand whenever a Porter girl loses her virginity."

He seemed impressed by this, judiciously extending his lower lip. "If you go there," I said, "her hand is always overflowing."

Encouraged by his interest, I told him about Mr. Bell, who owned the hardware store, how he changed the stock so inadequately there were still packages of wire with pictures of men wearing stiff hats and paint cans with labels showing women wearing aprons and sausage curls. He talked constantly and once told me about a Klan speech he'd heard as a boy. A grand wizard stood up in front of a large crowd over by the courthouse and preached about the dangers of Catholicism, saying the nuns and priests held orgies and that they wanted the Pope to gain control of the country, take away our religious liberties and economic freedom for the sinister uses of the Vatican. The grand wizard was jumping up and down as he talked and said, "The Pope's going to start right here with Indiana because he knows we've got good people. In fact, the Pope himself is on that five-o'clock train," and he pointed toward the station. A crowd ran from the courthouse to meet the train. The cars were all empty except the last one, which held just one passenger, a man. The men rushed in and pulled him off by his coat collar, threatening to lynch him. I paused a moment, "He was a carpet salesman from Detroit."

Strom laughed, shaking his leg, letting the side of it graze mine. Jiggling the ice in his glass, he looked into it and finished off the last sip. "I get the feeling people can be happy here, but a lot of them must ferment. My brother will probably never leave now, but he just gets more and more bitter every time I come."

He didn't seem to feel my hand brush his knee, and this made me nervous. I didn't know what to make of it.

"You're not, I can tell," he said. "You've got a sense of humor about all this." He circled his glass around in the air. There was a song I liked on the jukebox, about black-haired girls and their blue eyes, and I felt myself humming.

The bar was filling up, and we had to lean in close to hear one another. I told him about my great-aunt Emily, who'd become famous as the window-smasher of Calumet, years before I was born. One day she left her husband with their three small children and walked into town with a shovel. She smashed the windows of a storefront, a lawyer's office, and a barbershop. Then she got on a train to Bloomington and smashed the windows of a beauty parlor, a hat shop, a feed store, and a bakery. She'd bought a cross-country ticket. She made it through Crawfordsville before they put her in jail and called her husband. As soon as they brought her home, she was at it again. She went on like this for three years, smashing windows in a pattern the police couldn't follow, sometimes three towns in a week, sometimes none for six months. Since her husband paid generously for the damages, no one pressed charges. It got to the point where people began to recognize her face from the newspapers, and when they saw her coming, they'd press themselves against the back walls of the room and protect their faces with chairbacks and catalogues. Amazingly, no one was ever hurt, and after a while she seemed to get bored with it. She sighed and shuffled along with the shovel slung across her shoulder as if it were her job.

In Marietta's house there were newspaper clippings of her sister in frames in the hallway. "Oh, there was nothing wrong with Emily," my grandmother would say. "She just got angry one day and couldn't stop herself."

"You inherit any of that?" Strom jiggled his leg, so his knee caught on my skirt a couple of times.

The whiskey sours twisted through my rib cage. "She's old now," I said. "I only see her at family reunions." (She'd been ill the day of my grandfather's funeral and hadn't been able to come.) I pulled at a strand of hair near my eyes. "But I can get reckless."

He told me about the basketball team he coached, the Wolves, and about Winter Garden, where he liked to go camping in Minnesota and the deer would come right to the flap of your tent. He was looking at my breasts as if he could see right through my dress, but of course he couldn't, or he wouldn't have begun to stroke the velvet against my arm. He turned my hand over and traced spirals in my palm. In the candlelight I could see my veins. Only skin set boundaries between me and him, just that thin, porous covering. It didn't seem like enough protection. He was too sober. Before I left with him, I wanted to see him trip and stumble, or tell me something he'd later regret.

Someone tapped me on the shoulder, and I turned around. It took a second for me to recognize my father's old friend, Mr. Schultz, he looked so out of place in that smoky air. His face wadded up awkwardly so his eyes turned to specks. "Ella? I wasn't sure if that was you."

I pulled my hand away from Strom's and sat up straight. "It's me." I felt my face redden.

He tried to smile. "Having a cocktail?" Placing his index finger just under his ear, he quickly glanced back at Strom. The linoleum floor tilted uncertainly, like a checkerboard someone had grabbed.

I tried to smile. "I was just about to leave, actually," I said, getting down from my stool.

"I've never been here before," Mr. Schultz went on. "I was just waiting for the train to come in and thought I'd pop over for a beer. Popular spot, huh?"

I blindly gathered up my purse and sweater. Strom threw a bill down on the bar and stood up, too. I wished he'd have stayed put. I didn't want to have to introduce them. "Well, nice running into you," I said, waving.

Mr. Schultz waved limply and turned back to the bar.

Strom followed me out. "Who is *he*?"

I thought I might vomit again, the whiskey sours suddenly swirling in my stomach like crazy music. I wanted to get away from Strom and be alone somewhere. "An old friend of my father's. I'm sorry. I don't feel well," I said, weakly. "I'm just a few blocks away."

He looked confused, and I realized he was shorter than I was, and when he spoke, his lips turned inward. "Aren't you going to invite me?" He seemed even easier to fool now, standing out here on the timid sidewalk, but I wasn't in the mood anymore.

▲   ▲   ▲

I hadn't seen Mr. Schultz in a long while. He taught math at Grace Lutheran school and used to go bowling with my father on Fridays. He was quiet as my father had been, with a habit of tugging on his earlobe when he talked, and he walked with a slouched shoulder, as if he were hiding something among the pens in his shirt pocket. Because Mr. Schultz had developed an appreciation for music in Cleveland, where he'd grown up, he loved the Bach my father played, and he came by the house often, saying, "I've got a problem for you, Louis," and my father would give him advice.

Once the two of them were in the living room, drinking beers. I was walking past the doorway to get a glass of water in the kitchen, and I heard Mr. Schultz mention his wife's name, Dorothy, a couple of times in this steady, subdued voice, but I didn't hear what he was saying about her.

As I was filling up my glass at the sink, I heard my father scream, "You what?" and almost dropped my glass. "You can't let that go on, William." My father's anger was always so sudden and strange, it seemed not to belong to him.

There was more talk, a mutter through the walls, and I was afraid now to go back to the book in my room, which would mean walking past the door near where they sat. I stood there in the kitchen, frozen, and heard my father's voice again, blunt and hard as a brick. "I wish to God you had never told me." And I wasn't sure, but thought I heard Mr. Schultz weeping.

My father had a happy, distracted way about him most of the time, a half smile on his lips, a busyness in his eyes, and this made his rage all the more frightening. It seemed to come from nowhere, like the twisters that picked at Porter in the fall and spring, and my mother and I never knew what to do, how to salvage the furniture he'd broken, how to calm him. She blamed his temper on the deaths of his parents in a car accident when he was a boy and the orphanage where he'd been sent to share a room with seven others, and said that after all he'd been through, we were lucky it happened only once in a while. But it felt strange to see Mr. Schultz have to endure my father's temper.

I didn't want them to glance up and see me walking past the doorway, furtive, letting my long hair fall over my ears, the glass of water trembly in my hand.

Sometimes my mother tried to goad him out of it. "Calm down, Louis. There's no need to make a fuss. Maybe we'll even laugh about this tomorrow."

Quietly, I went out the back door in the kitchen and sat in the
backyard tire swing, until I heard Mr. Schultz leave through the
front door and the hoarse start of his car.

Later, I learned from Jo, whose father was a good source of
gossip, that Mr. Schultz had ended an affair with the school secretary and she'd been following him around town in her car,
drunk, and had passed out more than once in the front seat of
her yellow Buick.

IV

When I let myself into my mother's house, I went to the kitchen. The sunlight, ruffled by the curtains, fidgeted on the walls and glanced off all the bright surfaces. I put the food I'd brought on the table and bent down to trace my thumb over the black heel marks in the yellow linoleum that curved and met to form a perfect wing. This was where she'd collapsed the day before and broken her ankle.

The stairs were steep and the wood worn blond in the middle, as if some milky liquid were running down them. I dragged my hand along the banister as I went up. There were photographs of me on the wall: one of me in a smocked white dress before the fire, my arms strangely unscarred and pale, one of me two years later in a green long-sleeved dress and a closed-mouth smile, and other tentative school pictures with a curtain-sky background, school-bright colors. In each of them I look as if I'm waiting inside the rectangular borders of the frame—calm, prepared, expectant— but waiting for what?

The bedroom door was halfway open, a crescent of light on the floor. I knocked lightly before nudging it open and going inside. The bedspread and linens were so smooth and sculpted, they had the look of stone. "Ella." My mother sat up quickly when she saw me and brushed back her loose hair. She was never as adorned as my grandmother, but now she looked pale and drawn, and the shadows beneath her eyes had darkened in a way that made me feel sorry for both of us.

"Thank you, I love daisies," she said, taking them from me.

I looked at the lump of her ankle under the covers. "Does it hurt?"

"No, sit down," she said. The mattress creaked when I sat down near her feet.

"I was just reaching for the flour on the top shelf when I fell," she said.

"I brought you some lunch," I said, getting up. I watched myself keep my voice light and casual, my smile steady, but her lie made me angry. The doctor had told me she'd fainted from hunger. "I'll go get it."

She pulled me back down to the bed. "I'll eat later. I can get around, you know." It was her plucky voice that she used to cover up sadness. "Sit down and tell me what you've been doing with yourself."

Tell her, I thought to myself. *Get her to eat.* "I want to find Hanna," I said. She let go of my hand and slowly stroked the brownish lids of her eyes.

"Now, why do you want to do that?" She looked around the room as if it were dark and she didn't know where I was. She hadn't always been this vague. She had sometimes fought back at him. *Whoever you're angry with, tell them, but don't scream at us.* I remembered how her mouth quivered and she punched lightly at her stomach, how my father went into the living room and practiced furiously for hours.

I said, "Grandpa died. She should know."

She shook her head. "If we knew where she was, we would have called her."

"You don't have any idea?"

She shook her head but wouldn't look at me. She used to go to lectures at the college and for a while talked of going back to school, but after my father died she gave all that up. I think she felt she wasn't capable of it anymore, and her voice got hoarser and less distinct. It was sometimes just a murmur. Her main activity was worrying, but my grandfather had come over once a week for dinner, and she'd asked him about small things, weather, the holidays, food, gardens, and that had seemed to soothe her.

"Mr. Schultz said he saw you the other day." She pursed her lips. "If your father were here, he'd know what to say. I know you always listened to him more than you have to me."

"That's not true." I stared down at my hands, thinking about how to weave our talk into something easy and trivial like wallpaper or shoes. I tried not to think about what Mr. Schultz might have told her. She pulled the blanket up over her arms, so it made a tent over her body. "You're a teacher, you know, not a hotel clerk."

"I won't be there forever." I looked away and saw that one of her pill bottles was overturned on the dresser. She shifted her weight in bed. Out of the corner of my eye, I saw her wince, but she hastily composed her face again. Her worry was fierce and persistent. Sometimes I thought I could hear it humming like a boiler. I searched her face, but I couldn't tell how much she knew. A flannel nightgown thrown across the back of the bedstead slipped to the floor.

"It's okay," she said. "Your father wasn't a big talker, but he always knew the right thing to say." She was shaking. "I never learned that."

I got up from the bed, went over to the dresser, and righted the overturned bottle of aspirin. *Say it,* I told myself, a wing batting at my throat. I turned, looked at her small, pert mouth. "Dr. Finch says you're not eating." My father would have taken her to the doctor long ago. Even my grandfather, who was sometimes too distracted to notice a person's appearance, would never have let her do this; he would have said fasting was something for movie stars and foreigners—it disrupted the natural cycle of things.

She shrugged and looked out the window, half her face clear in the sunlight, half of it in shadows. She wrapped herself in a cape of silence.

"What's happened to your appetite?" I asked, sitting down on the bed again.

She kept looking away out the window, blinking rapidly. I looked out the window, too, following her gaze into the field. I watched the wind comb through the corn leaves, a tractor inching in the distance, snaillike. I could hear her breathing. It had always been this way—she glowed with the pain she wouldn't admit to, her power over me all the more radiant; in fact, it was brightest when she seemed on the edge of collapse.

A few minutes later, I felt my hands turn numb beneath me and realized I'd shoved them under my legs, but I was afraid to stir. I wondered if I would ever be able to leave her. We were trapped in these poses for a long time, awkward and frozen like the glass swans joined at the neck on the curio shelf.

▲   ▲   ▲

There was a spitting, lonely rain the morning I went to Marietta's. Knocking on the door, I caught a glimpse between the living-room curtains of her regal silhouette. I waited. I thought she must not have heard, so I knocked again. She didn't answer. Rain pricked my face. I put my ear to the door and heard a sound like a spoon stirring. A lock of damp hair fell into my eyes. I kicked at the base of the door until my toes ached.

Finally she answered. Her hair was curled, her face made up, but her eyes looked strangely large and glassy. "Ella, honey, come in," she said, opening the door. "You want coffee?" She headed for the kitchen.

I followed her and sat down at the table still damp from being wiped. She took the cups and saucers from the cabinet. "My mother's not eating, Grandma. She fainted. That's how she broke her ankle."

"I knew it," she said, calmly pouring cream from a carton into a pitcher. "She's upset, but she just has to eat. Maybe now she's learned her lesson." The coffee began to perk in the big silver pot. "I'll bring her a casserole, something you just have to warm up in the oven. That will make it easier for her."

After my father died, Marietta's thick casseroles accumulated in our refrigerator, plastic tubs and foil-covered plates of heavy, gelatinous food that my mother couldn't keep down and reminded me of tumors. Marietta must have noticed we hardly ate any of it but just didn't know what else to do. We finally threw the casseroles away each day, so that we could give her back a clean container.

She seemed distracted by something outside. "All those times we were down to our last cent, eating beans, there was money in that bank. Never a word about it." She'd just had the lawyer take my grandfather's will out of the bank deposit box, and I knew she was angry not because he'd kept the money a secret from her but because it was only one of many, and he'd died keeping most of them. If people found out how he'd died, some of them would unkindly say she'd driven him to it, but what looked like snobbishness in Marietta was really a shyness, born out of her inability as a girl to talk past her own beauty, and he'd tunneled into those dark silences long before he married her.

"And there was that one time the doctor thought my heart should be tested. Henry said we couldn't afford it and the doctor didn't know what he was doing." Since I could remember, there had been a lot of worried talk about Marietta's heart, though the fear seemed disproportionate to its mysterious defect. Did she have a hole in her heart like the one Cornell claimed Hanna had?

When the coffee was ready and she poured it into our china cups with hummingbirds painted on the sides, I said, "Well, I'm going to look for Hanna. You don't know where she is, I know, but you must have ideas." Her name swung in the air between us.

Marietta's lower lip trembled. "Oh, no, honey. I wish I knew." She shook her head daintily. Hanna was suddenly a far-off song, some barely remembered tune about making a fortune, sailing away to an island.

"What about the police? Won't they look for someone who just disappears?"

Her thinly plucked eyebrows creased. "You think I haven't asked them?" She hung her head and retreated, embarrassed, then pounded her fist on the table. "She's a grown-up, and if she doesn't want to be found, she can't be found." Her gaze trailed toward the window again, and she jumped up. "Don't do it," she hissed. "That crow again, eating my birdseed." She grabbed the broom and rushed out the back door. Through the window I watched her scurry around the feeder, swatting at the crow as it skittered up into a tree.

I looked down at my forearms. The skin was thick and resilient, but I wanted to be thin-skinned at that moment, to be bruised by my grandmother's loss. When had she given up? When had Hanna's absence become a thing she fought less than her crows?

She walked in past me to put the broom back in the pantry. I asked her where Hanna had lived the last time she wrote. "She must have left a forwarding address."

"Oh, that was such a long time ago when we were writing letters. That wouldn't be any help." A thin wire of grief trembled in her voice. "I just don't want to see you waste your time. She'll come back when she's ready. We can't force her."

"We won't have to force her," I said. "Her father died."

She looked away again. "Ella, you don't really know her. You think you do, but you don't. Decide what you're going to do with the money your grandfather left you. That's something."

▲   ▲   ▲

Those flames passed before I could hold them, make them lie down and stroke their grain. They slid through my fingers and trilled into the ceiling. When I caught them in my fist, they evaporated. I wanted to press them into balls I would save in a tin box and take out to roll in my palm and study their color, cut one open to see the roiling interior like an intestine or a heart.

▲   ▲   ▲

Franco's was a dark pizza parlor with sparkly dioramas lit up in its corners. Jo and I sat in the wooden booth next to the stuffed sheep that stared through the glass at us, its one leg lifted apologetically from the green carpet and silk flowers strewn among its hooves.

When the pizza came, I slid a slice from the pan and nipped a string of cheese between my fingers.

"I had a fight with David." Jo slipped a disc of pepperoni in her mouth and chewed.

"About what?" I didn't know him well, since as a couple, they preferred to be alone. He was the kind of boyfriend who bought her yellow sweaters because the color suited her, and if he thought she looked weak, took her immediately to Pete's and watched her eat a hamburger.

"He wouldn't ask his boss for a raise, and we've been talking about it for weeks. He just lost his nerve."

I nodded, not knowing what to say. She was only twenty-three and engaged, and though plenty of girls got married at that age, I didn't think Jo should. When she talked about it, her face cramped and she held this weak, trembly smile.

Through the glass, the sheep in the diorama stared at us with its curious face. While we were eating and drinking red wine, she told me about the fight, how he'd slammed the car door in her face and then come back, sorry, how he'd kept burping because he'd drunk so much beer, and that she noticed he'd begun to wobble his chin like a puppet and that was a habit of his father's she was most afraid he'd inherit.

Jo shook her head slightly and gulped at her wine. "Sometimes I wonder if I want to marry him just to get out of the house." Though her dad drank so much he sometimes couldn't go to work, she usually liked to tell me how smart he was, if he only had more self-confidence, or about the gifts for her he bought through the mail and couldn't afford—a pearl pendant and Italian leather boots. They took care of one another, in their way, and this was the first time I'd heard her talk about him as a burden.

"Do you?" I said.

"I don't know."

"Maybe you should get a place on your own first. David's got his job at the *Vidette*—he's not going anywhere."

Her eyes teared up. "I couldn't do that."

"Why not?"

"I don't have the money."

"How much do you give him?"

"About half." Ever since she'd taken up bookkeeping at the Linden Hotel, I'd suspected she'd been supporting her dad, who seemed to work less and less.

"When did that start?"

"I don't know. It just happened gradually."

She looked radiant in the red light of the candle, with her pale skin and dark lashes. "David thinks he'll be better off on his own after the wedding. Because he'll just have to be."

She sat upright, and her neck seemed to lengthen, and I could see behind her eyes, how she was putting things in order, even if it meant squeezing wishes that didn't exactly fit into boxes of plans where they belonged.

"It's not the only way," I said. "What about your viola?"

She shook her head and made a dismissive tsking sound. "Haven't even practiced in months. I don't have the discipline for it anymore."

"Maybe if you tried harder . . ." I said.

"Will you shut up? I'm not going to college, okay?" She turned her head toward the black-and-white photograph on the wall of a Porter basketball team from twenty or thirty years before. "What good did it do you?"

The muscles in my face tensed. If I pretended this didn't hurt, it almost didn't. "I haven't finished yet," I stammered.

She nodded, still not looking at me. "Look, you go off if you want to. I like it here."

It sometimes seemed the one thing about herself Jo was sure of—she was born and raised in Porter, Indiana, home of Umlacher's popcorn factory and a five-time state championship basketball team. If I at least knew where I belonged, like her, it would be less frightening at those times when I didn't know who I was.

▲   ▲   ▲

Jo never had any patience for my fascination with Hanna. She was "just crazy" or "*some* woman" to her—anyone who had abandoned her family (as Jo's mother had) wasn't worth her time.

Hanna last visited the month after my father died. She'd heard about it too late to come to the funeral. I was fifteen, still immature enough to believe that if she liked us, she'd keep coming back. It was during the period when my mother was keeping me home with her, and it was such a relief to have someone else there with us in that cavernous house.

She wore a black skirt with embroidered white lassos and a black chiffon scarf over her birthmark. I was so excited to see her I tripped over a chair as I led her into the living room. "Mother, look who it is."

My mother came out of the kitchen and her mouth dropped. "You!" For a moment I couldn't tell if she was happy or annoyed, but then she walked over and gave Hanna a hug.

Hanna said, "Are you all right?"

My mother made an "mmmm" sound and pulled away. "It was sudden."

"Catherine, I'm sorry." My mother's face was open, not the way it looked when she'd accepted other people's condolences, smiling and gritting her teeth as if she were enduring punishment.

Hanna looked at me and didn't say anything, maybe because she only seemed comfortable acting cheerful with me, or intimate in a theatrical way, but I thought I knew what she was thinking. *It's awful. There's no way around it.*

She wouldn't try to cover his death with some platitude meant to make you cry or stop crying. She understood the heaviness of things. I stared at her green eyes, her pointed chin, the hair pulled back from her face. I studied the tap dancer's way she maneuvered between the coffee table and couch to finally sit down, crossing her legs. She was wearing black high heels.

"How can you walk in those?" said my mother.

"They *are* wobbly." Hanna extended her foot and circled her toes. She shrugged. "If I fall, at least I'll be well dressed when I do." Her large green eyes were strikingly clear against her aging skin. "Ella," she said, "I saw it beginning the last time I came, but how old were you then, fourteen?"

"Thirteen."

"You're a young woman, my God. I forgot how quickly it happens."

"It's been two years, Hanna," said my mother.

"Two years?" She looked at me, her eyes distracted. "Two years is nothing to us anymore, Catherine, is it?"

I wanted to impress her. "The year after next I'm going to college," I said, ignoring the alarm in my mother's face.

"College?" Hanna said, straightening her skirt. "Wonderful. All that reading you did will pay—I wish I had gone myself now. I would have liked to have studied astronomy or botany."

My mother interrupted her. "I think Ella will go to the teacher's college."

Hanna's face seemed to lose focus, her eyes wandering away from me to the wall, her mouth pulled down. "Here?" The truth was, I hadn't decided where I would go, though I knew it depended on a certain amount of money my parents had saved in the bank, but in that moment, it was all decided for me, and in a way it was a relief to give up the part of myself that would have had to leave her.

From the look on Hanna's face, I thought she would protest, but she just nodded and said, "Oh."

My mother straightened a vase on the table and changed the subject. "The college library asked for Louis's music compositions. He would play there sometimes."

Hanna put her hand on my mother's knee and leaned forward

so that her shoulder touched my mother's. It was an unfamiliar intimate gesture. My mother rubbed her eyes. I always forgot that Hanna was the older one. "You're going to be okay," she said softly, rubbing my mother's knee.

Hanna talked about her job as secretary for an eye doctor, about the apartment building where she lived in Des Moines. "I noticed the Dixie Diner is gone," she said sadly, and we talked for a while about what else had changed since she'd last seen Porter. The air in the living room suddenly seemed hot and close. I rolled up my sleeves, barely glimpsing the leaf-shaped scar as I leaned back into the chair.

"You can't see the moraine from the road anymore either," said my mother.

Hanna suddenly leaned over and grabbed my bicep. "My God, what did you do?" The scar whitened around the edges. I didn't understand at first. She stared down at the scar, squinted. How could she not know what had happened so long ago? No one— not my mother, not Marietta—no one in my family had told her?

My father had a rational way of explaining things, moving his hands flatly in the air, and I might have learned that from him if he hadn't died. It would have been useful—I never knew how to tell people what had happened and hated watching their eyes veer sideways, thinking it had hurt them just to see.

The three of us looked down at the leaf-shaped burn. It gained focus and a frame like a picture on the wall. Gently, I took Hanna's hand off my arm. "It happened a long time ago," I said.

"What?" said Hanna.

"The fire," I said. My mother picked at her forehead as if she were trying to peel it off, then moved sharply to stand up and knocked a crystal dish off the table onto the floor. "Ella, please, go in the kitchen."

I sat down at the table with my biology book, stared down at the scar. I'd thought it wasn't very noticeable, and I rubbed at it hard and tried to imagine it gone. How could my mother not have told her? This new anger seesawed under me. In order to stand steadily on it, I would have to blame her, and even if it had been her fault, even if she had slapped me so hard I fell into the flames, or chased me into them, I couldn't do that.

The pages of my biology book seemed to absorb all the light in the room. I wasn't going to be able to do any homework now. I took the sharp tip of my pencil and poked holes in the diagram of the frog.

Hanna's mistake must have made her want to leave, because I heard the door slam and went to the window to watch them. The wind blew their skirts tight against their legs, and I noticed they had the same figure—slim long legs, a small curved torso. Soon a yellow taxi rocked down the driveway. It had to be from out of town, because Porter's two taxis were blue. Hanna walked across the yard, the tree shade blinking over her. Just before she stepped inside the car, she reached to fix the scarf in back, and the rhinestone button at the nape of her neck caught the light. I wanted to be wearing that dress, stepping into that yellow taxi.

▲   ▲   ▲

The air was powdered with cold that night I drove to the corner of Willow Street, parked away from the streetlight, and walked through the damp grass, past the houses with their sly shutters. I'd been inside the shack behind my old apartment building once before, and knew it would go quickly.

Even though I lived at the hotel now, I was afraid I'd never leave it, that I'd grow old as a night clerk with a postcard collection, an award for reading the most library books, and a habit of drinking a bottle of bourbon a day. But I was also afraid that if I did leave, my mother would let herself waste away to nothing.

She seemed so fragile and disappointed, as if she were waiting for me to do something about it.

The shack wasn't locked. The door groaned open, and a mouse careened past my foot on the gritty floor. There was that smell of dry dirt and chemicals, and I knew it would look accidental enough for the insurance to pay. The landlord had threatened to evict me the third time he smelled smoke lingering on the stairwell, but this wasn't about revenge. What pushed me forward was just the thought that after I saw it, the thrill would be enough to put me to sleep later, and I was so exhausted it was as if I were watching myself from the distance of an arm's length.

I walked in, found a can of paint thinner, and tipped it over near the open window. The sharp smell whirled up to my tongue and nostrils. From the apartment building thirty yards away, the blare of a radio voice startled me: "Ladies, if you think you've found happiness, wait till you hear this—" Somewhere down the block, a car horn bleated. I began to tremble and sweat. As I stood up, the scars on my torso twisted and tingled like separate limbs, with their own nerves and mysterious functions. Picking my way over a lawn mower and rake, I went back outside into the clean air.

A cat with a tail like an antenna ran through the tall grass. I could see into a few of the windows in the apartment building: a lamp on a desk and an arched bedstead, the wavery blue square of a television, bras and slips hung to dry above window-ledge flowers. As I went around the corner, arrowweeds pricked my ankles; then, steadying myself on the shack's grainy wall, I reached the open, paint-flecked window.

I struck a match, let it bud into my fingertips, and dropped it over the sill. Finally. The oily surface of the paint thinner crumpled and sighed. A white flare ribboned the darkness. I ran back, and my heel slipped in the mud as I pivoted around to look.

My scars seemed to shake and cartwheel apart from my will, stinging pleasantly like the first sense of sun. My breathing slowed as the fire's prism colors emerged, twirled and bending. Fuchsia, green, and lavender swam up like fish and gradually disappeared again. I backed away as I watched the walls gently fold in on themselves. A sheen of blue slithered between them, and I held out my hands to feel the strokes of heat. Finally I'd got it started. In the center, near the door, red puckered and grimaced, and the flame pierced the air, split it open like a ragged makeshift mouth.

V

Though it was my job to inspect the rooms each week, the hotel was so old that dirt wasn't easily detectable, but since the funeral I'd noticed more of it, mildew in the seams of the bathroom tiles and handprints on the white walls, rust marks in all the sinks. Dirt was everywhere when your job was to keep things clean. My mother was fierce in her housework. She scrubbed the corners of the kitchen with baking soda and an old toothbrush, she burned evergreen candles in all the bathrooms. The walls, counters, tabletops, were all smooth and bright, but worn down from rubbing like the inside of a shell.

I was writing a quick note to the housekeeper, a matronly woman with cow eyes who called me "honey." "Rug in Room 7 stained." To every problem like this she said, "Oh, dear," as if it were an emergency.

I looked out the window and saw a man walk by with a puppy balanced on his shoulder. A girl swinging a baton skipped up behind him. I went back to my note. "A guest found mouse droppings in the corner near the window in Room 9."

The bells on the door tinkled, and a slant of light skidded on the ceiling. I looked up to see who it was. He stood there holding a tool box and smiling crookedly, a person I'd never seen before, who nodded and threw back his head in this "Aha" way as if he'd been looking for me. "I'm here to fix the sink?" He had a blunt, round nose like the toe of a shoe, blue eyes hooded with dark, spiky lashes, and a very red mouth as if he'd been biting it.

"You must mean the one in the cafeteria," I said, because it often overflowed when the drain got clogged from bits of food.

He raised his eyebrows and looked around at the lobby walls. "Mr. Linden didn't say which one. Could it be one of the sinks in the rooms?" The plaintive lilt in his voice wasn't American, but I couldn't tell what it was. I wanted him to talk more so I could place it.

"Not if he didn't give you a number," I said. His jeans faded around the muscles in his legs, and he wore a clean white shirt with a collar. I'd known only two foreigners in my life, a Mexican woman who worked as a nurse for one of Marietta's friends, who was an invalid, and Mr. Botticelli, my Latin teacher. I'd envied their apartness, a certain lack of history and family that made them graceful in the weightlessness pulling up any strings that had once tied them down.

"The one in the cafeteria backs up a lot—you have to go through the other door." I pointed past the painting of the clown in the toy car.

"Right. This way," he said, turning with a grin. He went through the cafeteria door, whistling in a minor key, something that sounded like a Bach hymn my father had played.

I folded the note to the housekeeper and tacked it to the bulletin board next to the key boxes, where she'd see it in the morning.

A teenaged girl with black hair floated down the stairs to the lobby, rubbing her eyes. She wore a pink bathing suit and rubber sandals and went to look out the window. She slumped down in the green vinyl chair, lifted up her foot, and began picking at her toes. She had the most beautiful skin: pale with shadows of honey and pink in the apples of her cheeks. Just a fine blue vein stalked down her neck, no freckles or moles anywhere, no scratches or bruises or birthmarks. She had the skin of a girl who'd just been born, freakishly pure and creamy. The more I looked, the more her flawlessness seemed impossible, and I wanted to scratch it to see if it was makeup or powder. I was glad when she jumped up, snapping the elastic at the bottom of her suit and bounding out of the lobby.

Just as I was counting the money into the change box, he came back and stood sheepishly at the cafeteria door. He let the door swing closed behind him and walked purposefully up to the desk. I let the quarters slip through my fingers in twos, but he didn't seem to notice I was counting.

"I'm Paul," he said, holding out a hand black with grease. His white shirt with the sleeves rolled was miraculously still clean. I looked up but didn't move. He glanced down, pulled back his hand, and wiped it, front and back, on the seat of his jeans. Even this gesture was tapered and formal as an old-fashioned suit. "Pardon," he said. "I'm pleased to meet you."

I opened the desk drawer, pried loose two old butterscotch candies that had melted into the wood, trying not to meet his eyes. Their unwavering gaze made me uneasy. "Where are you from?"

"My accent isn't gone yet, eh?" His voice was warm and had the fullness of a man much older than he.

I sorted through a handful of pencils and pens, testing the inks on a scrap of paper.

"Poland," he said. "Kruszwica. And you?"

I made piles of stubby pencils and pens that had gone dry. "Porter," I said. It looked as if his deep set eyes could see something in me he wasn't supposed to, and I was relieved when his glance moved to the bank calendar on the wall.

"I was hired yesterday as the security guard. We'll be working together."

I tore the old page from the guest registry and threw it in the trash. It wasn't that I disliked him, but I enjoyed the long, drifty nights at work alone. "Why do we need a security guard? No one's going to try to break in here."

His smile cracked. I watched his lips and tongue turn his words. "Mr. Linden has a new insurance policy."

I got up and wheeled around to pin two bad checks to the bulletin board. I didn't want to be rude, but the situation seemed tricky to me. I didn't know how to take his formality, it could so easily have been sarcastic. When I turned around, he picked up his tool box from the desk and looked at me uncertainly. "I suppose I will see you again—" he said, parting his lips.

"Ella."

"Ella." He nodded as if to agree the name suited me, and he walked out the door, the tools in his box clanking against one another.

The sheen of his foreignness had surprisingly tarnished when I learned he'd be working at the Linden. I took the candle from the old conch on the wall and set it on the desk in front of me. It would be a tricky situation. I fished out a book of matches from my pocket and lit the candle, watched the flame tremor. There was always a blue pearl in the middle, draped in a thin gloss of orange, a pale yellow cowl around that, and then the light. I licked my finger, ran it through the flame, first at the very tip and then lower. Then lower. I didn't feel anything until the wick. The flame stuttered. When I pulled my finger away, I stared, satisfied, at the seared black tip of my nail.

I kept humming to myself the tune Paul had whistled, which sounded so much like a hymn my father had played. Was it Bach? My father had always said his name the way other men said "Lincoln" or "Robert Miller," the local Porter man who had died a hero's death in World War II. "Bach," he said, his mouth and eyes serious as if I could learn something important just from the name.

I hummed the tune again. What was it? The hymns were confused in my head. *Our shelter from the stormy blast . . . And take they our life, goods, fame, child, and wife, they can harm us none.*

Those nights my father walked the two miles to the church alone, even in the snow, he must have heard the rhythms in his steps, in his breath, going over the music he would play in the dark, empty church.

I still couldn't place the tune, but it sounded like that part of the hymn just before the refrain, when you could hear the return to the familiar words and the relief of this made people sing louder.

A sturdy-looking woman in sneakers and stretch pants came down the stairs then and said, "Hello there, young lady. I'm going out now, but we need some more tissues there in Room Four." The way she said "there" as if it were a comma or a throat-clearing let me know she was from Wisconsin. *There* and *and that* had special uses in Wisconsin.

"I'll bring a box right up," I said.

I went to the shelf in the back of the closet for the tissues, climbed the stairs and walked down the hall. My ears were overly sensitive to tics and slips of the tongue, from all those years listening for (and often dreading) the notes my father missed. If he made a mistake on Sunday morning, he'd ask my mother and me in the afternoon if we'd heard the missed note and didn't seem to believe us if we said we hadn't. If we said we had, though, he'd berate himself for it all day until he was too depressed to eat dinner.

I used to go to the church with him sometimes when he was practicing and sit beside him at the organ, turning the pages of his sheet music (I could read music, even though I didn't play an instrument). The empty sanctuary below us was strange and dark, except for the small votive lights between the stained-glass windows and the overhead light shining down on the cross. I liked the church empty and secretive like this, with the pews vacant, the candles unlit. There was a kind of wise calm in its waiting to be filled.

As my father played through the following Sunday's music, I secretly listened for the wrong notes that might slide through the smooth seams of melodies, because they gave me something to count, though I kept the numbers to myself.

I knocked on the door of Room 4, and when no one answered, put the box of tissues on the floor just in front and walked back down the hall.

Music chased the devil away, Martin Luther had said, and I believed it when I looked up at my father, small against the panel of organ pipes, his mouth grim with concentration, his face in profile as serious as if the church were a ship he was steering through a storm. Not everyone appreciated his fervor. He favored stark harmonies, which made the people singing sound out of tune, and he liked preludes and interludes that sometimes made people stumble over the words. Most of them would have been just as happy to let their voices follow Mrs. Eckhart, one of the Sunday-school teachers, banging away on the piano.

Quietly, he composed his own music, but he only occasionally played these pieces at the college chapel, or at home for my mother and me. He wore a small defeated smile, staring down at his hands on the keys, hunched over them as if he were bowing down to this exquisite, odd music like a wordless foreign tongue, and I always wondered where he'd got the ideas for these melodies, where they'd come from.

When I got back downstairs, opened the gate, and went behind the desk, the phone was ringing, each timid shriek annoying me, and I didn't want to answer it. Upstairs I heard the regular thump and clap of someone doing jumping jacks, and the whine of water in the pipes.

▲ ▲ ▲

After the night I saw Mr. Schultz at the Paradise Lounge, I stayed away. But sometimes at work, I'd change into one of my dresses, and I'd happen to meet a man, bleary-eyed from driving or from drinking in the dining car on the train. They'd see the dress and offer some edgy, offhand invitation to watch the late movie on TV, or they'd ask me to bring up extra pillows, and when I got to the room, they'd invite me in for a drink. It became a kind of game. The dresses, like the camouflage fur of certain animals, blended me into the group of other women. When I didn't wear one of them, nothing happened.

Once I took off the dress in the dark, a man could easily be blinded by the softness under his hands and some image of big breasts and rosy flesh he'd seen somewhere. As long as the lights were off, I could have been anyone. My skin would turn numb and smooth as a mannequin's, and a covering like a small, warm washcloth settled between my legs.

I was trying to lose this part of myself so I could get on with my life without it, the way humans now get along without tails and a sixth finger. I'd been thinking I could evolve. I'd been thinking what the scars really made me was a species of one, but then I realized I'd begun to hate this paper doll I became whenever a man touched me. This imaginary piece of skin. Unless I could work up some courage, I knew I'd only become more flimsy and numb.

There was one young businessman who was very skinny with a long, stalky neck. He nervously said he'd heard there was a good late movie on that night. When I went up to his room, I saw that he'd barely touched anything; his suitcase stood upright on the floor. Luckily, the streetlight outside the window had blown out, and the room was dark. We sat side by side on the bed watching an old western for an hour or so, and then turned it off. He leaned into me with a dreamy and distant expression around his lips. He felt fragile, smaller than me, like another woman or a child. I don't think he saw any of the scars, not even the ones on my arms, because he kept his eyes closed or looked at my face, his fingers furtive and light like the feet of a squirrel. He wanted me to sleep there with him and kept wrapping his arms around me every time I tried to get up. "I have this asthma," I finally said, wheezing. "I can't breathe in here." He was so gentle he frightened me.

A couple of weeks later a banker with pouty lips and a vain way of pushing his hair back from his forehead invited me up to his room for champagne. "A customer of mine gave me a whole bottle," he said, winking unevenly. "I can't drink all of it by myself."

After I locked up the desk and turned out the lights, I went upstairs. He filled our plastic cups so the champagne spilled over the edges and was sipping as he brought mine over to me. "Good bubbly," he said.

I looked up at the painting over the bed, a water mill and a sorrowfully laboring horse. The streetlight was right outside the window this time, glaring under the half-drawn shade, and the lamp was on, too, on the bureau all the way across the room. I started to stand up so I could turn it off, but he slung his arm across me and held my hip. "What do you need? Let me get it for you." He was less drunk than I'd first thought.

"I was just going to get that light."

His teeth were yellow, and so were the whites of his eyes. "What for? It's not too bright, is it?" He edged in close to me, and I glanced down at his stomach, pouching over a narrow black belt. I decided not to test whether or not he noticed the scars, so I yawned dramatically. I was about to tell him I had to go when his mouth slammed against mine, his tongue jabbing at my teeth. He quickly unbuttoned my dress, hooked his fingers under the strap of my slip, and yanked it down to my waist. I wrestled away from him, covered myself as best I could, and said, "I have to go."

"No you don't," he said in a gravelly voice and swallowed. He grabbed my shoulder and pushed me back on the bed. He pulled down my slip again. My skin felt hard, as if it were cracking. The red horsehead under my breasts reared up in that harsh light, and the thorny vines unfurled, very red and raised, almost as if they were growing.

He sat back on his heels and combed his fingers through his hair. "What's this?"

He got off the bed and stood looking down with his mouth drawn into a stupid O. I pulled up my dress and shakily buttoned it.

"What happened to you?"

"I was burned."

"You might have told me," he said, as if I'd offended him.

"I might have," I said, standing up. "If I hadn't already decided to leave." He had a heavy face full of cheap longing. Deep bags purpled under his eyes.

He stepped closer and put his clammy hand around my waist.

"Okay, honey. Let's turn out the lights and start all over," he said, nudging me toward the bed.

I pushed his hand away and ran for the door, afraid he'd grab me again. "Poor girl," I heard him say before I closed it behind me. I wanted to kill him.

Halfway down the hall, I saw Jo carrying the books; it was the end of the month, and she was working late. "I was just—" She looked down at my half-buttoned dress, the slip hanging out from one sleeve.

"Don't worry," I said hoarsely. I couldn't bear to look at her fluttering eyelashes, her pink, shocked mouth. This would only make her pity me. Wiping smeared lipstick from my mouth, I said, "I left before it got out of hand."

"Ella," she said softly, shaking her head. "What are you doing?"

The ice machine clattered and hummed. I couldn't think of any way to answer this, so I slipped past her against the wall, went down the hall to my room, and locked the door.

▲   ▲   ▲

If I could remember the fire, I wouldn't need to test the men anymore, and if I could remember, I could help my mother forget, help her lose that guilt, and maybe leave Porter without worrying about her. I couldn't remember the fire any more than I could remember being born, but I wanted to believe the memory lay buried somewhere at the bottom of a box filled with tangled jewelry, that if I searched long and hard, I would find it.

When I closed my eyes, there were flames against the skin-dark of my lids. It happened when I was four. What was fire to me then? Not dangerous, but bright and watery as a reflection; vulnerable and nervous as a cat; amorphous, half hidden, a brilliance rising up out of sleep.

Maybe early on, something had told me there was a way to go

through fire, a way to not let it touch me. There was a stained-glass window I must have seen, held in my mother's lap in the front pew—three bearded men standing calmly in a furnace, the flames at their feet and heads like a frame of poinsettias. Or maybe, as my father read aloud, I'd seen a picture in the *National Geographic* of the Indian men who walked serenely through burning coals, their mouths and brows drawn back as if facing a strong wind.

I rolled over on my side to look out the window near my bed. A bright streetlight turned the dust on the glass white, shadowed the stiff, dead moth between the windowpane and screen. Insomnia was always easier than sleep, but tomorrow I'd dread the guests asking for glasses and soap, the ones who'd have to be turned away, and the tedious job of counting the money.

I pasted details onto the facts I was sure of. We still lived in the white house with the trellis. It was fall. A day when yellow leaves lay thick in halos around tree trunks, and the shivering leaves still on the branches made a sound like falling water. Behind the house, there was a wooden duck whose wings spun frantically in the wind. The wheelbarrow and rake would have looked heavy and immovable the way objects do on overcast, empty days. There was a garden inside a scalloped wire fence. When my mother bent down to pull up a weed, I saw the arched wires bend in against her ankles.

I wasn't sure what was invention or dream, but a few things always came back to me: the breeze under my dress, the way I'd turned out my ankle and stood on the side of my foot, the veined crest at the back of my mother's knee.

Then there were speculations. My mother might have been reaching for a soft, overripe tomato, her face hidden in the plants. She might not have heard me walk away, because of a freight truck that clattered by or someone blaring their radio. I ran toward what must have looked to me then like bright birds rising into the trees, that lacy flutter of shiny feathers, and when my mother saw me fall into the neighbor's burning leaf pile, the flames were struggling and had almost gone out. I always stopped there.

I pulled the blanket around my body, drew up my knees, and curled around them, cocooned the scars as if they might unfurl into something else by the morning: strands of pearls, scarves. Sometimes this was how I tricked myself into sleeping. A dog was barking somewhere down the street, and the small ring swayed at the end of the shade pull. I thought of that banker again, his wheedling voice, *poor girl,* his eyes shallow and dull as old nickels, *she'll never get anyone.*

I tossed to the edge of the bed. The bedsprings squeaked, and the mattress sank in beneath me. I heard a scratching noise in the next room. It was an old hotel; there were mice and spiders, small, thick ones that looked like metal rivets.

As I burrowed under the covers, the scene assembled again in my mind, though the structure never held; it would fall in on itself in a second. Maybe: At breakfast, my parents had argued. My mother had that tight half smile as my father screamed at her. Her hand would shake as she poured the coffee, and when it spilled, he'd get up to leave for school. After lunch, we would have gone outside. Strolling the yard, she picked up dead leaves and crumbled them in her hand, letting the pieces fly behind her. The grass scratched at my ankles. My mother had become a stranger with a hard mouth and a stiff walk. As I moved into the neighbor's yard, I would look back to see if the stranger was still there, if it was she or my mother. Surely my mother would have noticed by now how far I'd gone. But it was the stranger with her head bent toward the ground, her lips moving slightly. Her hair flagged in the breeze, and then I lost her in the smoke.

On the walls of the room, the moon cast a filmy green light.

Under the weight of my head, my arm had grown numb. I let the stiff hand drop off the bed, and slowly the blood prickled back to it. Somewhere down the street, a car horn blared. I squinted to see the hands of the clock in the dark: 5:10. In three hours I would get up and dress. Dark pants and a red sweater, comfortable shoes.

Each time I thought of the fire, the picture was new, pieces of other memories constellating around the things I was sure of, rearranging themselves and then shaken up and scattered again like the designs in the end of a kaleidoscope. I wanted to remember so my mother could forget. It was unseasonably cold, the sunlight brittle. A thin frost on the water spigot. I tried to turn it on, but the metal handle stung my fingers. My mother moved hurriedly because she wasn't wearing a coat. She was taking the shirts down from the clothesline, the sleeves frozen into odd, grand gestures, and she piled them in a basket beside her.

There was that musky smell of dead leaves, and the frost made the grass blades crumble like glass. I was pretending to fly. Running as fast as I could, I leaped into the air and threw up my hands, so that I felt temporarily weightless (that feeling I had in elevators, swimming pools). As I came down, the grass splintered under my feet. When my mother called, I looked back and laughed. I kept running until the air looked watery, as if the light had melted, and I was coughing and suddenly warm and falling.

When I couldn't sleep, it was as if my body had to call me back to it, arms and legs tensed up and sore from the effort. In the morning the sheets would be kicked to the bottom of the bed and tangled around my ankles.

▲   ▲   ▲

Paul started work in November. Each hour he made the rounds of the hotel, checking the locks and windows, often stopping at the desk to ask me a question. "What's the word in English," he asked, "for a point like this in a building?" He drew a roof in the air with his finger, curved tendrils on each side.

"Alcove."

He nodded. "There's an alcove over the soda machine outside. It would be easy for someone to climb up on it to reach a window." His accent was rich and polished like a piece of antique furniture. "I'll check that on my next round."

I wasn't worried. "Fine."

His heavy, careful footsteps and the strict click of the locks as he checked them made me feel watched, studied, and what I liked most about working at the Linden Hotel was that I could often lose myself in the anonymity of strangers. Many times, I would have to go into their rooms to deliver towels or check on a complaint, and if no one was there, I'd sometimes go in and study the suits and dresses hung on the hangers in the bare closet, the scatter of pills and coins on the dresser, the rumpled look of the bed, and the scents caught in the curtains and sheets, and I could enter another life for a while in those vacant rooms. But now that Paul was there, of course, it was impossible.

"The door's ajar in Room Nine," he said. "Is there a guest there?"

I explained that it was a signal to the housekeeper that this should be the first room she cleaned in the morning.

"It's not safe," Paul said, straightening his collar. "Anybody could walk in. Why not put a note up for her?" There was something so earnest about him, as if he were trying hard to make up for something he'd lost—money? a girl?

He put a stick of gum into his mouth, and despite the desk between us, I could smell the spearmint caught in the white of his teeth. I wanted to tell him to relax, that it was nice of him to try so hard, but he didn't need to prove himself to me, and we didn't really need a security guard anyway. "What did you do before?" I asked.

"In Poland? I was a messenger. I delivered things on a bicycle." He was used to worrying about being on time, doing exactly what someone told him to do. That was the problem—he wasn't used to walking up to a door and finding no one behind it, he was used to urgency. But I wanted him to stop asking me so many questions.

When he left the lobby to check the grounds outside, I took out my plastic-covered library book, a biography of a school-teacher in Africa, but couldn't concentrate on the black lines floating in the yellowed pool of the page. It happened sometimes that the very act of looking at a page abstracted me, took me someplace else. I started thinking about Hanna, how she had a habit of drumming her fingers on her lips as if to make sure her mouth was still there. She'd once come back home with a geisha doll for me from San Francisco, a bald white girl with a set of ten black, complicated wigs, each one as exotic as a hothouse flower. "In Japan," she told me, "men pay women just to look beautiful and converse." Because she wasn't meant to look anything like me, the doll, with delicate painted features and a body of sticks and a cushion, didn't seem as sinister as most dolls, and I liked playing with the wigs. Another time when I was small Hanna brought me red sequined slippers with heels like Dorothy's in *The Wizard of Oz*. After she left, my mother looked strangely hurt when she said, "Those aren't for little girls."

But if Hanna didn't always know what was appropriate, that was part of her appeal. When I was only eleven, she'd sent me a bottle of expensive perfume, Joie de Paris, and a pair of dangling rhinestone earrings that I hid under my mattress as soon as I unwrapped them.

The dull-faced clock on the wall clicked, and the hands shifted as I looked up, surprised at the time. Absently, I'd slipped off my shoes, unpinned my hair. This homely lobby, with its clown painting and trophy case and worn gold carpet, was as familiar to me by then as my bedroom in my mother's house, and sometimes, if I hadn't slept the night before, I could even put my head down on the desk and doze off.

Paul came back and sat in one of the fat vinyl chairs against the wall. He tapped the heel of his boot against the floor and looked up at the glass trophy case. "Mr. Linden must have been good. My soccer team, we never won." I imagined Paul running in shorts and knee socks on an impossibly green field, a cardboard-looking castle in the background.

"He made the basket that won the state championship," I said. "All the way from the other side of the court. People still talk about it, and if you look behind the trophies, you'll see the newspaper articles." Paul's busy feet and eyes reminded me of a landscape passing through a train window, his features rushing and changing, and I couldn't quite look at him. "He spends most of his time at the golf course now," I said. "Once in a while he checks on us." It was true. There were long hours when I had nothing to do, and sometimes I finished a book in a night, or spent an hour talking on the phone to Jo. "The only reason he keeps the place open, I think, is because it belonged to his family."

Paul raised one eyebrow as if he didn't believe me. Almost no one could tell when I was lying, but sometimes people thought I was lying when I was really telling the truth—when my guard was down, some of the falseness must have seeped out.

"Is it always this quiet?" he asked.

I leaned forward over the desk and finally looked straight at his face. His eyes were dark blue and clear, defined as an actor's in a silent film. He stopped chewing his gum. "Sometimes even quieter," I said.

▲　　▲　　▲

Setting a fire was like making a summer from childhood, the way the sun winked at you in the trees, scattered sequins on the surface of the lake, and made its rays walk over to you and back in the water. All that wind and shine—that feeling of leaning toward something.

Sometimes I thought I could travel through fire if I was careless enough. I could walk straight through it and feel its silk, its nervous light on my dress, until I got to the other side: Paris, China.

▲　　▲　　▲

Jo lost her usual precision when Paul was around, dropping pencils, fiddling with the ends of her cropped hair. He told her that Polish women cut their hair short only when someone had died or when they'd given up on love, but he liked hers. "It stays out of my way at least," she said, uncomfortably shifting her feet.

The only rule he broke was taking milk from the refrigerator in the hotel's small cafeteria. After it closed, no one was allowed inside, but he had a key. I imagined him alone in the dark there, steering past the chrome table and grill to the refrigerator, where he'd rummage for a bottle, his face and fingers numb with cold. As he walked back out toward the door, only a little guilty, potato peels and bread crumbs would stick to the soles of his shoes. The first sip would taste chalky and sweet, and as he walked through the door to the lobby, it would loosen his tongue.

His hands were long and tapered, and he moved them in the air when he talked like a professor or a magician. His features were an odd mix of the fine and the coarse, dark-blue eyes, wide round nose, thin light-brown hair, lips that looked painted. The two sides fought with one another, and it made his face hard to pin down.

On his breaks, he'd bring a glass of milk to the lobby and sit down in one of the vinyl chairs, red or forest green. I was usually reading by that time, and though we set up fragile pieces of small talk, the conversations didn't stand up. In the silences between us, we'd hear fragments of talk from the rooms upstairs. The voices wafted down to us, faint and blurry as sounds dropped out of a dream. After a few nights, Paul tried to catch my eye when this happened, but I ignored it. I didn't want to be his work buddy. I wanted our familiarity to remain utilitarian and slight, nothing to worry about. Still, he insisted on stopping by the desk every two hours, as if I were one of the things he was supposed to check on.

▲   ▲   ▲

I was five or six when my father explained it to me. "You don't remember. I was at work." He bent down until his face was even with mine, and as he spoke, his voice held each word like a broken bone. "Your mother was in the yard with you. Next door someone was burning leaves. You were always curious and wanted to see things up close." He wasn't looking at me but at the laces wrapped several times around the ankles of his boots. "It was an accident. If anyone asks you why your skin looks this way, you just tell them that."

I was sitting in the tire swing and put my hands into the darkness of the tire until I couldn't see them anymore, and imagined what it would be like not to have them. I leaned forward to look at the dirty ribbon of white paint around the rim of the tire, circling me in a way that made me feel chosen. "If anyone asks," I said, "I'll tell them once I flew up to the sun and got burned."

He kissed me on the cheek, stood up, and walked away toward the house. It was hard for him to tell me things. I pulled up my blouse to examine my stomach, touched the silky, finned ridges of the scars.

▲   ▲   ▲

My father was right, the children would ask. Even though my parents sent me to Grace Lutheran, the school adjacent to our church where my father taught music. "What's that melting on your arm?" And it wasn't usually enough to tell them it was an accident. To avoid the questions I didn't say much to anyone, and this made me seem strange. On top of this, I had an exaggerated way of walking, with my head raised to look above the heads of other children, dragging my feet in long slow strides. It was the way I'd imagined Cleopatra or Mary Magdalene would have walked. I also had a habit of pretending to be different characters from the comics and would sometimes refuse to say anything I couldn't imagine inside one of those clouds over their heads. This rule often excused me from talking, but made the other children think I was even weirder.

In grade school I had one friend, another outsider, a skinny black girl with red hair named Anita. Her family lived in Gary, but her mother drove her to Porter each day so she could attend a good Christian school. She was hoping to protect Anita, as my parents hoped to protect me, from the cruelty of children who didn't know they should act like Jesus. And though we probably weren't teased as much as we would have been at the public school, we weren't well liked or included either: Those children were afraid of us. In the end, our parents' efforts only allowed us to put off for a little while the inevitable, and when it came to me at least, I resented not being better prepared.

Anita and I spent all our time together: We pretended we were

refugees escaping a war and hid under the clamoring gym bleach-
ers; we pretended we were peasant girls and knew how to make
poisons or potions with dandelions from the playground; we pretended we were missionaries in India feeding the poor and starving (squirrels). When Anita moved to Michigan in the sixth grade,
I begged my mother to let me come home for lunch so I wouldn't
have to eat at a table alone, but she wouldn't let me. "You'll make
another friend," she said. Every day I wore the green ribbon Anita
had given me tied around my neck.

One afternoon I sat at a desk in an empty classroom reading
when Scott came in. He was a boy with an elfin nose and bright
eyes who already, at ten, walked holding his arms away from his
body, so his biceps would look big. "What are you doing in here?"
he said, poking his head in the door.

"Nothing." My father was in a meeting, and he'd asked me to
wait for him.

Scott grinned with small even teeth. In the bathroom there
were hearts drawn around his name in the stalls. "You're a brain,"
he said.

I closed the book and put it in my satchel, trying to be friendly.
He came inside the classroom and grabbed a piece of chalk from
the tray under the board. "Let's see," he said, as he began writing
on the board. "Ella sucks . . ." He turned around. "Who do you
like?"

No one. I like no one. A lump swelled in my throat.

"Barker?" He was a large, slow boy nicknamed "Injun" because
of his size and olive skin. "He likes you, I hear." He wrote in
Barker's name, then slowly erased it. Late-afternoon light razored
against the window. Ouside, a ball bounced against pavement.

"What's this?" My father was at the door. Scott threw down
the chalk and quickly erased the board. "Get out of here," my
father said in a voice so low you could barely hear it, his knees

popping in and out, his hands pressed flat in his armpits as if to keep them from flailing out.

It wasn't that I resented him for coming into the room and seeing that—what I regretted was that I couldn't have scared Scott away myself.

My father was especially worried about me that year. I was at the age he'd been when his own parents had died in the car accident, "smashed into a tree in the rain" was always how he put it, specifically, as if he still had to rehearse the details to himself. Driving me to school in his truck, he would offer me a lot of advice out of the blue. He'd be listening to the crackly news on the radio and suddenly say, "If you smile and look people in the eye when you talk to them, they will always like you." Or he'd be quizzing me on history dates or spelling words and interrupt to say, "As long as you're honest, people will listen." I think he didn't have a clue how to help me.

What had saved him, he believed, from a life as a meatpacker or farmhand, was the library, and he began to take me with him more often to the one in Porter.

There had been a library down the street from the orphanage in Munster. He'd gone there almost every day after school for seven years, and when he graduated, won a scholarship to IU in Bloomington, where he'd studied music. "Without that library," he used to say, "I would have just shrunken up." Every year he donated money to the Porter Library, and because of this, his name was engraved on a copper plaque near the entrance.

"It's for the invisible part," he would say, pointing at his head, when we stood at the circulation desk. *The part no one can see. The place that's not scarred.* Wilma Kohl, thumping the date-due stamp on our cards, would smile with her little red mouth. She wore bifocals on a string of bright Indian beads and had a mole on her neck like a pendant. My father would lean toward her with a snappy word about the weather or the popcorn festival, and she would say something like, "I couldn't agree with you more."

He had to keep renewing all the lengthy books on philosophy and history he liked, because he could absorb only a few pages at a time. He would hold a book open with one hand and peer into it, one hip elegantly jutted to the side, the brick-colored spines accordioned past him on the shelf. Even when boys ran and slid on the slick floor, or a mother scolded her girl for ripping out a page, he didn't look up.

My favorite books that year were romances, and except for the ones in the "Classics" section, they were kept on stacks behind a curtain in a section marked "Adult." If my father was preoccupied, I could sneak behind the curtain, read as much as I could, sweating in the close air, then mark the page where I'd left off with a bobby pin. If he'd caught me, he probably wouldn't have minded, but I didn't want him to know I thought about those things and would have been mortified.

I remember one book about a beauty with a port-wine stain on her forehead. A handsome doctor fell in love with her and discovered a way to remove birthmarks, but after he removed hers, she fell in love with a race-car driver, an arrogant man, whom, in the beginning, she hadn't liked at all. Almost all of the heroines, in fact, fell in love with the very men they'd loathed in the beginning. This happened so often I began to think this was the way love worked, and wondered if my mother had begun by disliking my father when they'd met at that picnic, and if I would end up with Russ, the bully who called me "Chicken Skin."

Coming out from behind the curtain I'd see my father in the aisle stooped over a book, his small shoulders shadowed, and when I came closer, his frown of concern.

VI

▓▓▒░▓▒▒▓▒▒░▒▓▒▒▒░▓▒▒░▒░▒▓▒▒▒▒░▒▒▓░▒▒▒░▒▓▒▒░▒░

Sadly fiddling with the button of her blouse, as loose on her now as the white choir robe she used to wear, my mother had asked me to go to church with them that Sunday and to lunch afterward at the Housemans.

We sat near the front, behind the Zeitlers with their six combed and curled children, each holding a small toy. Pastor Beck looked surprised when he saw me from the pulpit. He closed his eyes and prayed for a moment, then rose up on his toes and blossomed, as if God had made him taller and brighter. I'd always liked him because he'd denied ever hearing my father miss a note, knowing, I thought, how much it upset him.

While Pastor Beck preached, a horn of light blasted through the high, square windows near the ceiling. I looked over at the stained-glass window with the Holy Spirit dove arrowed down at the apostles with serrated flames on their tongues. Finding it hard to listen, I thought about the time a man stood up in the front pew, though the directions in the bulletin clearly said "Congregation remain seated." All around him, people whispered. Pastor Beck had made an odd motion with his hand, pushing it down as if a little dog were jumping on his leg and he were slapping its head. A few people, unsure who was right, stood up with him, then sat down again, like children playing musical chairs. The man stood there, stiff as the prow of a boat, one tail of his suit jacket stuck to his waist with static, and my father chuckled so loudly from up in the balcony that people turned around and looked up.

The only time he had sat next to me was the service when one of the steward's sisters-in-law was in town and wanted to play the organ. He was so upset at her mistakes, he tore his bulletin into little squares that he let snow on the floor below us.

Even now the lack of him made it hard for me to concentrate, and the high-school girl's pedantic jag through the first hymns had annoyed me. Halfway through the sermon, I stood up, wriggled past knees and dress shoes to the side aisle, and walked out to the narthex. Staring at the cluttered bulletin board, I waited for Marietta and my mother to come out.

When we arrived at the Housemans', my mother leaned her crutch against the wall and sat down in a rocking chair near the table. No one had said anything about how thin she was, though I'd noticed the shock in Marietta's face when she'd got into the car, her red dress hanging from her bony limbs like a deflated balloon. Erma Houseman must have assumed it would be rude to notice a woman's thinness when her father had just died.

None of the Housemans' clocks was set to the right hour, and whenever I was there, I felt time getting heavier, this humid thickening in the air. Erma had hair dyed the color of molasses and an aggrieved voice, as if life was simply too hard for her. She said I should go say hello to Fred Houseman and Russel Frye, and as I walked into the living room, I heard Marietta and Erma begin to argue about how long the pie would take.

Fred was standing at the fireplace, and Russel Frye sat in a chair. The tiny cottage of a cuckoo clock perched on the mantel. Against the wall stood a grandfather clock with a stern face that I'd always thought of as Fred's twin brother. He had a tall, square body, his eyes and mouth thin, even lines. Russel and Fred were talking about the tornado that had touched down the week before. Russel Frye pushed his glasses to the bridge of his pink nose. "We were lucky that time," he said. "No one was hurt."

"I can hear it when a twister gets close," Fred said, jiggling the change in his pockets. "I'd know it just from the sound—that high-pitched whistle—whether or not to go down. And that one was at least five miles off."

I told him I'd stayed at the front desk, even when I'd seen the hail balls, that I hadn't taken shelter in the basement with the guests. Russel's ruddy face looked stricken. He was a pharmacist and valued caution the way an athlete values strength or speed. I traced a leaf pattern on the couch.

"The problem is, you don't have enough respect for the weather," said Fred Houseman. "You have to know it. When you're out in the fields and you see a storm blow toward you or when a drought turns everything to stone, then you see how small we all are, how insignificant." His son had died in Vietnam, and he always seemed sorry that he himself hadn't yet collided into a danger big enough for him.

Russel turned to me. "Henry taught you better than that." He clicked his tongue and crossed his legs so that his pants hitched up to expose the white patch of skin over his black sock. I wondered if he'd meant more than what he said, if he'd heard about my trips to the Paradise Lounge.

I started to agree and shake my head at my own carelessness, but something stopped me. "My grandfather worried too much," I said. "He had too much on his mind all the time."

"You'll see," Russel said. "The older you get, the harder it is to avoid." Erma called us into the dining room. He uncrossed his legs and heaved himself up from the chair.

Erma had made German food, as always, heavy dishes the color and texture of rocks. We sat down around the steaming platters and bowls. "Shall we pray?" said Fred. We bowed our heads as he recited the prayer in an even voice with an undertone of anger, his awkward imitation of authority. "Come, Lord Jesus, be our guest . . ."

He served the beef roladen from a large silver tureen, and we passed around the potatoes and sauerkraut, the buttered green beans, and the small, heel-shaped rolls. "You look pale, Catherine," said Russel. "You'd better take seconds today," said Fred, chuckling as he spooned meat onto her plate.

It's not a joke, I thought. *She's starving.* At first, the polite clattering of yellow silverware on china plates muffled any conversation. Food was the one vice the men allowed themselves, and they cut, speared, and chewed greedily, as if it provided them with some answer to a question that had been dogging them for a long time. If my grandfather had been there, he'd have nodded in thanks to Erma with each bite of a new dish. They all tasted like pickles to me. I kept looking at the place where he usually sat, where Russel was now. It made me angry to think they might have invited him to make my grandfather's absence less obvious.

My mother smiled at whoever was talking, pushing the food around on her plate as if she were looking for some detail in the china pattern underneath. Fred and Russel were complaining about Plymouth Steel, how it would bring blacks closer to Porter. The buttery string beans began to make me nauseous, and I wished I hadn't agreed to come, or that I could leave. "People just aren't going to stand for it," said Fred, lifting his chin. As I watched them talking, the skin on their faces seemed to slide forward and, in that dim light, dripped a little around the stubble of their beards.

I untied the little purse of meat in the beef roladen, scraped the pickle and bacon from the inside, and took a bite of bland meat. Marietta and Erma started to argue about which was better for you, eggs or oatmeal. "Eggs are the purest kind of energy," said Erma.

"But they're bad for the blood," said Marietta. I looked at her rouged high cheekbones, the skin above them sunken, at her wide-set eyes thickly mascaraed in crinkled lids, and the wrinkles pursing her red lips. Old people still talked about how beautiful she had been, but it had somehow misshapen her, I thought, twisted her faculty for empathy and swelled the muscle that protected her heart. Why wasn't she more worried about my mother?

I pushed away my plate and folded my arms over my stomach. "The spooks tried to buy that house on Locust," said Fred. My father wouldn't tolerate this kind of talk. His best friend at the orphanage had been black. His name was Roger, and he'd gone on to become an engineer in California. My father would have said something like "They have as much right to live here as you do," and Fred and Russel would have resented him for it, maybe even nodded to one another in confirmation of his pretension.

"Ella," said my mother, "do you eat enough eggs?"

I shrugged. They were putting up a smug gate, a white fence with a stubborn lock, defending themselves from fear. But fear might have made them humble; it might at least make them feel something. "Before you know it, we'll have South Chicago at our doorstep."

I looked down at my plate, at the smear of potato salad, the flecks of pink bacon, the sauerkraut that reminded me of worms. I wondered if this was how my mother had lost her appetite, disgusted by all the endless chewing and talk.

Erma was blinking back tears. "When we were girls, Porter was a hundred-percent American. When we were young, something

like this would have been taken care of. It wouldn't have been
allowed to happen."

My mother was trembling, trying to look at anyone's face but
mine. Erma smoothed her hair and bobbed her head. "I want to
show you something, Ella," she said. She got up from the table
and went over to the closet. While she rummaged in its cluttered
darkness, Marietta tried to change the subject again. She laid her
voice out over the table like an extravagant piece of purple velvet.
"Of course, we had things like diphtheria to worry about when
we were girls, too. They called it the monster. It was so sad to see
the little coffins, the tiny blue fingers and noses, as if they were
turning into china dolls, these beautiful little children."

There was an old photograph on the wall—a spirit picture—
of a mother and father sitting in front of a house. Next to them,
the giant cut-out figure of a toddler in a christening dress floated
over the yard, one of the Housemans' dead siblings.

Erma came back to the table, holding a book with yellowed
pages that had to be unlocked like a diary. She took out a tiny
key, turned it in the lock, and unhooked the clasp, opened it in
front of me to a creased poster that said, "Churchgoers, the
Women of the Klean Up Society of America invite you to a social
followed by a rally for America." She turned the page. There was
a newsbill that said, "Go to Church Sunday—One of the Fore-
most duties of a Klanswoman is to WORSHIP GOD. Every Klanswoman each Sunday should attend the Church of her choice."

Marietta cleared her throat and fidgeted in her chair. Erma
smoothed down a wrinkled corner. "Isn't this something?" she
said affectionately. She turned the page to a photograph of a
crowd in white robes, a large cross burning beside them. I noticed
the big bows on some of the shoes, the two pairs of high heels,
and it suddenly hit me that *these were women.* My face and chest
got hot. Erma started singing, "Beneath this flag that waves above,

This cross that lights our way, You'll always find a sister's love, In the heart of each Tri-K." I turned the page, and though they were much younger, I recognized them: Erma Houseman and Marietta and three others. Then the same crowd, but without their masks, their faces solemn and plump. My mother got up and began to clear the table. "It was a delicious dinner, Erma. Thank you."

"Mother," I said, before she got to the kitchen, "were you one?" She didn't answer, and the door swung closed behind her.

"Oh, she doesn't remember," said Erma Houseman. "But she went around with us to the rallies, to potluck suppers, and when we had sewing circles. Marietta carried her in a little sling."

Marietta put her hand over the photo album so I couldn't turn the page. She tried to sound teasing, but she was too nervous. "That was so long ago. It's all supposed to be secret. You know, you're breaking all the codes."

"What difference does it make? Practically everyone we knew is dead now anyway." Erma Houseman turned to me. "What I'm trying to say, Ella, honey, is if you get your girlfriends together, you can talk some sense into these young people, make them see the threat of the Negro, the Jew, the foreigner, make them see this moment of danger." She was more excited and animated than I ever remembered seeing her, and looking up, speechless, at her glinting eyes, I realized she'd made a career of this.

A short grandfather clock chimed grandly. "There's no danger," I stammered.

When I was a girl, the Klan ghosted among the people we knew like guilt. From the house at night, even safe in my room, I could sometimes hear their rallies in the fields, the men shouting and the singing that sounded like heretical hymns. I saw a burning cross only once. I was with my parents coming home from a potluck supper—and though my father cursed under his breath, neither of them said anything else. I could feel their hope that I wouldn't ask about it like a hand around my throat. I was very young and assumed it was a grave marker for a child who'd accidentally burned to death.

"Look how pretty your grandma looks," Erma said, pointing to a picture of Marietta in a white robe at a scene that looked like a wedding. She had a wreath of lily-of-the-valley flowers in her hair. Her face was unlined and innocent-looking, but I saw in the turn of her mouth, in the tentativeness and the way she held her body, an unspeakable fear. I'd seen a slighter version of it before and always thought it was fear remaining from those years when she was a beautiful girl, envied and hunted. Now I saw it was something else, too.

I barely remember what happened after that. There was some talk about the vacation the Housemans were going on the next day. My mother, despite her crutches, managed to clean up the dinner dishes before anyone else got up from the table. I made up some excuse about work so I could leave. "You're going already?" said Fred.

"Come back anytime," said Erma.

Marietta looked into my face and kissed me on the forehead, something she hadn't done since I was a girl, and my mother, hobbling, followed me to the door. "I'm worried about you," she whispered.

I looked at the pointed tip of her shoulder, the elbow, thick now in her bony arm. Her eyes looked scared but steady. I'd never find out how much she knew about me, and now she pretended we'd just heard and seen something nostalgic and incidental, though she couldn't have done it if my father were there; it would have enraged him. There was a new hollow, lower in her cheek, just above her jaw, where I wanted to slap her, see her shocked into pain, but I didn't touch her. "Don't worry," I said. "I'll be okay."

"I will worry," she said. "You know that."

▲   ▲   ▲

That night all the lamps in my room seemed to ooze light, and I preferred the dimness, with its blurry outlines and shadows, where my thoughts could remain clear and bright. What had my grandmother done? I tried to picture her in that white robe, holding a torch, marching in a parade, but her face disintegrated in these scenes. I saw only robes and K's and crosses. What must she have thought of my father, with his black friends from the orphanage and the way people minded what they said around him, and my girlhood friend Anita with her shock of reddish hair—had Marietta grown out of that hatred, or had she been holding it back?

What bothered me most was that I'd fallen right in step with them, my silence complicit—as if I'd marched up behind them in that photograph in a matching white robe—when the whole time I'd felt about to combust with everything I didn't say, arms and legs blown off from the pressure, head stuck up in the ceiling, my insides strewn all over the table. They probably would have found a way to ignore that, too. I saw their calm faces again, their averted eyes, the visible relief when I left, and knew what it reminded me of: each time Hanna had said good-bye to us.

The next night I drove down Lincoln toward the sign for the drive-in, a twirling root-beer mug with foam (where beehives supposedly nested), and I turned down Locust toward the Housemans', naming to myself the items probably in their cluttered garage: their dead son's limp-necked rocking horse, the clocks Fred couldn't fix, household cleaners, boxes of nails, seed

packets and fertilizer, paint remover and bent rakes—all of it
tinder.

I parked at the corner and walked to the house. There was a
light on in the picture window, a lamp they must have set on a
timer while they were away in Wisconsin. Laughter and the idling
snores of cars wafted over from the drive-in beyond the trees.

I tried the door on the side of the garage. It was locked, so I
used a stick to break one of the windowpanes and reached
through the broken glass to the door handle, heard it click open
from the inside, and pulled my hand back through the broken
glass. I went in and flipped the light switch.

Two hollow grandfather clocks leaned against a wall near a pile
of gray wood scraps. In the corner, cans of paint with crusted lids
crowded against paintbrushes and a rusty bucket, next to bundled
piles of newspaper. A mop and hoe poked out from the center of
three stacked old tires, and next to the garden hose tangled high
up on hooks in the wall, an old white shirt with brown stains
hung over the top rung of the ladder. The lawn mower leaked gas
next to the wheelless bike with bent handlebars.

Jittery from not being able to eat all day, I went over to the
front garage door, unlocked it at the side, and helped it slither
into the ceiling.

Spilled oil mottled the concrete floor, which would probably
make it look accidental. A power saw lay on its side, still plugged
into its socket near the front. Crouching so I could see its yellowed
cord, I dropped a match into a fold where a hair of gold wire
pricked through the rubber. It sputtered out. I dropped another
match in the same place, but it went out after a couple of seconds.
"Stubborn," I heard my grandfather saying. "Obstinate."

Rummaging in my dress pocket for another match, I heard a
rustle, a flounce, in the bushes. Hurrying to the back, I flipped
off the light and held myself against the wall. *I should have waited,*

I thought. *I should have been more careful.* Footsteps swept the lawn. I studied the megaphone of streetlight at the end of the driveway. *Someone's been keeping an eye on the house. They wondered why the garage door was left open. Someone spied a light from their parking space at the drive-in.* I listened so hard my ears began to ache with the march of my eardrums. I hallucinated a figure that disappeared, heard the hard thrum of silence like the wheel of a record after the music. I pressed my fingernails into my palms and squeezed shut my eyes until they spasmed, sure I deserved to be caught. Standing there counting to myself, I willed my body to be still and tried to blanket my mind as if it were a torch they might see. It took a long time for the fear to lift, for my heart to stop racing so I could tell myself it was nothing, a cat, a branch falling from a tree.

What I had to do was get the thing started. There were several theories for why I had to do this tangled and swirled in my head, but what I remember most was how I wanted to make the Housemans lose their smugness. I had this idea that they wouldn't be able to hide their regrets anymore in the garage with their son's old toys and the cabinet that Fred had never finished, because all of this would be burned up and exist only in their minds, so they'd have to think of it all, their long pasts, and the things they worked so hard to ignore and the things they should have been ashamed of but weren't—all that history, the full weight of it, the things that made them just as human as the black people they hated, would come crashing back, I thought, when they came home to find their garage burned up. And they would know that keeping certain people out of town wouldn't be enough to keep them safe, because no one was safe.

I turned on the light just long enough to find the can of gasoline near the lawn mower. I took it out the front and spilled it all over the bushes and lit them. The waxy leaves rustled as they caught fire. I went back in and threw two matches at the electrical socket where the saw was plugged in until it sparked and exploded up the wall. The whole front of my body felt hot.

The fire rolled along the cement floor and weaved among the limbs of the bicycle, then hid behind a pile of cardboard boxes. I waited. I could hear it breathe back there before the boxes began to glow.

At first it was a little like drinking—that bitter release of yourself into alert oblivion. I went out the front and down to the end of the driveway near the mailbox to watch. My eyes teared up in the brightness. In the back of the garage, the fire trailed among the paint cans, until one by one they burst into dandelions, their ragged petals quivering in the hot wind that blew over the clutter. The left side of the garage roof shook, then tore off and flipped onto the holly bushes, and the branches turned to orange wires. All the flames rippled over the walls, scrubbed them until they collapsed. "Bowled over." I heard Marietta's voice. Had she ever watched a black family's house burn?

A high tree branch caught fire, and a garbled screech and flapping went into the tree with the popping of wood. Beside me, the grass whined, and a ball of flames darted up to a branch, jerked at a fork that caught fire, then fell down, and the whine stopped just before I smelled the squirrel's burnt flesh.

For a while I lost myself in the shirring of flames and the cackle of wood. When I looked down again, I was surprised to see that dress, those arms, those laced-up shoes. "You're not yourself," my mother had said, even the time I'd come home with blood dried on my leg, smelling of tree bark, and it was true, just as it was true now. I didn't dare look to see who it was I was.

Watching the flames shore up the empty flowerpots and the path of round stones that led to the back door of the house, I was struck with awe—this force was miles beyond me, and there was no way to tame it. Was that what made me so unsteady? I lay down in the grass while a car passed behind me on the street.

Loud cracks caught in the wind. From the ground, I looked for the red heart where the fire lived, and the flames wrapped around one another like veins, and they braided so tightly it made it impossible for me to see inside them to what I had to see.

I stood up, ran down the street, then walked through the scrawny trees to the pickup window at the drive-in. A few cars were parked in the slanted spots next to the intercoms. I peered inside the window, ordered a soda, and turned to watch a young couple in a station wagon, purple and pink smoke strung up in the trees behind them.

"See that?" I said to the girl behind the counter, pointing.

She gasped, and I felt short of breath, a tingling under my fingernails. "Something's on fire."

▲   ▲   ▲

Not wanting to go home to the hotel yet, I got back in my car and drove to the liquor store, bought some bourbon, and parked in the empty lot on Lincoln. Crumpling the bag around the bottle's neck, I gazed across the street into the lit windows of the Big Wheel Restaurant. Two waitresses glided in and out of sight, and a heavy man in overalls guided himself to a booth. I took a long sip, felt the bourbon blanket my chest. Now, after I'd heard the sirens, it seemed I'd seen a knowing look in the counter girl's freckled face—she'd smelled the smoke on my clothes, spotted a scab of soot. She knew. After she called the fire department, she'd called the police. "There was this woman," she'd said. "Long, dark hair, her eyes a little too bright." I smelled the sleeve of my dress, talcum powder. I searched my skin for black marks.

I looked at the car next to mine with no wheels and a FOR SALE sign stuck to its windshield and drank until my eyes burned. Loud guitar music splashed out of the window of a passing car. The parking lot of the restaurant began to empty, and the street lights cleaved the empty black asphalt. I felt a certain shimmery void—a longing, as if I'd forgotten something back there at the House-mans'.

The air inside the car had a stale, sweet smell, dirty hair and sweat. I found some crackers to eat among the frayed maps in the glove compartment. Already my memory of the fire was fading, and that panicked me. It didn't usually fall apart so quickly.

The salt tasted good after the sweetness of the whiskey, and I listened for more sirens. The yellow spokes and red rim neon around the Big Wheel sign began to spin around the white-lined rectangle that said: BEETS WINGS, and slowly, the warmth I'd wanted seeped into my arms and legs. The green of my car floated over the tables in the restaurant window.

For a long time I concentrated on the hypnotic revolutions of the neon wheel, the movement of a circle: whole and empty. I must have been drunk or strangely dreaming, because the wheel began to lower itself slowly. When the rim hit the ground, it broke off the stand, dragged itself upright, and tilted for a moment be-fore there was a break in traffic and it weaved its way between cars. Some horns honked, but no one crashed, and in a minute the wheel careened into the distance, spinning so fast its yellow and red lights formed a brilliant orange ball.

▲   ▲   ▲

Static crackled on the radio. A tap on the window. I woke with my face pressed into the ridged vinyl seat and saw a man staring in at me. He had a stern, angular nose—three lines like the ones children draw—and in the flick of light that hurt my eyes, he tapped his fingertips against the glass, looking as if he thought I might be dead. I tried to raise myself up, but my shoulder caught under the steering wheel. He ducked low to see farther into the car. My blouse had come unbuttoned, and my black skirt had bunched up high on my thighs. I flinched to cover up the scar under my bra. The man tapped again on the window. Swallowing hard, I struggled with buttons as I maneuvered around the steering wheel, felt a swell of nausea as I unwound the window handle.

He was wearing a little gold cross pin on the lapel of his suit, and I thought it must be Sunday. "Have car trouble?" he asked, grinning.

My voice was hoarse. "No, I just fell asleep. . . . I was waiting." I rubbed the heavy bones around my eyes, too tired to make up an excuse. If it was Sunday, that would have meant I'd slept two days. "What day is it?" There was already traffic on Lincoln, the hot morning sun eclipsed by the Big Wheel sign.

He must have smelled the bourbon then, or heard me kick the bottle on the floorboard. His lip curled in awkwardly. "Saturday, the fifteenth."

"Thanks." I turned the key in the ignition, my fingers weak and shaky. "I need to get home."

He gathered his eyebrows in a way that ruined the symmetry of his face, nodded so the top of his balding forehead turned shiny. "Can I help you?"

I looked beyond him at his blue Lincoln, where his wife with thin red lips watched out her window.

"I don't think so," I said, feeling feverish and wanting to get away. "I'm just going home."

He put his hand over mine on the steering wheel. "Are you well enough to drive?"

"Of course." His hands were soft and firm, and something in his timid grip, something about the tension in his fingers and the way he seemed to want me to tell him what was wrong reminded me of my father. He took back his hand and nodded. I rolled up the window, and after he turned away, watched him walk back to his car.

I bent the rearview mirror so I could see my sleep-swollen face. A grid of lines pressed into my right cheek, and green shadows cusped beneath my eyes. *If my father were alive, I wouldn't be like this,* I thought.

Something webbed in my throat. When he thought something was bothering me, he'd wait to ask me about it in the morning in the truck as he drove us to school, the flat road pulling under us, his fist working the gear shift. I took several deep breaths, then backed out of the parking lot, a dark lace of leaf shade sweeping the windshield.

VII

Two guests had just checked out, and after I returned the keys to their dusty boxes, I sat down to glance over the reservations for that night. The day clerk's ladybug cursive was almost indecipherable. I worried it was only a matter of time before someone asked the right questions of the neighbors or the girl at the drive-in counter, and discovered the fire at the Housemans' wasn't an accident.

Jo, wearing a sweater with a yoke of flowers, came in through the side door, pushed through the gate, and sat down purposefully beside me. She heaved her chest and sighed. "I'm not leaving until you tell me what's wrong." We hadn't spoken since the Wednesday before, and guiltily, I thought about how she'd never told anyone but me how her father sometimes cheated on his bill and drank whiskey in his truck when he was supposed to be fixing someone's stove. I tried not to look in her eyes.

"Why do you always think something's wrong? I'm okay."

She leaned back in her chair and cleared her throat, staring at the desk drawer in front of us. "Why are you sleeping with strangers? You think no one else would want to?"

My chest unclamped. I'd forgotten. Of course she didn't know about the fire. Not yet anyway. "Don't be ridiculous," I said, getting up to walk around her. She grabbed my arm and squeezed it. Jo didn't understand how much control I had over the situation, how they didn't see me at all, how it wasn't a question of my sacrificing myself for them the way she assumed. I felt my voice go calm and small. "I know what it looked like, but we just had a drink and talked. He needed to know some things about Porter."

"That wasn't it." She pointed her pretty chin at me.

I closed the guest registry. "You don't have to believe me."

"Ella, you have to be more careful. I don't want anything to happen to you." She was blinking rapidly, her hair stuck up in three tiny horns near her forehead. She reminded me of cotton dipped in antiseptic, soft and stinging.

"Leave the worrying to my mother," I said, trying to laugh, but coughed instead. "Believe me, she does it enough."

She raised her eyebrows. "You didn't even know him. Was he so irresistible?"

I'd blotted out the banker's face by then and could only remember his sticky, damp hand. "He was all right."

She leaned forward, rested her chin on her fist, so her cheekbone jutted out. "Ella, people are talking. David says they're getting the wrong idea. And I don't know how you can do it, when there're plenty of nice guys here in Porter who'd—" There she went again.

"I don't want to go out with any of them."

"Why not? Tell me that." She smelled of deodorant and toothpaste, her pale complexion blank as silk.

"Because they're here, and they're happy." She drew back and shook her head. "Because they know too much about me already. A thousand reasons. Don't you ever do something you know you shouldn't? Are you so good?"

She puckered her lips, pushed them to the side, and got up. "If you're going to be like that, I'm going up to Seven to finish the books." She slid the key from its box and went up the stairs, stamping her feet. I heard her unlock an empty room and slam the door.

If there was gossip about me, there would soon be gossip about her, too, and she worried about those things more than I ever did. She pretended she didn't care about popularity, but one of her favorite things to do when we were twelve and had just become friends was to play popcorn queen. Because of Umlacher's popcorn factory, there was a popcorn festival and parade each October, when a high-school girl was crowned. The game embarrassed me because I thought we were too old for it, but to please Jo, I dutifully played. We made a crown out of a headband and some of Marietta's jewelry and took a tablecloth from someone's garbage for a cape. We filled paper bags with as much popcorn as we could make, and when the queen was crowned, the other one showered her with popcorn as she walked, lipsticked and rouged, down the street.

Jo went moony-eyed to the popcorn parade and studied the queen's every move, how she stood and waved as if she were wiping a mirror to see herself better, how she smiled, how she'd done her hair, how she laughed. Jo's mother had been a queen herself, years before she'd married, had Jo, and finally left for New York.

About an hour later, Jo finally came slowly down the stairs, slapping her foot deliberately on each step. "Ella, I'm sorry." She was near the bottom. "I shouldn't tell you what to do, should I? Just be careful, will you?" She swung around the banister's last curve and landed squarely on the lobby carpet. "You're not yourself these days."

I heard someone singing in the shower in the room above us. "What's that supposed to mean?"

She gave me a wary, sideways look, then came toward the desk. "You look more nervous or something. Tired. And you've been snapping. Ever since the funeral. Snapping." She pulled her sweater tightly closed in the front. "I know you're worried about your mother being skinny and all that about finding your aunt, but don't get carried away yourself."

It occurred to me that Jo was the kind of person who would know what to do immediately in an emergency, that I'd never asked her, but she probably even knew CPR.

"I'll try not to," I said, putting my head down on the desk. She'd even told me three or four times about the hotel's plan for a fire escape.

"Just try to calm down," she said, coming through the desk gate. "It doesn't do any good to worry. That's why it's a sin."

▲   ▲   ▲

By the time the firemen got to the Housemans', part of the kitchen had burned. "Apparently caused by an electrical malfunction," said the *Vidette*, alongside a picture of the house with what looked like black teeth marks. Fred was quoted, saying he was just grateful not to have lost his home. "In the face of forces like this, electricity, fire, you realize how small we all are, almost insignificant," he said. He almost sounded grateful for the lesson.

When my mother came to the hotel to tell me the news, her face sagged, but the edge of her skirt and the collar of her blouse were so precisely pressed they looked like tin. She ran her gaze over the sparkles flecking the tight dress I wore and said calmly, "There's been an accident. A fire." I think she'd wanted to make sure I heard it from her first.

I folded my arms and squeezed my shoulders to keep from shaking. As she spoke, running her fingers over the sash to her skirt, her voice trembling, it was as if she were telling me about the first fire I couldn't remember and she pretended to have forgotten. "It seemed to start in the garage and then spread to the house. I don't know all the details." Her ruby ring flared as she opened up her pocketbook, rummaged around for a moment before she clapped it shut again. Narrowing her eyes, she said, "They were on vacation, you know, in Door County. Don't worry, no one was hurt."

I didn't want her to have any part in cleaning up the cinders.

"That's a shame," I said. "At least it wasn't the whole house." In that instant, it seemed only vaguely connected to me.

"That's right." She tried to smile and fixed her collar. I could see her nerves strung tightly beneath her papery skin, and I knew, at any moment, one of them could snap.

"And thank goodness no one was in there," I said. I meant that much—I had only wanted to scare them.

▲   ▲   ▲

Fire is meant to be stolen. If we'd been born with it, as a natural secretion from under our fingernails or from the moisture in our lips, if it were an element tricked from the rub of skin against skin, or some electricity in our hair, if it ignited our livers, or trilled in our blood, no one would bother hoarding it. If it couldn't burn us, it wouldn't kindle happiness either.

A window eave browns and curls into a witch hat, a brass doorknob blackens to a crusty rock, a doll's head melts into a perfect pink puddle. No matter how morbid my mood, afterward I always feel nimble, quick, and light, a phoenix flapping over its spoils.

▲   ▲   ▲

I began to listen for Paul's footsteps. They creaked in the hallway upstairs, and his boot soles tapped on the pavement in the side alley, but in the lobby, silenced by the carpet, he startled me. It amused him to see me start or gasp, and he never warned me.

Until he'd come to the hotel, we'd never had any trouble. Two weeks after he started, a brawl broke out between a couple of drunks—they danced down the stairs holding one another by the shoulders. A few days later, I saw a block-faced man, his hair greased boyishly into his forehead, staring at me through the window. Paul calmed the drunks and chased off the Peeping Tom as if we'd needed him all along and had just been lucky nothing bad had happened there before. It made him happy, I thought, to feel that he was protecting us.

He slid into the lobby three or four times a night for his break. The blue of his uniform would catch at the edge of my field of vision and, as he stepped closer, magnified the blue of his eyes, which were deep and intense, but he had the squat nose of a boy. I'd find some work to do then—dusting out the key boxes or polishing the keys, re-counting the money in the change box. I didn't want to be drawn into another one of his spiral-staircase kinds of conversations. He asked me once or twice if anything was wrong, but I just said there was a lot of work to do.

Whenever he got up from the chair to get ready to do another round, he had a way of opening and closing his mouth as if he were tasting something. He'd stuff his hands into his pants pockets, jiggle the change and keys. Except for the times he sneaked up behind me in the lobby, he usually made as much noise as someone walking alone in the woods, trying to make the wild animals aware of his presence.

After a few weeks I noticed his walk began to slow down. He seemed to pause more on his rounds—at the curb outside, at the window on the stair's landing—and I wondered what he was waiting for, at these points without windows or locks, if he was just resting, or had heard something suspicious, or was only hoping for company.

▲   ▲   ▲

When they burned witches at the stake, it was proof of their guilt if they didn't ignite immediately and tried to get away, or if at the end, anything was left besides charred bones. These things meant they'd publicly demonstrated their magic, but only because they'd been forced to. I wondered what they said about the ones they'd burned who'd proved innocent?

There was a charmed part of me it would never touch, because unlike most people, I hadn't learned to fear it. You heard mothers hiss Hot! *to their babies when they crawled near a stove or an iron, but I must have confused this warning with all the others. This was one way I had to escape the guilt—a heavy door that opened to a small, cool cell with bookshelves and then locked behind me.*

▲   ▲   ▲

I waited in the sewing room while my mother finished talking to Marietta on the phone. She was making a dress for me, and she'd asked me to come to the house for a fitting. There was only one window, its blue gingham curtains drawn above piles of fabric, a box of old patterns, round tins of buttons and thread, a pair of scissors. The sewing machine sat on a table pushed against the wall, its needle lifted, poised and expectant.

Pattern pieces crinkled in the draft when she opened the door. "Why don't you take those off?" she said, nodding to my skirt and blouse. She held up the bottom of the gray dress. "Here's the skirt. I want to measure how long to make it."

I went into the bathroom, took off my clothes, and pulled the gathered fabric to my waistline, then went back into the sewing room. She rested her wrapped-up ankle on a chair as she bent to fiddle with the gathers. "You're getting thinner," she said, holding the fabric against my body expertly. She rarely touched me, and so her soft hands startled me each time she took my measurements.

She belted the tape measure around my waist, then glared down at the markings. I felt the pad of her finger in the small of my back. "Almost twenty-three and a half," she said. "I'll have to take this up a little. Let me measure for the bodice while I've got you here." She ran the tape measure from my waist to my shoulder, then wrapped it around my ribs, just below my bra, over the pink terrain of scars. "Stay right there," she said. She sighed and studied where each of the seams should be, whispering to herself, "Oh, here," and then moving around to my back, placed a cool finger against my neck and murmured, "there."

I stared at the austere cross that hung over the door. The hard, plain geometry of it reminded me of a plumb line, some kind of tool. In my mind, I automatically replaced the suffering face and wasted body, the nailed feet and hands. Without these the cross seemed too efficient, as if we couldn't afford to think about Good Friday, only Easter.

My mother was on her knees, pinning the hem. "Grandma and Erma spent all day yesterday picking out a new wallpaper for the kitchen. They got rid of those awful brown pears." Her worn hands neatly turned the frayed edges of the material. "Staying busy, I guess."

The words seem to shoot from a tiny hard spot between my eyes. "Is that what you did after the fire? Stay busy?"

She pinched up another section of fabric, turned me a little. Her thin arms were working fast. "What?" I knew she knew what I meant. She stopped pinning and looked down at my shoe.

"There was a lot to do," she said in a flat voice. I looked down at the top of her head, the gray hairs dulling the brown. Something prickled in my chest.

"Salt baths," I said.

Her voice flickered. "Yes. We had to give you those." She began pinning the hem again. I could hardly bear to think of them and wondered why I couldn't remember what must have been more painful than anything I'd ever felt since. Sometimes I thought the numbness began with those salt baths. When she'd finished pinning the hem, she sat back and studied the evenness of it. She looked girlish and frail, kneeling there on the floor.

"That was a strange dinner Sunday," I said.

She looked up from under a gray strand of hair. "It was, sort of."

"Did you go to those Klan rallies with Grandma? Did Hanna?"

She stood up and went over to the table where the pattern was and looked down at a diagram, placed her finger on it. "Oh, that wasn't the *Klan*," she said, making a tsking sound. "My father always said you couldn't make him put on one of those ghost costumes, even if it was Halloween."

"Didn't you see the pictures?"

She squinted to read and looked away. "Of course I saw them, and I'd seen them before, but it wasn't the same thing. It was just an old-fashioned ladies' auxiliary, Mother told me. They had quilting bees and bake sales. Same crowd as the Rebekah Lodge."

"You believe that?"

"Of course." She came over and knelt in front of me again, put a pin in her mouth, and said through clenched teeth, "Put your arms up."

She shied away from saying anything critical of her parents, even if it was obvious (like her mother's vanity, which must have sometimes wounded her). Their frailties seemed to panic her—

she got this look on her face as if she were being chased. "Did you see Mr. Schultz again?" she said finally. "He's such a nice person. He told me he was worried about you, working all alone at the hotel." There it was again.

"I'm not alone. There's a security guard now."

She pinched a few straight pins from the table and laid them in the palm of her hand. "I never liked that place."

"It's a perfectly good hotel." With something like a razor, I cut away the memory of the men's hands, though I thought she could see this, or anyway suspected what I was doing. "Didn't Grandpa and Grandma stay there after they got married?"

"That was before. Aunt Emily stayed there on one of her window escapades, and they wanted us to pay for it."

"Really? For the windows or the room?"

She sighed. "The room." She slipped a couple of pins into the red pincushion tied to her wrist. "Oscar paid for it in the end, as always. Hanna was running over there to see her every day, and we didn't even know about it."

One of the pins in the bodice pricked my stomach. This was what really bothered her: Hanna going to Emily without her, Hanna doing what she didn't have the courage to do herself, Hanna the prettier one.

"Well, that wasn't the hotel's fault," I said. My great-aunt Emily's mind was going, Marietta said, and she didn't like to have visitors, so even though I thought she might have heard from Hanna, I'd dismissed the idea of going to her for help. But that was when I still hoped my mother or Marietta would give in to the pressure of our lie and help decide to me find her.

"Nonetheless . . ." My mother's ruby ring sparked in the window light. Her skin was a bluish color, her wrist thin and knobby.

"Have you eaten yet?" I asked her. She looked so vulnerable

and thin. It was as if her dead father were pulling her flesh to some other place, wherever he was.

"Of course." She stood up and adjusted the collar where it was basted at my neck. "Tuna-fish sandwich. Now, take this off, but be careful not to rip any of the stitches."

VIII

▮▮▮▮▮▮▮▮▮▮▮▮▮▮▮▮▮▮▮▮▮▮▮▮▮▮▮▮▮▮▮▮▮▮

Emily's house in Plymouth was pink with green shutters. A plastic canary that Marietta would have said looked cheap perched on top of the mailbox. When I explained who I was to the nurse in the blue uniform who answered the door, her voice took on a canned sweetness, and she ushered me into a sunlit and dusty room with an orange velvet couch worn sheeny. Emily sat with her hands on the wheels of her chair near the window in the sun.

"Emily," said the nurse, testing the unstable surface of her, "Ella, your niece is here."

As she turned toward us, the end of a white lace scarf around her neck twisted under her arm. "Ella?"

"Catherine's daughter," I said, taking a few steps closer to her. "I haven't seen you since the Kestler reunion." She craned her head to look behind me at the track I'd made on the wood floor, and I glanced back, thinking there must have been mud on my shoes, but the floor was clean.

"Yes," she said finally. "You were born just before Robert, Earl's son."

I nodded, but didn't know who she was talking about.

"You're the swimmer, aren't you?"

117

I nodded, though of course I wasn't. I'd never even owned a bathing suit. "Used to be."

She had intense, bright-blue eyes, but her gaze wandered in and out of focus, alternately alert and bored, like sunlight clouds were blowing through. When I took another step closer to her, wavering over whether or not I should hug her, she drew back and patted the windowsill with her palm, precisely, as if she were keeping beat with a record. "Have to make sure it's still there." She clicked her tongue. "Catherine's daughter all grown up." She said it as if imitating a grandmotherly voice she'd heard some-where. She held out a small hand powdered with freckles, and I took it, squeezed it, and kissed her lightly on the cheek. "It's so nice of you to visit," she said in that strange voice.

I sat down on the limp, fleshy couch cushions. "Marietta says hello."

She tilted her head, but her tight gray curls didn't move at all. "Is she well?"

"Yes, she is," I said, a little too brightly, "considering . . . I mean she's still spending a lot of time alone." I thought of Marietta circling the birds in the feeder behind her house, trying to get a particular yellow-and-black jay, of her putting on lipstick in the mirror, looking longingly at the reflection, trying to fish up a younger version of herself. "She's keeping busy, though." *We're all busy,* I thought, *busy as ants in a trampled hill.*

She nodded. "I was so sick myself I couldn't get out of bed that day, or I would have been there. He was never healthy, that man. Don't know what he would have done if she hadn't taken care of him. Always going to bed, it seemed like, saying he didn't feel well when it looked like nothing was wrong with him." Her eyes glinted. I wondered if she suspected the truth. "My mother says hello, too," I said.

"Oh, how is Catherine?"

Starving, I thought. "She broke her ankle last month," I said. "Nothing serious, but she's having trouble keeping her mind on things. It was so unexpected."

"Terrible thing, losing your father," she said, twisting the white scarf in her lap. "You know that, sweetie," she said, and it surprised me that she remembered this. "Your father was a fine man," she said, sitting up straighter. "Talented. I liked to hear him play at Grace Church. It was magnificent."

He used to sit in his black church coat up in the choir loft, and sometimes during the service I saw him fold and unfold his sheet music, as if each time he smoothed it out, it would contain some new secret.

Emily's gaze turned suddenly distant, and she methodically touched the wheel of her chair with the ball of her hand. I watched her lips move, counting. In that precise afternoon brightness her palm ticked against the wheel, and a shadow slanted on the floor. If only I could get her to rummage around in her memory, I'd find out where to look for Hanna. "We had dinner at the Housemans' last week. Do you know them?"

"Erma," she said, nodding. "Marietta's friend. Has a whiny voice."

"She showed us pictures of them when they were young."

Emily smiled and nodded. "You see me, too?"

"No. At least I don't think so. They were in their Klan uniforms."

Emily straightened her mouth and looked at the wall. I asked her, "Was my grandfather in the Klan, too?"

Her face came back, and she waved her hand. "Pfshh. Did she tell you that? That wasn't the *Klan.* It was the Women's Klean Up Society for America. We didn't have a chapter in Plymouth—we had something else called the Queens of the Golden Mask, but it was the same thing. They had the hoods and all, but it was a group for *ladies*. It was just a way to see your friends."

"They helped the men?"

She shook her head and looked out the window, distracted by something she saw there. "Your grandfather didn't do anything like that. He was too weak, too nervous. Wouldn't have known what to do with himself." Marietta hadn't liked Oscar, Emily's husband, either; she said he wasn't good enough for her. Each of them must have seen the vulnerabilities in the other's husband, no matter how well he'd hidden them. The sun lay over Emily's shoulder like a pale drape and lit the fuzz on her cheek. She surveyed a spot somewhere above my head. Suddenly that strange, familial voice was back. "How old are you now?"

"Twenty-two."

"I had children when I was your age. You shouldn't wait too long, honey, or you'll regret it."

"But I'm not married," I said. "I don't even have a boyfriend."

As she nodded at me and looked away, the flesh under her chin wobbled. "That's too bad, honey. Time's a-marching on."

The nurse brought in a tarnished silver tray with a teapot and clover-shaped cookies and set it on the table. "I thought you might be peckish. Emily bought these from the little Girl Scout across the street."

"Thank you," said Emily.

The nurse asked if I lived far from there.

"It's a few hours away."

"Then you should come more often." She put her hand on Emily's shoulder. "Right?"

"She's a busy girl," said Emily, pointing as if it were obvious from my looks. The nurse studied me a moment, nodded, and left the room.

Emily wheeled herself closer to the table and poured us each a cup of tea. The teacups had delicate flowers and a thread of gold around the rims, just like Erma's and Marietta's, such delicate cups, and each of them had managed to keep them unchipped all the years since her wedding. I sipped at my tea and held the bird-bone-fragile handle. "Have you heard from Hanna?"

"Hanna," she said sweetly, leaning back and smoothing the pink blanket over her legs. "She was here for my birthday. Where is she now? California?" She tapped her forehead. "Did she go on that tour? I'm trying to remember."

I thought of Hanna in a white bulky sweater, her hair gone naturally white, walking out on the porch of her little stone house to look at the sea.

"When's the last time she came to see you?" I asked. "Does she come often?"

"No," she said, as if it were a question. "She doesn't come often. She was here for my birthday, was it this year or last? Where is she now? I'm trying to remember. Someplace warm. I knitted her a scarf."

Hanna and I would drink champagne in the lobby of an extravagant hotel. In the hallway, men in suits would look worriedly at their watches, expensive luggage piled high on wheeled carts. "I'd almost given up on you," she'd say, sipping from a fluted glass.

"When's your birthday?" I asked Emily.

"June. She had a new hairstyle. A flip at the ends like the first lady's. I always told her what I told you, that she might as well get started having a family, and now it's too late." Her eyes were alert again, pressed open.

"She got married?"

She looked doubtful, her voice high and stuttering. "Oh, no. Oh, no. She's too busy." Something fluttered in my throat. "I sent her a scarf to go with the jacket she was wearing." Emily's fist was punching the wheel of her chair in intervals of seven. She seemed impatient to go somewhere.

"Grandpa left her some money," I said.

"Is that so? She'll be happy to hear that." She punched the wheel seven more times.

"She doesn't know he's passed away."

"Of course not." She lowered her eyes and looked at the pointed toe of her shoe and then, after a few minutes when I thought she'd nodded off, said, "A shame they never got along. A shame not to get along with your father."

I leaned forward, took a sip of lukewarm tea. "Why do you think that was?"

She sighed. "I don't know, but it made her wild." Her words were beginning to slur, maybe from the fatigue of talking, but she also began to say things with more conviction. "I remember I could tell what was going to happen even when she was a little girl and she was twirling around in a circle asking her father questions, you know, like children ask. I remember we all laughed because she asked what color God's bed was." She still didn't look up. "Children made Henry nervous; he always wanted them to be calmer, and children aren't calm." He used to threaten that if I didn't quiet down, he would send me away to China, where they let children run naked in the streets. Emily wiped her forehead with the sleeve of her dress and went on. "He didn't pay much attention to her questions, and she was twirling in a circle, asking about dying, about why so-and-so had died, and she knocked over a jar of milk, and of course it made a big mess. Henry screamed at her to be still, grabbed her and set her down in a chair, and I could see in that little girl's face right there that she wanted to keep twirling." Emily looked up, and her eyes twinkled in the sun. "She wanted to knock over every damn bottle in the house."

I was getting close to the truth. "So you could tell what was going to happen, even before it did."

"Yes. Goodness, there's nothing wrong with asking questions." I nodded.

"And then when she was older and everyone acted like it hadn't happened. You know, she came to live with us for a while after she started having the trouble. She stayed with Oscar and me six months." She'd hit an untouched piece of memory and offered it. "Marietta told everyone I was sick with cancer." This was long before anyone knew anything about my father's, before we'd all pretend such a disease didn't exist and it was still a good lie. "People thought she'd gone away to nurse me when they sent her off to get her away from those boys." For a moment I thought she'd said "bowls."

"Boys?"

"Those miserable boys down by Lake Eliza." She'd said it as if I knew what she was talking about, looking down at her finger, tapping at the arm of her chair. I suspected she really remembered this. "I went along with it for her sake. Oscar was worried I'd lose my wits then, so I had to stay inside most of the time anyway, or he'd have put me in the state home." She looked out the window.

I was trying to imagine what had happened with the miserable boys—was it just that she'd started dating older boys who worked in the mills?

"Why didn't they just let her stay home?"

"Oh, she couldn't go to school after that, with everyone knowing. She had to stay away long enough for us to take care of her." One of them must have got her pregnant. That was why she'd gone away for six months. But why hadn't she married the father, or just come back afterward? And it didn't quite make sense, because my mother had always said that after me, she couldn't have any more children, and it was a sad thing for my grandparents since Hanna had taken a fall as a girl that somehow made it impossible for her to bear children. Emily had the aura of conspiracy again, and I knew if I let on that I didn't know the details, I'd never get her to tell me them.

"That's right, I guess."

"We got to be real close. She was moody, but we had fun. I remember we baked a lot of cookies and she wanted to hear all about the windows." She drummed her fingers against her lips as if she was sorry for telling me so much, and we sat there quietly for a while. She tucked her chin into her neck and looked away, shrugging. More fell out in a steady stream. "I made Oscar wait for me, and he never forgave me for it. By the time I was your age I had two children. Most of the girls I knew had four or five. For two years I didn't want him to touch me. And I was afraid of my food. It seemed like if I swallowed too much, it would eat me. And then after the children came, I had my spell. Did you hear about that?"

"I've heard stories," I said. "I've seen the pictures."

She smiled and settled her hands in her lap. "I was famous." She nodded to the pictures on one wall, the same newspaper clippings Marietta had saved: A younger Emily with a hoe slung over her shoulder. A barbershop's window shattered into a web. Emily, with her curls piled high on her head, holding up empty hands. Emily in a button-shaped hat being handcuffed by policemen. A jagged hole in the window of a department store, a knocked-over mannequin in a wedding dress, broken glass caught in the veil.

"Why did you do it?" I asked.

She smoothed the lace scarf around her neck and fiddled with the ends. "Because glass will shatter. Air won't." I knew what she meant, that stillness can choke you. She wheeled herself a little closer to me. Her eyes fixed on me. "I couldn't take that quiet." She said it so emphatically I had the feeling that when she'd told this to people before, they hadn't believed her. "I remember being at the Eau Claire train station, sitting up all night on one of those benches, and in the morning, when I realized I didn't have any money, I went up to the counter and I demanded that they send me to Bloomington. I knew I had to go there next. He hemmed and hawed, and when I could tell he wasn't going to give it to me, I took my shovel and went right up to the depot's window. He came running over and said, 'Whatever you want, whatever you want.' That was a good feeling, before they arrested me. Suddenly everyone was listening."

I reached to pat her hand. "No one holds it against you now."

She arched one eyebrow. "But they did then. You betcha." She wiped a cookie crumb from her lower lip. "It got to be expensive."

Later, the nurse came in and said it was four o'clock.

"Sue, bring me my book," Emily said. "I've got Hanna's address in there somewhere."

When the nurse came back with it, Emily opened it up for me. "Oh, yes, here." She pointed. "Right there, honey," she said. There were three written in Emily's spindly writing: one in Sunnyside, California with a pencil mark over it that looked unintentional, but it was hard to tell, one in Washington, D.C., and one in Indianapolis.

"Which one is it?"

She looked bewildered as she studied the crowded page and pointed again. "Right there."

"There's three, Emily," said the nurse. "Three addresses."

"Oh, really?" she said, shaking her head, "I didn't realize."

"That's okay, I'll try them all," I said.

When Emily lay down for her nap, I got ready to leave. As I was putting on my jacket, the nurse said, "Tell her to come visit more. And you, too. Don't be a stranger." Her voice was eerily intimate. I looked at this wiry woman in her uniform, the moles starring the hollow of her neck and her chin, someone's daughter, someone's niece.

▲   ▲   ▲

Watching Marietta in front of the mirror, I got the idea. She was fixing her curls, and the hair spray smelled like wet, bottled smoke. I sprayed it around the electrical outlets, or near exposed wires, so the fire looked accidental, the result of some mal-function.

And there was a kind of glue I'd sometimes sniff first. It gave me an airy headache, made my body move one step ahead of the direc-tions I gave it. I'd dab the glue onto some old wood. I wrote words: PARIS, LOOSE, and lit the glue so the words blazed up for a minute like a marquee.

And there were more ways to look accidental than I'd used—a candle near a curtain, a piece of fat in the oven, a mouse and a peanut-butter-coated electrical cord. I could harness chance and stay as unseen as something forgotten, something misplaced.

▲   ▲   ▲

We were sitting in Marietta's living room. "They saw the smoke, thank goodness," said Erma. "We might have lost the entire house, all the clocks, the piano, the boys' pictures."

A finger of sunlight shot through the window. I took one of the peacock feathers from the tall vase beside me, separated the wet-looking strands, and spread them in my palm. Because I was afraid they might find out some other way, I'd told them that I'd been the one to show the counter girl where the fire was.

"Why didn't you say that before? You weren't working that night?" said Marietta.

"It was just before my shift," I said. "And I'd gone for a walk. I thought I told you."

Marietta sucked in her breath and shook her head, an embarrassed pull at the corner of her mouth.

Erma smoothed the arm of her chair as if she were petting a dog. "It was so unlike Fred to leave the saw plugged in like that, but his mind hasn't been on work lately, you know, since Henry's been gone. He doesn't talk about it, but he misses him." Her mouth twitched.

Marietta clicked the back of her house slipper against her heel, still smiling slightly as if she hadn't noticed the mention of his death.

"We miss him, too," I said, thinking of the powder lacing the saucer's rim, his stiff clenched hand, the torn envelope with his hastily erased note. I understood better now why he needed to escape. "I keep thinking about his stories. What was that one about the man in the burlap suit?" The walls seemed to tilt in slightly, distorting my voice as if I were talking into a tunnel. It was a shaggy-dog story about a man who couldn't hold on to anything, not even the clothes on his back, but it was funny and had a happy ending.

"I sure don't remember." Erma laughed, but her smile lingered a little too long with her gaze.

Marietta shrugged. "He had a lot of those."

Erma was still smiling. She leaned forward, fiddling with her clip earring. "All those good speakers used to come to our meetings, remember, Marietta?"

Marietta faked a laugh. "Oh, not that old stuff again. Don't start with that."

Erma went on. "I still never thought I'd see the day we'd have a Catholic president, did you? If they would've known that was coming, it would have made the best story in the world. Forget what they said about the Pope."

Marietta pointed her toes and slapped her slipper against her heel. "It never made sense to me. In the beginning, all we had were the Catholics. Now, Fred would be glad if we just had them."

"Well," said Erma, "that was before they moved a black family in here in a makeshift house on a street that didn't even have a curb."

"Erma, those were church people," said Marietta. "It was Christian charity to get them out of that slum in the city."

Like sharp rocks crowding up against me, their talk trapped me in a place I couldn't stand. "How could you belong to the church and also the Klan?" I said, my heart pounding. "Wasn't there a rule against that?"

Erma was shaking her head and pressing her lips together. My grandmother moved to the edge of her seat. "Why, no. See, we didn't work back then. There wasn't any Ladies' Guild." For Marietta, a club was a necessity.

"We had a lot of oomph for a bunch of women, though," said Erma. "And—"

Marietta interrupted her. "It wasn't anything serious. That was for the men. We just got dressed up, had baptisms, showers, gossip. We needed a reason to get together." It was the cheerfulness of the group that was its measure, even if that meant spreading hatred for people you didn't know here and there, even if that cheeriness was a cover for a violence only the men were allowed.

Marietta had to keep telling herself that it was only a club, only play, not real enough to hurt anything. That stunned fear on her face in the photograph and the one burning cross I'd seen kept fusing in my mind like a holograph card. Were the fires I'd set some kind of legacy, some fear passed down in the genes? "Grandma, how could you?"

Acid raked up in my throat. Marietta and Erma sat woodenly, each staring at the space between her feet on the floor. Erma started shuffling her clunky orthopedic shoes, and Marietta's long fingers fluffed at her hair. Their faces turned worn and yellow, as if they'd suddenly become ill, and I realized that was exactly what I'd wanted. The clock that played "Let Me Call You Sweetheart" on the hour clicked into its tune.

Erma raised her head to the ceiling. "Pfish. You talk some sense into her. Those hippie professors did it to her. You can't send girls to college anymore, or they come back like this." And she marched out of the living room, slamming the kitchen door behind her.

Marietta gave me this weird, compromised frog smile. "Honey, we only had our mothers and fathers to teach us. Erma's own father believed the Klan was called for in the Bible. We did what we were taught."

"You didn't have to," I said.

"No. But we were poor. A disease could sweep through town and kill a whole family of children."

"What does that have to do with it?"

"We did what we were told because that was how people got along. And we had to. People need others around to help, especially when you don't have much." She muted her voice and looked at me again with that frog smile. "Later on when I got married it was different. I started with the Ladies' Guild, but you know what, we still wore white dresses. We still wore long white dresses because we liked them, and I tell you, it wasn't much different from the way it was before. Just no more parades. No men around. I had this pretty white dress I remember with French lace on the skirt—Emily gave it to me—and it looked a little too much like a wedding dress, people said, but I didn't care."

The dream of my grandmother's lost, fragile beauty had often made me sad, but now it irked me and somehow fed my fury at her.

"Do you think that just because someone looks different from you they're any less?" I yanked back my shirtsleeves. "Look, my skin's not the same as yours."

Her mouth tightened. Her blue eyes rounded under her pink, wrinkled lids, and I caught a glimpse of her younger self. Of course, there was nothing for her to say, because she had believed she was better than other women, and the gaze of everyone around had confirmed that. "Honey, you are special," she said, grazing my knee with her hand. "Anyone with half an eye can see the beauty in you." I couldn't let her get away so easily. The rocks were too sharp, and I was losing my footing.

"How can you be friends with a bigot?" I said.

"Of course she doesn't think of you in the same way as those others."

"Maybe she should."

"Oh, she just gets going sometimes," said Marietta. "You can't listen to half of what she says. Even she knows that. She used to tell me your grandfather was a coward because he wouldn't join the men."

"What did you say to her?"

"I said that was one of the reasons I married him." She shook her head, rearranging the candy dish on the end table. "Look, maybe back then I didn't think for myself, but later I did. I changed with the times."

"I never heard you contradict Grandpa."

"I did, a little, at home. I couldn't tell him anything, though. He didn't listen to me." She looked down, and her mouth trembled. I thought how easily inertia could rot a person's integrity, but I wanted to believe her. To do that though, I had to fill in the story, imagining she and her friends had made their white Ladies'

Guild gowns out of silk instead of cotton sheets, that they burned
those awful masks at a party, and after that, sabotaged the Klans-
men's efforts, and finally withheld sex and hot meals to help per-
suade the men out of their fervor.

"And what about Cornell?"

"We never even met that man."

"Did you tell anyone he was Jewish?"

She lifted her chin and said incredulously, "We didn't know
that."

"She never married him. I went to see him in September to see
if he knew where she was."

Marietta stood up and circled herself with her arms around her
waist, began to pace. "Well, then, he was a common-law husband
anyway." She looked at the ceiling. "Thank God Henry never
knew that. That would have been all we needed. . . ." She bumped
into the mantel and stopped herself, not looking up.

"He seemed to be a good person," I said. "A piano player." It
didn't really describe him, but I couldn't think of what else to say.

When Marietta turned around, her face was composed again—
it was amazing how deliberately she could do this, as if she were
arranging her features on a plate. "So you reported that fire? Why
did the newspaper say it was that girl at the drive-in then?"

Gratefully, I noticed it was already five o'clock, and I had to be
at work by six. "I told her," I said, feeling exhausted when I got
to my feet.

▲   ▲   ▲

Jo sat beside me at the desk, finishing up with the books. I
swiped the polished dark wood with a rag and tried to speak
calmly with a man who was complaining about the lack of heat
in his room. It was an old hotel, and the radiator heat was temperamental, but he seemed one of those people so beaten down

and sad that they took complaining seriously because it was the only way anyone would listen.

"I'm very sorry, sir," I said, in my best night-clerk's voice. "I'll have to call our maintenance people about it. In the meantime, would you like to move to another room?" He shook his small head uncertainly. His hair had thinned in patches, and he had a wrinkled brown circle in the middle of his forehead, a dull parody of the bright red dot Indian women wear. "Or can we bring you more blankets?"

"More blankets, yes." He nodded, looking relieved and a little guilty.

"We'll bring them right away."

When I came out of the back closet holding two neatly folded and stacked wool blankets, Jo said, "David put money down on a house." She shrugged. "It's nothing special."

I looked at her diamond-shaped face in profile and thought of her mother, singing at that nightclub, Blue, in New York. The color rose in the apples of her cheeks like the blush on peaches.

"You don't have to do it," I said. There was a small scratch on her cheek.

She shook her head, so her short hair fringed out around her face. "It's an ugly green one on Washington Street, but we're going to paint it." She slid the books into the drawer, took her little key from her skirt pocket, and turned it in the lock.

"I have to take these upstairs," I said. "But don't leave yet, okay?" I carried the blankets up to 9, and when the man answered, he was already in his pajamas.

"Thanks much," he said, taking the blankets from me. The tiny diamonds on his pajamas reminded me of Jo and her mother, both diamond-faced women.

"Do you need anything else?" He looked away and shook his head.

When I got back downstairs, Jo was staring into the desk with her arms folded in front of her. She didn't look happy.

"What happened at your grandmother's today?" she said, sticking her pencil behind her ear.

I'd already told her about Erma's photo album and those pictures of Marietta and her friends in Klan uniforms, and I was surprised how lightly she'd taken it, saying, they probably just needed an excuse to get away from their husbands once in a while.

"I found out you were probably right. At least that's what she claims," I said. "But my grandfather didn't have anything to do with it, I guess. He wasn't a joiner."

She traced a finger over the desk. "That was all such a long time ago. Who knows what people really thought? It was all crazy."

"I want to know," I said.

She tapped her knee against the side of the desk. "Sometimes you just have to let things go." She was turning the tables on me, wanting to give me advice so I wouldn't think anymore about what she might be about to let go. "For example," she said, "there's a reason, and you may never know it, why no one knows where your aunt Hanna is."

"But what if I think I can find her?"

She sighed through her teeth. "And then what? She's just a person like anyone else. She's not a princess. She's not wanted by the FBI."

"She should know her father died."

"Believe me," Jo said, scratching her nose, "she'll find out when she needs to." She was determined to undo what her mother had done, move into a home instead of abandoning one, marry a man she wasn't sure she loved instead of leaving him. She wasn't a leaver, like her mother; she was a stayer, and stayers had certain beliefs that helped them remain in a place: *Let things go. Be real-*

istic. Don't expect too much. For all her pessimism, there was a tenacity in it I admired.

Hanna had once said to my mother, "I don't know why anyone would want to live in Porter." She hadn't meant to be cruel, but the ineptness of her words didn't seem to occur to her until my mother's mouth clamped down, suddenly the little sister, dutiful, a stayer.

Jo ruffled her hair in the back. "Remember when we found all that stuff under the train platform?"

"Yeah," I said, not knowing where this would lead. We'd discovered these objects we hadn't even known we'd wanted until we held them in our hands: a Zippo cigarette lighter, a miniature scissors, a jade-and-pearl earring.

"That doesn't usually happen," she said in a clipped voice. "You have to accept things as they are and make the best of them. Things don't usually just come to you by accident or because you're looking for them."

How had she become so dark-spirited? Did she really believe that? I decided she had to be just trying to convince herself that she would make the best of marrying David and all he had to offer her. My grandfather had been a stayer too, though, leaving finally the only way he could, and this made me frightened for her. That fear must have made me blurt it out, "My grandfather didn't die of a heart attack. He killed himself. He put arsenic in his coffee."

The pencil fell out of her hair and bounced onto the desk. She covered her mouth.

"I'm sorry I couldn't tell you before. I barely believed it, we'd lied to so many people."

"Why?"

I gazed at the scratched and ink-stained blotter on the desk, crazy cacophonous marks. "We just did."

She nodded, so her eyes enlarged. "Why do you think he did it?" The real question. The chasm in the ground we'd been cautiously stepping around with our lie.

"You saw how he kept to himself." *Though if I'd been braver, I might have been able to draw him out, keep the bitterness in him from turning to poison.* "That's why I want to find Hanna. I thought she might know."

Jo's stricken face was white, and the cords in her neck stood out. "It's awful," she said, pressing her hands together almost as if she were praying, with her thumbs touching her chin and her eyes lowered. "Who knows why people do things?"

▲   ▲   ▲

The first time it happened I was sitting in a restaurant eating a piece of lemon pie. A man with a high forehead and little curls by his ears sat down across from me at the table and asked how old I was.

"Fifteen," I said. I wasn't afraid of strangers anymore. I wanted to know the places they were from.

He puckered his lips in a fake whistle. "Too bad," he said. "Are you sure?"

I nodded.

He licked his lips and shook his head. "They must grow pretty cute fifteen-year-olds around here," he said. "Something in the water." He put his hands on the table and pushed himself up, went back to his stool at the counter, glancing coyly over his shoulder at me, and paid his check.

I was stunned, and felt myself blush deeply. This had happened before to Jo, and she'd giggled and posed like a movie star when she'd told me about it. But I thought it had only happened because he was a stranger, someone who didn't know me well enough to know I was scarred. I looked down at my navy skirt and white blouse and realized he'd seen just enough: long, shiny hair, pretty eyes or mouth.

I followed him out to his car, and he opened the passenger door. When he kissed me, that flowery, tannic fume of booze overwhelmed me, and I thought to myself, *That's right. There's not any reason he should know.*

▲   ▲   ▲

Paul circled the hotel on the hour, careful to give space to the talks Jo and I had. Sometimes he sang songs to himself in Polish, and sometimes I caught him talking to himself, usually going over in his head what he had to do. He wore these heavy, steel-toed boots he'd bought at Orion's, the farm-equipment store, and his footsteps were so loud you could hear him everywhere he went, except when he was closest to me, in the lobby. I thought he wore the boots to feel stronger—he was tall, but not muscular, not the sort of man a criminal would fear. His uniform was a pressed dark-blue twill. LINDEN in bold black letters marched across the back.

IX

████████████████████████████████████

Marietta came to see me at the hotel. She was sitting in the lobby in her suit, her pocketbook on her lap and her hair curled into little springs at her ears and neck. She'd had her house painted purple. It stood out on the street of white porches like a wound, and against the purple paint, the pale-green curtains in the picture window looked sick. The three or four times I'd stopped by to visit she hadn't been there. When one day I noticed the newspapers piling up in the driveway and the lawn and rosebushes gone ragged, I knocked and even kicked at the front door and, not seeing any light beyond the curtains, imagined that the entire house had been filled in with cement. She was twittery now, batting her thickly mascaraed eyes and demurely tucking in her chin. "I've been waiting for you."

"Well, here I am," I said, taking my coffee behind the desk. She chatted while I counted the change into the money box and looked over the guest registry.

It was as if she wanted to make up with small talk for her frankness the last time I'd seen her. She told me Erma had chosen the most beautiful wallpaper, a design with little hummingbirds; there was a squabble in the Ladies' Guild around a woman who claimed that she spoke in tongues ("Lutherans don't do that,"

137

Marietta told her. "No one will know what you're saying"). She'd
bought apple strudel with nuts, for a change, almonds. The
woman who did her nails was pregnant. She was considering
painting the living room lavender, too, and what did I think of
that?

It was flashing behind her chatter and gestures—what she'd
come to ask me. I could see the glint of it, the sharp edge. I had
to keep my hands busy so I wouldn't have to look. I paper-clipped
two weeks together in the guest registry. I polished the numbered
disks attached to the room keys. It was coming, I knew it.

She'd seen a robin, though it was usually too cold for them in
February; Harry Wise fell down drunk at his wife's birthday party;
Bertha Raddis had to give up her Sunday-school class; and she
was thinking of painting the living-room walls lavender. Her
pocketbook strap flipped like the wing of an injured bird, and she
looked guiltily around the room. The velvet curtains had ripped
clear up one side; the man who owned the new ice-cream store
on Lincolnway was from Hammond, and he knew the Muellers;
they'd caught a Peeping Tom around the girls' dormitories—you
had to be careful about your windows. The living-room walls
really needed painting. Was lavender a good color? Almost blue,
but not quite? Her gaze following some phantom trapped butter-
fly, she said, "Did you find her?"

I was polishing the wood on the desk in hard circles. "I think
so. I went to Aunt Emily's."

"She's seen her?" Her face turned very stiff and pasty, her pos-
ture a flat board.

I nodded.

"Well, what do you know," she said, her voice trembling. "Emily has seen her and not us."

I pressed my fingers harder into the dustcloth and made a

squeaking noise on the surface of the desk. "She had three addresses for her, but I don't know if any of them are right. Emily was confused."

Marietta's shoes shuffled on the floor. When she didn't say anything, I looked up from my dusting. She wiped her cheek as if to get something out of the way, sniffed, and then it came out in a blaze: "Henry sent her away."

"I know, Grandma." I set down the cloth and went behind the desk again, began to sort the checks into envelopes.

"I didn't want her to go."

"You couldn't stop him." I licked an envelope flap and wrote a date in the corner.

"Heavens, no, I couldn't stop him." She swung the orange-stockinged leg that crossed her knee. She turned to face the wall and shook her head slightly. "I didn't think it would last this long."

"I know," I said, getting up to pull the broom from the corner.

"I thought she'd be gone for a few months and then he'd forget about it. But then when she didn't come back, it made everything worse. She wasn't, I know, but it made her look guilty." She rocked the pocketbook handle back and forth, and her mouth closed unevenly as if she was about to cry.

I began to sweep the floor behind the desk. "Guilty of what?" Of letting herself get pregnant? If that was it, why couldn't she just say it? The bristles whisked against the polished floor. There wasn't any dirt, just a safety pin, a penny. Of course, she'd have given the baby up for adoption (was that the fear, that the child would one day come back and knock on Marietta's door?), that was if she hadn't been unable to conceive, as my mother had said. Or was the child with Hanna now? Was that why she had stayed away?

Her eyes went blank. "I can't talk about that," she said.

I pushed the broom harder against the floor, so the bristles fanned out, and tried to scratch the gleaming surface. "Didn't you ever write? Didn't you visit?"

Her mouth moved mechanically. "After a while it was her fault as much as his, you know. She wasn't really here when she was here half the time. She pretended to be someone else. She came home when she wanted. I couldn't help it that she stayed away most of the time. That was Henry's fault."

I pushed the broom into the corner, stabbed at a tiny cobweb.

"I told him she'd taken after me, and it was natural for a girl like that to get a lot of attention. She was popular, but he couldn't see it that way. I convinced him to let her go away with Emily for a while, and I hoped when she came back, it would all be over, but—"

"You lied about it," I said. I leaned the broom against the wall and looked at her face, which threatened to fall down, but she propped it back up.

"Don't you know how hard this is?" I remembered her fear in that old Klan photograph and suddenly felt sorry for her.

"All this time you've hidden it," I said. "What did she do?" I wanted to make her say it.

She shook her head, and her face looked haggard. "In the end she wasn't— Henry couldn't take it. You know how some days he wouldn't even be able to get out of bed. He was fragile for a man."

As I ran the cloth over the edges of the square boxes that held the keys, I thought how my grandfather's washing his hands could put an end to any conversation, how his fists never seemed empty, how he'd liked to say, "These years aren't coming back" when he was talking about working and saving money, but I thought he secretly longed for some pleasure in a particular year that had run away on its long, lithe legs forever. "No he wasn't," I said.

Her voice was tight. "Anyway, I'm glad you found her," she said, but she didn't seem glad. Her eyes looked terrified.

I made some coffee, and we sipped from Styrofoam cups, changed the subject to other things, the color she should paint the living room, the blue dress I was wearing. After she'd finished, she put her cup down and said, "You should go to Chicago, somewhere nice."

I hesitated, wondering how she'd known exactly what I wanted. "But I'm worried about my mother right now. You see how thin she is. And you want me to find Hanna now, don't you?"

She waved away my words so casually I thought she'd misheard me. "Oh, you're young. You'll make new friends."

She was talking the way she used to goad me about finding a boyfriend, and there was something similarly unsettling about it. "What's in Porter for you?"

"Well, a job."

"This?" She opened up her pocketbook and took out her compact. "There are a hundred better ones you could get in a heartbeat in Chicago. And there's the money from your grandfather, don't forget." It was as if she wanted to get rid of me.

I said I'd been thinking about moving there. She smiled slightly. Peering into her compact mirror, she said, "You're not an old lady like me. You should be seeing the world." She put her hand on one loose cheek and lifted it a little. "When I was young, I used to look at old women like me and wonder how they could stand being alive, they were so ugly. I'd look at women ten years older than me and say, 'I could manage that face, but not that one.' I let age creep up on me little by little. It's a horrible thing, getting older. You have to trick yourself."

I hated it when she talked this way, as if finding yourself pretty was the only thing worth living for. "You're seventy," I said. "You have two daughters. That's something."

She shook her head. "Hanna had beautiful skin," she said. "Isn't it funny, we had exactly the same complexion." She closed her compact nostalgically, as if she'd been looking at an old photograph. "I remember there was this old man, Mr. Hamburg, who was dying. He wanted Hanna to visit him at the hospital. He said just to see her face would make him feel better. She didn't know him really, just from church, but she was so outgoing she went as a favor to me and brought some of your grandfather's roses. His wife said he couldn't speak at that point, but he smiled when he saw her, and she sat with him awhile. A little later he died. Isn't that nice? She didn't really understand it when it was all happening."

"Understand what?"

She shook her head and lowered her eyes.

"We'll see her soon," I said. "Maybe you can explain it to her."

Marietta scraped her high heel on the floor and stood up, looked nervously around the dim lobby.

▲   ▲   ▲

I'd written letters to all three of Hanna's addresses, and two had been returned "Address Unknown." Only the one to Indianapolis still hadn't come back. I thought I should wait to hear from her before I just appeared unannounced on her doorstep, not just as a matter of being polite and giving her fair warning but also because I wanted some signal, maybe a Polaroid snapshot from her new life, or a friendly phone call at least, so I'd have some idea what to expect. I'd put so much of myself into looking for her, I couldn't really consider the possibility that she might not want to see us, but she had made a life far away, with or without a child, and Jo was right, she'd kept it that way for her own reasons.

After a month when I didn't hear from her, I thought maybe

I hadn't sounded urgent enough in my letter and she'd been too busy to reply. I also thought that the letter might have been lost or accidentally delivered to her next-door neighbor. I decided to go to Indianapolis even though it would be a shock. I'd try to convince her to come back to Porter for a few days, we'd all sit down in Marietta's lavender-lit living room, and I'd say, "He poisoned himself. Who can say why?"

▲   ▲   ▲

On all those rural roads with fields marked out like window-panes, I imagined how she would look, though it was diffi-cult to age her. I had to remember all the former Hannas with their different hairstyles and makeup and wait for them to assem-ble. I had changed my mind and felt certain that her gray hair would be dyed—red, probably—and she would have developed that nervous way of hurrying her walk that you see in certain small-boned older women. Her voice would sound from farther down in her throat, more crisp and definite. And her full cheeks would have dropped a little; she'd look tired.

I got to the city in the late afternoon, driving past scribbled neon signs and dusty storefronts to the tarred, mildew-colored street. When I couldn't find the number, I began to worry that Emily really had lost her mind. There had been three addresses, after all, and she hadn't even realized it.

I parked on a corner near a playground and got out to look at the numbers more closely. On a building at the end of the block, I saw how the brick shadowed where the numbers had hung be-fore: 172. That was it.

I looked up at the ashy brick, the smudged windows, the laun-dry line tied from the fire escape. It was unmistakably a city house, just as I'd imagined, and from the sidewalk I heard the cadence of her breath, saw the chair beneath her scraping the floor.

The door opened quickly when I knocked. She looked even younger than I'd thought, and wore her hair curly and long, black. She had the same pink Cupid's bow mouth and long curved neck, the same thin figure. I felt something in me expand when she looked up, a lightness. But the eyes were someone else's, narrow and brown. It wasn't Hanna.

The woman became a wall, just drab stone I had to get past. I asked her if Hanna Kestler lived there or if I had the wrong house.

"Oh, did someone send you to get her things?" She smiled. Her teeth tilted inward. There was a lift and then a heavy sinking in my stomach. Hanna had moved again, but maybe the woman would know where she'd gone. "I wrote to someone over there in Porter," she said. "You must be family."

"I am," I said. "Where did she go?"

Her eyes were very clear, but strangely twinkling and unfocused. "Go? Oh, no, she died." Her voice skittered into the breeze. The dry grass in the yard buckled and waved into a lake of needles. The clouds in the sky collided. There was that time she came home and collapsed on my grandparents' couch, and I watched her sleep for hours. "You didn't know? I'm so sorry. I just assumed because I wrote her mother in Porter. It happened a few months ago, in August."

I couldn't look at her. A cat suddenly appeared at my ankle, its fur spotted black and white like dice. A pink moon shape curved on its nose. I could have counted each whisker, separated each sharp, fine strand of fur.

This woman who should have been Hanna but wasn't put her small hand on my arm. There was a tight, salty ring around my throat.

"She was a nice lady. I only knew her a little, but she was nice." The cat arched its back, and I counted the ribs, the vertebrae in its spine, watched one paw lift and spread out like fingers. "They found some medication in her room, something wrong with her heart, they said. She was too young for that, a stroke. Her friends from the stationer's found her, you know, where she worked. You're family?"

The cat's ears tilted back and sharpened. It seemed I'd forgotten something important Hanna had told me, something I needed to ask her.

"Come on," she said, opening the door wider. "I'll take you up to the room. You'll want to arrange for someone to get her things, won't you?" She led me up a staircase with a pink-and-green banister. I hadn't been far away all that time, going up and down another set of stairs, in the Linden Hotel.

"It's an old-fashioned rooming house," the woman said, "for girls only." She unlocked a door at the end of the hall and let me in.

It looked like a room someone had left in a hurry. Scattered bottles and cosmetics tripped across the bureau, and the curtain sheers had been splashed with what looked like coffee or dark red wine. I could see the gauzy print of Hanna's fingers all over. I didn't touch anything," the woman whispered. "Take your time," she said, slowly closing the door. I wanted to cry, but couldn't with that salty thing choking me.

I thought of what Cornell had said about the hole in Hanna's heart—it must have been a real defect, not just something he'd dreamed up to make himself feel better.

I went over to the window and opened it. I had to get some air. I pressed my stomach over the sill and hung my head out in the cold. "She's dead," I said. A silver candy wrapper cartwheeled over cracks in the sidewalk, the green gate perkily blinked in the windows of a parked car. Everything was maddeningly unmoved, even glossed with a faint cheer, shapes curved into smiles. I pulled back in, scraped my spine on the bottom of the window.

I had trouble believing in it. When I turned around, the room enlarged, traces of her everywhere: her fingers spread in the Japanese fans on the wall; the dent in the silk pillow from her head; the soles of her feet leaving their marbled prints in the dusty floor; her green eyes peeking between the stalks of dead daisies in a vase; her shadow on the walls.

On a table in the corner there was a portable record player and a stack of jazz albums. Had they been Cornell's choices, or hers? The record on the turntable was "Ladybird," and the needle still rested on the disc, so I turned it on, listened to a couple of seconds of a frail horn. I pushed down the lever, scratched the needle across the disc over the hair-thin ridges, then the horn blared back again. Damn her. I hated her for not coming back. How could Marietta and my mother have lied about her dying? I scratched the needle back the other way to the papered red circle in the center. The needle whined, then stopped in a stupid "whoops."

I lay down on the bed, picked up the piece of newspaper folded on the pillow. There was a picture of a beautiful woman holding a bottle of perfume. "Life's pleasures," the ad said. The mattress was firm and smelled of lilacs, the pillowcases embroidered with spoked flowers. I closed my eyes, combed my fingers into my hair, and saw her face, wide green alert eyes, a small uncertain mouth. That was her. You had to make up what you didn't know or remember and believe in it. There wasn't any choice.

I got up, went into the bathroom. The tiles lining the wall and floor were the colors of dinner mints, and a scent of vinegar and roses lingered around the tub. I tried to overlook a bottle of henna and a bottle of peroxide on the lid of the toilet because not knowing the color of hair distorted the face I'd just settled on. I picked up a bra from the floor, elastic flailing around my wrist, and smelled her talc and lemon scent in the nylon. I opened the medicine cabinet and looked in the shelves: aspirin, lip balm, creams and oils in almost-empty tubes with dirty caps. She'd worked in a stationer's. I focused on this fact. What friends found her? They should have contacted me. Didn't they know I was her favorite niece, that she would have wanted me to know?

After I slammed the door of the medicine cabinet, my face in the mirror looked strange, the dull whites of my eyes cracked with red, my lips laced with chapped skin, a thin red sickle on the side of my nose where I'd scratched myself during the night. It meant Hanna had never mentioned me, or talked about home only as a place she was glad to have left. I opened the cabinet again, just enough to grab a lipstick, and drew a cross through my reflection. Something dark and ropy chafed inside my chest.

I went out of the bathroom and studied the objects on the bureau: a tarnished key, a tin ashtray, a Kleenex flecked with mascara. I opened the drawers, rifled through her tangled stockings and lingerie, her pastel sweaters and socks. I found only one photograph, a picture of Hanna and my mother when they were girls, but it was blurred from her turning her head so that Hanna seemed to have two noses. I riffled through some bills and papers, a few letters addressed to people I didn't know, and found a letter from my mother. There was some news about my grandparents, my mother's friends at church and then this:

Ella's taking some time off from college before she decides what she wants to do, though I have a suspicion she'll go back to teaching. You're right about her. She's a shy girl. I hate to think of her living around people who don't understand her. The other day she told me she was having trouble sleeping, and I can't help thinking it's because she's given up going to church. She says it reminds her of Louis. I don't to want to upset her, but I can't help thinking church would help. I may ask Pastor Beck to talk to her.

There was more news about the weather and then: *Come visit in June. And I'll mention to Ella your invitation.* But Hanna hadn't come, and my mother hadn't passed on the invitation, whatever it had been. It was like her to think church was the answer for something she couldn't answer herself. What had she been so afraid of?

There was a dress stuffed into the bottom drawer like something put away to be mended. I shook it out. It was a blue silk dress with a chiffon scarf around the neck and tiny pebblelike buttons down the back. I held it up to my shoulders, then on an impulse slipped off my skirt and sweater. In the bureau mirror the scars looked pink, like very pale satin ribbons tied up all around me, binding my arms to my sides, the tops of my legs together. I didn't move for a few minutes, looking at them.

Finally I stepped into the dress and buttoned as many of the buttons as I could reach. A scar trailed down from one sleeve. The dress was out of fashion, and a little too long, but it suited me. I smoothed the wrinkles around my waist, and my breasts pressed up against the tight darts in the bodice.

Here was the invitation: I could live in this room, wear her clothes, get a job at the stationer's, and begin to write in a little, gilt-edged book. There were novels to read in the closet and boxes of photographs or buttons pushed under the bed. I turned, admired the curvy profile of the dress, the fine blue sheen. I'd dye my hair and read movie magazines, I'd listen to jazz. I'd eat in restaurants and never go back to Porter. Then I remembered. The landlady had sent the letter to Marietta in August, the month my grandfather had died. He must have known about it when he took the arsenic.

The delicate buttons popped off as I pulled the dress up over my head. I had matches in my purse. If the house had been empty, I would have set the room on fire. Still in my stockings and bra, I took the dress into the bathroom, shoved aside the shower curtain, and dumped the dress in the tub. I struck a match to the hem and watched the flame waver before the skirt kicked up orange. The bodice and sleeves jerked, then slumped over to the side. The silk turned a coffee-stained blue, then blackened in a coast and shrank under this fire that splashed the edges of the porcelain. *What was fire anyway, what was it made of?* It lapped the bowl of white and the chrome faucet. *Grief,* I thought. *Grief.* Sitting there on the edge of the tub, I watched the flames burn up into the tile.

I finally had to turn the tap all the way up to drown them and scrubbed the ruined edges of the tub with a washcloth. Washing the soot from my hands, I tried to calm down so I could wipe my eyes and go downstairs and thank the woman, tell her someone would be there soon to pay for the damage from my dropped cigarette and to get Hanna's things.

On the way back to Porter, straining to see in the highway dark, I beat at the steering wheel. He must have heard the news not long before he went into his bedroom. How long before, I didn't know. A week? An hour? He'd been writing to her and then erased most of what he'd written. "I'm not saying it's your fault, but you should have come back. Love," "I'm not a real father, after what I put you through. Love," Not. Your. Love.

Near Plymouth, I hit the wheel so hard the car swerved onto the shoulder, spitting up gravel behind me. I had to stop, because I was trembling. I thought about dropping matches in the gas tank and watching the car explode from the field. They'd assume I was dead, and then I could walk away. I could go anywhere. I could leave, just as Hanna had always said to me. But I'd wasted all my matches on the dress.

The fields around me were flat and still, ragged and drifting. When I finally felt steady enough to drive again, I pulled onto the road, waiting for pale lights to comb up in the distance.

A flame is a briny syrup that catches in the teeth and lingers more than a day. You can smell it on people's breath unless they've rinsed their mouth with alcohol or lemons. There's always the one taste, but a thousand forms: the bubbling orange foam, more air than substance; the spiked red tongues that slip under doors and in cracks; the gorgeous pinks and purples that rise with chemicals in a fire that shimmers like glass or oil; the bark made of gold that constantly peels away to itself; the massive fires like mountains, barely moving. Each one has its own face, its own clapping voices.

▲　　▲　　▲

That week I got a postcard from Cornell, and I wrote him a quick, terse note telling him Hanna had died. I didn't think he'd write again. She was the only link between us, the real reason we'd come together in the first place. Marietta had gone to visit Emily, my mother told me. "She said she kept touching things, and she had the same twitch just before all that business with the windows." Had Marietta gone to tell her, I wondered, or had Emily known all along and only told me what she could?

People made up all kinds of things to get by—diets, prayers, and regimens; animals in the stars—all these arks in a flooded world. Even if that thing had holes in it, if you clung to it, it helped you float along.

Marietta hired someone to put up a hurricane fence around her yard and to paint all the windows lavender. So that no one could surprise her, she hung ribbons of bells from every doorknob in the house. She talked more about the birds she'd seen at her feeder, and the feathers she'd collected lay in bowls around the house, waiting to be mounted under glass. The walls were filling up with them. She said her heart was fine, remarkably better, and whenever she checked, it was beating regularly, not skipping the way it used to. And she couldn't stop smiling. In a housedress she swung around the room with her duster, so frantic I thought she might hurt herself.

"Henry was never well. He wasn't lazy, he just couldn't get out of bed sometimes. He was too skinny, don't you think?" She looked at me. I couldn't see any dust, but she swished over every surface with the fury of someone on a search. I looked at the pile of *Reader's Digest*s in the corner. "But he was gentler than the rest. That's why I married him." She stood in front of an opaque window, ran her index finger over the sill. Lavender, a color that made you want to sleep for hours and hours, days, even.

"Isn't it a little dark in here for you?" I asked. I hadn't told her that I'd gone to Indianapolis.

"I think she'll be back soon," she said, and her optimism knocked over anything that might shake it, seemed to trample the framed pictures of my parents' wedding and my mother's graduation.

"I don't think so," I said.

"If she knows how much we want to see her . . ." She narrowed her eyes and came closer to me. I hated it, but told myself it didn't matter. So what if she lied? Hanna had been more of a wish than a person to her for a long time.

▲   ▲   ▲

My mother was so thin she couldn't get out of bed. She was making her body into neat angles like wire bent into an absurd shape: a coat hanger, an egg cup. It looked as if her teeth had grown; she couldn't quite close her lips. She said she was sick, and when I brought her a plate of dry saltine crackers, I remembered giving the same meal to my father at the end.

"Thank you," she said, her voice hollow.

She's known all along, I said to myself. *That's why she's been doing this to herself. It's too much for her to hold in.* She couldn't have told me, any more than she could have told me about the fire she'd watched me fall into. She felt too guilty. She thought she should have been able to see that Hanna's death would be too much for my grandfather to withstand, that if she had said the right thing, been a better daughter, he wouldn't have done it.

The room was dusty and cold. Outside, an ocean of snow and a white sky that looked unreal until you got used to it, the world as a clean cotton sheet. The heater sputtered on, and there was an unpleasant grating in the pipes. She must have known by now that there was something wrong with me. I couldn't put the words together—they scattered in my head like glass thrown against a wall—but I wanted to tell her I'd set fires and seduced men, all because she'd taught me to be such a good liar.

"I'll finish your dress as soon as I feel better," she said. She wanted me to look like her, to wear simple, practical clothes, to stay in Porter and go back to teaching first grade. She would incinerate me with safety.

X

Paul set a plate down on the desk in front of me, a tangle of noodles with a pink meaty gravy poured on top. "I thought you might be hungry," he said. The steaming plate smelled of dill and pepper. "It's Stroganoff. My aunt used to make it." He nudged it closer to me.

"You can cook?" I picked up the fork.

"I broke the rules," he said. "They'll probably notice some things missing tomorrow." His hooded eyes looked even deeper-set, a dark blue the color of bruises. "I couldn't find any celery, though. It's better with celery." He pulled the vinyl chair up to the desk and sat down across from me. I wound the fork in the noodles, and he watched me take a bite. "What do you think?"

It had a strange sour-milk taste that I liked. "You didn't make any for yourself?"

He shook his head. "I was concentrating. Is it good?"

"Delicious."

"You don't look well lately," he said.

I took another bite. The meat was heavy and tender and weighed pleasantly in my stomach. Then I took two more bites and pushed the plate over to him. "Have some."

"Has something happened?" He looked at me, and when he

could tell I wasn't going to answer, he put a forkful into his mouth and smacked his lips. "Needs celery." He got up and walked inside the gate behind the desk to the closet and came back with a bottle of bourbon and two thin plastic cups.

The bourbon calmed me, and I sank down in my chair. His accent was so familiar to me now, I knew how to read the low hollows and peaks in his voice.

Two small boys were running up and down the stairs, counting them and making a slurping sound with their lips every third one.

"What is it about what they're doing that's so fun?" Paul smiled. "They know, I guess." Watching them, he said, "When I was that age, I climbed trees. No one understood."

"Lots of boys climb trees," I said.

"Yes, but I was always in a tree, as much as possible. I ate my lunch up there," he said, laughing. "I would have never come down if it weren't for the problem of sleeping. One time I fell out and hurt my neck. As soon as the doctor put on the brace, I went right back up in that tree. My mother couldn't stop me." He shook his head and smiled in that way he often did, waiting for me to reply.

It came out awkwardly, as if I meant to tell him about a practical joke, but said this instead: "When I was three, someone was burning leaves and I fell into the fire." His smile closed up, and I wished I hadn't said anything, but knew why I had—I could tell he liked me, and I wanted to make sure to head off any disappointment right there. "I have scars from it on my arms and legs and across here." I drew a loop around my torso and back. "Most people don't know," I said, trying to make my voice go light again, "unless they went to school with me."

He didn't smile. He had an intent face I couldn't interpret, as if he were figuring a math problem in his head. "Children can be nasty," he said.

I looked down at my shoe. "I didn't mean *that*. Everyone gets teased."

I told him about the time I went with the Turner twins behind some bushes, agreed that we'd all show one another our stomachs. I'd unbuttoned my blouse and pulled up my undershirt, and they touched the scars gingerly as if they were still hot, the pads of their fingers cool and moist like dogs' noses. "It doesn't hurt or anything," I bragged. Sonny looked envious, as if my stomach bore the marks of a sin he wished he were brave enough to commit, but he sounded disappointed when he said he thought the scars would be black. Later, Susan and I cracked open a golf ball with a hammer, pulled out the long rubber cord, and said it was a tapeworm we'd pulled out of her stomach.

"I was a curiosity," I said. "I got a lot of attention for it, that's all. People thought I was brave."

He closed his eyes for a moment, rubbed his chin, and looked away at the trophy case.

▲   ▲   ▲

Sometimes a fire flies up out of nowhere, and sometimes it must be coaxed or torn out of air. There's a sense of it dormant and cocooned, waiting for a spark or flint to undress it, waiting to wildly unfurl and color. If it's windy or damp, you have to whisper, cajole it out of hiding, throw yourself at it so it feels wanted.

▲   ▲   ▲

Jo needed boots, so we went to Orion's. They sold everything— baby clothes, toasters, and tablecloths on the same crowded aisles as rifles and bags of seed. Tents and lawn mowers and stuffed animals hung from the high beamed ceiling.

We found boots she liked—knee-high black leather ones with shiny toes for professional equestrians—and she sat down in a chair to try them on. "It's obvious Paul likes you," she said, smirking. "What do you two do all night, anyway?"

"Shut up," I said, hitting her lightly on the arm. "We work." Since it was Saturday, there was a lot of commotion in the store, families with small children wheeling full carts of merchandise through the narrow aisles and high-school boys unpacking boxes and straightening the shelves. Jo zipped the boot up her shin and gave me a sideways glance. I could hardly hear her. "There's no work after ten o'clock."

"Well, someone has to be there," I said. "Okay, we talk, I guess."

"You guess? About what?" She stood up and seemed to be wiggling her toes inside the boot. "Have you told him about Hanna?"

I'd put a heavy blanket over the thought of her, like the dustcloth put on furniture to protect it when you move. "Of course not."

She came back to her seat beside me and unzipped the boot. "Why not?"

"It's none of his business. I only told you. I haven't even told my mother and grandmother about that trip." Hanna's vacant room meant that I didn't have to hope for anything from them anymore, but I was still furious about their lying to me.

Jo blinked her dark lashes and put her hand on my shoulder. "Ella, they know, remember?"

"But they don't know—"

"They don't know, or they're just not asking?" She took off the boot. "They know you were looking for her, don't they? Sooner or later you were going to find out. You're just as bad as them, not saying anything, even now."

My eyes stung. A little girl in black patent-leather shoes skipped screaming over the cement floor, a cowboy hat on her head and a toy gun in her hand. Jo was right. I'd been so angry about their secrets, and there I was dancing along with them as if I didn't know anything.

"How are the boots?" I asked.

She tilted her head, said "Too small," and put them back in the tissue-paper-lined box. The lights above us in their cages blotted brighter once and hummed. "I'm sorry," she said. "But think about it. They must be waiting for you to say something."

▲   ▲   ▲

Rain nailed down in the window like tiny bars someone pushed from the sky. My grandfather's room was airless and neat, the walls bare, a single blue blanket folded at the foot of the bed. It was as if he hadn't wanted to be distracted by anything extra, any decoration that might make him careless about germs, or the roses and his house. Marietta was napping across the hall, lying daintily in her housecoat.

I'd told her I'd go through his closet and change the sheets, because she said she couldn't set foot in there, it reminded her of him too much. She'd let six months go by already without doing anything about his things, but now she wanted to donate what she could to the church. On the nightstand there was a Bible, a coaster crocheted into a pink-edged snowflake. He didn't save what he didn't need, so I knew I could finish quickly. "There's no sense in keeping things you can't use," he'd said. "You'll weigh yourself down with clutter." Clutter hadn't bothered Hanna, though. When I finally went back to get her things, it would take two full days to sort through the records and jewelry, the paperbacks under the bed, the perfume bottles and silk scarves. I wondered what had made Hanna and him so different in this way, and if it could be as simple as not having much besides blood in common.

Though it was the middle of the afternoon, the room went dim. The suits in the closet still smelled of his limy soap and hair oil. I took them off their hangers and folded all three over my arm, gray, black, blue. They would sell them at the church rummage sale this spring. The dress shoes on the floor were worn down at the heels, the leather smelling of sulfur, wrinkled at the toes. I laid these over the suits in a cardboard box and set it by the door.

I opened the middle drawer of the bureau, filled with mothballs and dark wool socks rolled and tucked into knots. I tossed them into a paper bag and went on to the next drawer, where bleached T-shirts and boxer shorts lay tightly folded in rows. These would become rags, or we'd just throw them out, but they seemed too personal to touch. He was such a private person, someone who held himself in, it felt wrong to be going through his underwear, even if he was gone.

I heard the hum of the refrigerator in the kitchen, my cobbled footsteps as I dragged bags and boxes near the door. The house felt hugely empty, yawning, and the metallic smell of rain blew in from the window.

In the top drawer of the bureau, I found four ties, a tin of loose change, and a useless thing I was surprised he'd kept, a glass paperweight with a moth inside of it, wings frozen in an icy light. I tried to see the insect face, but it was smashed.

As I swept the floor, I thought again of Hanna and how he'd hidden his love for her, every single time she tried to come back. He must have had some rationale for it. She was like the blackspot he had to regularly spray off his roses. He wouldn't forgive her until she asked for forgiveness (and for what?). Or he'd forgiven her, but only as one has to forgive another human being, all of us sinners. I could see him holding that frame of an argument in his heart, propping it up like the trellis that held up his one Lysistrata rosebush, and then when he heard Hanna had died, it must have collapsed.

I didn't know if my mother had always been her father's favorite, or if that had only come later, after Hanna left, but all my mother's attention couldn't have made up for Hanna's absence. How had he come to the point where he loved her absence more than her?

She'd said to me once, when we were in Marietta's kitchen, rinsing the dishes, "When I was your age I was so bored, I felt like a weed, just stuck here growing, and growing ugly. You'll do better than that."

I took my time rubbing the rag over the spindly legs of the nightstand and the knobs of the bureau, the plain handles of modest furniture, grotesque only when you looked at a piece and forgot the rest of the structure, this squat mushroom knob, this oddly bulbous leg, objects you didn't notice unless you stared too long at them, things that had dumbly surrounded him as he poured the arsenic into his cup.

Standing up, I dropped the rag on the bureau and glanced at myself in the mirror above it. My father's old flannel shirt gaped open near the tail of a pink scar, a line like a piece of barbed wire. I moved closer. If I looked hard enough, there was a way to dismiss the longing, like studying a picture or a rock that had nothing to do with me. This mark was as definite as paint or ink, fake-looking. It stung as I stepped back, then throbbed as if all the blood I had were rushing into it.

I went down the hall to the kitchen and poured myself a glass of water from the tap. The water, cool in my throat, traced a blue mark down to my stomach. I turned on the faucet, filled the glass again, and drank, as lightning sheeted over the kitchen. It was so pleasant to be leaning against the sink, drinking water in that flash of light, I thought I should feel more and try to see less. The rain suddenly quickened to a sound like gravel nervously pouring onto the roof, and I went away from the sink. I struck a match on my jeans and felt the ecstatic heat brush my fingertips before I threw it out the screen door into the rain.

I went back to my grandfather's bedroom. The last thing to do was to change the sheets on the bed, and I'd be finished. I pulled the pillows from their cases and peeled off the blanket and sheets, uncovering an old ticking mattress. A pink scrap of paper hung out from the corner of it. I ripped it off, and in my fingers held a pearly arm. It must have been the work of the children Marietta sometimes baby-sat for, I thought. Lifting the edge of the mattress, I found the rest of the body, a fleshy girl eating grapes, a paper doll without her clothes.

The rain began to stop, and the musty smell from the closet mixed with the scent of clean linens. I heaved the mattress back, then pushed it off the box spring.

A crushed pile of paper bodies lay tangled there. I knelt down to look closer. They were all naked women, their limbs bent back, arms, legs, and heads crinkled together. One with her inner organs diagrammed, a mermaid with teacup breasts, a Venus cut from her shell. I got dizzy when I saw how many there were and picked up a picture of a woman in red high heels and an apron, her breasts like frog eyes. A creased one of a brunette wearing stockings and a garter belt, a gun held at her thigh.

I saw the shapely holes in the library's medical and art books, the *National Geographic*s and photography magazines, my grandfather lurking nervously in the stacks, one hand stuffing the paper figure into his pocket. He'd spent a lot of time alone in his room, and he'd washed his hands sometimes until they bled. He must not have known what to do about the lust in himself any more than he'd known what to do about Hanna. Something like a thick oil formed on my skin. No one should have seen this. No one.

One round paper breast had withered from moisture. I thought of those silences he tunneled into, and Marietta's careful lipstick. My eyes teared up, and all the skin blurred and gleamed on the paper like sweat. He'd cut each one out so carefully, the tips of long fingers, the complicated hairdos, never a trace of the original background—part of me wanted to save them. They were flat, paper women, just flimsy, shiny pictures and low voices spun out in his head. I got up, swept the whole pile into a box, and pressed the lid down over legs, arms, stomachs, all those breasts, all those pretty faces.

Why hadn't he thrown them out? Maybe he wanted Marietta to find them, to punish her for her vanity, her withholding of sex. It seemed more likely, though, that he'd forgotten about the paper women, the way something you've never told anyone eventually loses its realness, and you're grateful.

I carried the box out the back door and dropped it on the wet ground near the garbage. It would have been too easy to blame the church for this. *If your right hand causes you to sin, cut it off.* It was deeper than any kind of righteousness or shame, whatever it was that had made paper less troubling than flesh. *Something bit him,* my father once said, about his silences. *I don't know what it was, but a long time ago, he got bit.* A kind of poison, maybe, had made it unbearable for him to touch another's skin.

The sky was gray and the air still damp. His rosebushes were brown and scraggly. A single gray bird tapped its beak at the water in the feeder.

He must have been lonely. When you had a secret life, you wanted it discovered just as much as you feared its being found out. It made me sick to my stomach to think about his collection, and I knew I'd try to forget this just as he must have each time he pushed one of the paper women under the mattress, just as I tried to forget that I had been one of those paper women, lying in the dark with a man, my skin slick and flawless, not feeling anything, not even knowing who touched me.

My hands were cold. I took the matches from my pocket and lit one. I held it there a moment before dropping it. The smoke was chalky black, like a rinse of coal, and smelled of cinnamon. I thought of us all burning in that box, breasts, hands, feet, thighs, burning up for him, all our bodies ghosted up in the smoke.

▲   ▲   ▲

What lies inside a cage of flames? The truth, the heart, but burned up before you can see it. Only traces remain in the ashes, a pattern you guess at or invent, an intangible thing that might leave a mark, but could just as easily blow away.

▲   ▲   ▲

I couldn't lie still, even when I tried to think of the mild smell of daisies or the rub of fleece. I threw off the sheets and blankets and sat up, holding my chest. I felt a combination of infinite tiredness and the desire to get up and run. My legs felt disjointed and loose, my stomach hot. Hanna's face and my grandfather's clenched hands kept appearing in my head, and I was obsessed with trying to remember everything I could about them, things they'd done, the exact tone of their complexions, the gestures they made when they asked questions, but this only magnified the fact that my grandfather and Hanna, inside their skins, inside their heads, were enigmas. One day I'd be at home in a place like Marrakesh or Singapore, a place people here wouldn't be able to find on the map, because foreigners like them felt so familiar. And their pull on me had only strengthened since their deaths. Was it love, or was that just the word I reached for because there wasn't another word for it?

I got out of bed and changed into pants and a shirt. I grabbed a wool jacket. I thought a walk might be the thing to take my mind off them, no matter how long it took. I could sleep late the next morning, well into the afternoon if I wanted to. Down the hall I heard a guest turn on a light and cough, a toilet flushing. I took the stairs lightly and walked through the dark of the lobby, unlocked the front door, and then locked it again behind me.

The snow looked like sea-foam or soap, too airy to have a temperature. But the air was freezing, I'd forgotten a hat and gloves, and my jacket was too thin. I didn't feel like creeping up and down the stairs again for my coat, so I gave up the idea of a walk and decided to take a drive. I walked over plowed snow piles to my car, in a cleared space near the curb. I got in, and after a few tries the engine started and the heater blew at my fingertips as the tires crunched over the salt scattering the pavement.

I drove down Lincoln toward the train tracks. It was dark, but a film of light lay over the snow. I passed the train platform and the gas station, the long white fields fenced with telephone poles.

That uneasy, testing feeling came toward me. I recognized it, dissolute and just beyond my grasp in that dark, edging down the road in front of me, glinting and dancing over the snow, and I had been afraid of it so long I didn't chase it. I slowed down near Taft Way, a dirt road that wound past the Barr house to the edge of Lake Eliza. Someone had plowed the road, so I turned through the narrow gorge between snowdrifts, into the pine trees, and traced the shallow path swept by the headlights, pushing into the needly green dark. There was a static of false energy in my blood, but my eyes were dry and exhausted. My foot cramped on the gas pedal, frozen at a level to push the car at a reluctant speed.

The house popped out of the darkness, a wet gray of old wood and cinder blocks. The Barrs had moved out decades before, and no one had lived there since I could remember. I parked, turned off the engine, and blew on my hands. In the headlights, the front porch sloped over the mouth of the door. Old boards crossed the windows, and the foundation teetered catty-corner like the aftermath of an accident. Teenagers broke into the house on dares, and the police sometimes chased out vagrants, but most of the time it stood empty. I didn't understand why someone in City Hall hadn't torn it down or rebuilt it yet, why all these years it had just sat there, secret in the woods, as if no one could bear to consider it long enough to decide what to do with it.

I got out, went around to the trunk, and lifted the gasoline and flashlight out of the clutter. I sat on the fender with the tin between my knees, pointing the flashlight at a blue-flecked snowbank hunched like a shoulder. Then I shone the light at the crooked front porch, pushed the beam down to the place where it slumped and then up to the roof, blinking it past a small round window. I traced the house's outline, then swirled the light around, scribbling out the lines I'd traced.

These were thin and porous walls you could break through easily. My father had punched through the wall of our dining room like that. Two cracks rivered down and shakily met where the paint bulged, and when he'd come home, furious, screaming, I sidled into the doorway of the kitchen. His head rolled back, his hand fisted, and it went right through the wall. I remembered the astonished look on his face when he pulled his hand out from the plaster, scraped and bleeding, and he was quiet again as if he'd let go of his fury on the other side of that wall.

I pointed the flashlight at the warped grain of the house's wood. It had accumulated a history, punched walls and handprints, broken shutters, lost doorknobs, a foundation that rose on one side, sank on the other: all this time that a fire would collapse.

Jumping off the fender, I followed the path up to the front porch and warily went up the rickety steps. I turned the knob on the door and opened it a crack before it caught on the huge padlock. I walked around a hole where the porch was worn away and scooted along a lone plank until I got to the window. Through the X of two rotten boards, I pointed the flashlight inside the house to what once must have been the living room or dining room. All I could see was a lumpy floor. My cheek grazed a splintery edge of wood as I called inside, "Come out. It's an emergency!" Beside me wind flicked through the bare trees.

I leaped off the other side of the porch into knee-deep snow. The side of the house leaned in slightly, and there was a scrappy frilled curtain behind one of the boarded windows. Trudging through the snow, my feet and ankles numb, I squirted gasoline up against the white paint curling off gray walls, the tin burping in my fingers. I held the flashlight under my arm and saw the gasoline tearing down in rivulets as I went around to the back, grown over with vines and black with some kind of mold or moss. I squirted the gasoline so high up on the wall it fell back down and stung my cheek, and I had to wipe it off on the rough sleeve of my jacket.

I went on squirting gasoline. This felt proprietary somehow, like my grandfather's checking his roses each night for blackspot or red spider mites. My feet tangled in icy overgrown bushes near the last corner, where a stone jutted out that said BARR.

People would wonder what had happened here. In the morning the ground would be burned black, soot smoking in the snow— a startling blankness like the hungry nothing after a storm.

Only for a second did regret shake in my hand as I fished up the matches from my pocket. I tore one out, pulled it between the matchbook cover, and when it lit, I wanted to sing. I heard a cat meow inside. "Get out of there, kitty," I screamed. "Here, kitty, come out!" I banged on the window with my fist, not hearing it anymore, but not seeing it creep out either. The wind sheared over the trees. I tossed the match at a string of gasoline and it zigzagged the wall.

Lifting my knees high up out of the snow, I ran to the edge of the woods and swiveled around to watch. It was the pale yellow of a winter sun, wobbling like a reflection.

I tried to ignore the thing that itched, tingled at my wrist, a twig or a leaf caught there. I hoped the cat had got out somehow; it wasn't the point to burn anything that was alive, only what wouldn't move. On the roof a wave of fire arched back and whipped into another; the flames twisted and preened, then coyly shrank back. I looked down, and in a blurry second, I thought I'd bled it, the flame ruffling up my sleeve. I fell on my arm into the snow and tried to put it out. Yellow flicked at my elbow, and then the heat turned to ice. I lay there, my hair wet, my cheek numb in the snow, the pain in my wrist exquisitely strummed with fine nerves, an intricate musical torment that felt familiar. Beside me, the fire applauded, and I watched it from the snow, one cheek frozen, the other hot with firelight.

My father's rage was so separate from him: that voice as if it had been piped into his throat, the one time he hit me so hard I fell back onto the prongs of the steaming radiator, the backs of my thighs burned over the scars. When he played the organ, I heard the rage, pushed low in the sharp harmonies, then radiant as the melody rose to its familiar refrain. Those hymns. Something in him was trying to break through them.

My heart beat faster as the fire billowed at the trees. I finally pulled my hand out of the snow and clambered up to my knees. My pants and jacket were wet, and between my shoulder and hand an emptiness spread. Hot and cold scarves of air whirled against my face as the numbness in my wrist cut to pain. I packed snow against it and looked up again. The house's frame wobbled uncertainly, then collapsed, and the flames fell into the snow.

Slamming the door of my car, I heard sirens. I started the ignition with the hand of my unburned wrist and the car rocked through the white, sliding over icy spots, snowflakes salting the windows. I swerved onto the highway in the opposite direction of the sirens and drove without hearing anything for a long time, my head cold and unoccupied.

▲   ▲   ▲

The next day each time I touched water I thought I smelled smoke. I was coughing in the shower. My complexion paled. I wore perfume and didn't stand close to anyone so they wouldn't smell it. The weepy blisters on my wrist turned crusty and brown.

At work Jo was gathering receipts when my sleeve fell back and she saw them. "Ella, what happened?" she said, grabbing my arm and turning the burn toward her.

"I fell against the iron," I said, my heart like a caged mouse. "It looks worse than it is." I thought she'd never believe me.

"It looks painful," she said. "Have you put anything on it?"

Later in the lobby two women sat waiting for an old relative to come down from upstairs.

"I can't believe the Barr house is gone."

"I heard it was a firebug," said the one with thin strands of hair that clung to her face like paint.

"They call them pyromaniacs, Susan. They're not cute." I stood up and turned around, pretended to be checking the keys in their boxes.

On Thursday Jo and I went to the Big Wheel for breakfast. We were drinking coffee, and when Jo went to the bathroom I heard the men talking in the booth behind us. "I think there was someone in that house. A woman. He had a lover in there." The finely scrambled egss suddenly reminded me of the fuzz on baby chicks, and I put down my fork.

"That house was condemned. No one could live there."

"No, but you could if you were desperate to meet someone."

My coffee cup rattled in its saucer, and when Jo came back I was already at the register, the thin paper check wavering between my fingers as I stared down at the chewing gum and mints in the glass case.

I had to keep myself away from matches for a while, keep myself calm. Where it was easiest not to think about them was work, with Paul there to distract me. I made myself study his face, the wrinkles brooming from the corners of his eyes, the broad plush cheekbones, the faint parallel lines between his nostrils and his lips, the comma in his chin, and the sudsy stubble near his neck. His flesh began to look more substantial than anyone else's.

"When I was a kid," he told me one night—the word sounded ostentatious in his mouth—"I was growing unevenly or something like that, my eardrums before everything else. For about a year every sound I heard was magnified a thousand times. At night I could hear the bugs in the weeds outside, my parents breathing in the room across the hall from mine, my brother combing his hair in the bathroom. Even the flip of a card, the click of a checker on the board, was unbearably loud. I couldn't sleep. I was sure I was going to die soon, but I was too afraid to tell anyone about it."

I held two fingers against my mouth, knowing that fear of not being able to trust anyone but yourself.

XI

▌▌▌▐▌▐▌▐▐▌▐▐▐▐▐▌▐▐▌▐▐▌▐▐▐▐▐▐▐▌▐▐▐▐▐▌▐▐▐▐▐▌▐▐▐

A s I walked back from Marietta's the cold air had a fluted sheen. I wore the plaid wool coat she'd given me for Christmas, my gloved hands deep in the pockets as I picked my way tentatively over the ragged ice left in the furrow of plowed snow. This time of year, even in boots, it was easy to slip and fall. You could die that way if your head slammed back on the pavement, and they'd find you lying there on the sidewalk, arms and legs sprawled. Tonight there were lights on in most of the windows, a greenish tint to the snow.

I walked slowly, with cramped steps, curling my toes in the thick socks inside my boots. I'd almost blurted out what I knew to Marietta. I'd been a second away from saying, "Why didn't you tell me she was dead?" but stopped myself just as she held up a red feather and studied it. No matter what I said to her, she'd never allow the truth to stand up and breathe long enough for her to feel regret. It terrified her. She had her birds, her feather collection. She wasn't going to kill herself as my grandfather had.

I tracked through an untouched sheet of snow and tried to feel what lay beneath it with the soles of my boots. Was this the place with the path stones? It was always hard to remember what lay beneath snow with only a marker, a spigot, a mailbox, to direct you. It made you realize how much you knew intuitively and how much you didn't. I was wrong. I saw the warped wood bench and remembered this was the rough baseball field, where the boys practiced. I turned onto Washington and heard a dog bark somewhere down the block. Inside my gloves and socks, my fingers and toes stung with cold.

I was walking toward Grace Church, where the colors in the stained glass vibrated in the gray stone. I realized I'd been wanting to go back but while the church was empty, and remembered the door was sometimes unlocked for choir practice. I thought I'd just go in and warm up for a minute. I went up the steps and pressed my thumb down on the handle until it clicked open.

Closing the heavy door behind me, I stood in the dark hallway where Pastor Beck greeted people after services, took off my gloves and blew on my hands, listening for footsteps or voices. Moving through the dark, I bumped the table where they served coffee on Sunday mornings, and something fell over. I opened the door with a cross-shaped window and walked slowly into the sanctuary, where two lights glowed near the altar.

The pews seemed to multiply and the ceiling expand with the smell of candle wax and old paper. The wooden cross over the altar looked worn and functional, as if it had been cut from someone's dining-room table. The problem was that the church sometimes trained people to become only more still and solid, to use God as a fortress against the very breath of life which could change you, but I thought sometimes in hymns you could hear the desire to burn away to nothingness, to not cling to yourself so much. I edged into the third pew on the right and looked back at the balcony, where the organ pipes rippled familiarly out of the dark. I turned back around and opened a hymnal, staring at the black notes, tiny vines strung neatly on trellises.

No one had replaced the altar candles, and the crooked stubs made the altar look makeshift with its withered brown flowers. I draped my coat over the pew in front of me.

Marietta had told me that last week they'd prayed for Hanna. In the other stained-glass windows there was Jesus with a shepherd's crook, a few sheep nuzzling in the folds of his robe. FEED MY LAMBS, it said. In another, Jesus poured from one jug to another, turning water into wine, and beside that one, loaves of bread and a basket of fish waited beneath Jesus' outstretched arms. Miracles of feeding. In another window Jesus made the sign of the blessing over a sleeping boat of disciples. THE TRUTH SHALL SET YOU FREE.

I looked at the stained-glass window depicting Shadrach, Meshach, and Abednego in the furnace, their arms lifted into the triangle flames. For them, it had been a test of faith. Was I testing my own? Daring God to show me something? To let me get caught? I looked at the ascension window, where Jesus' feet were sunk in purple clouds, his hands outstretched to feel the breeze through the nail holes. The apostles *oh*ed around him, their heads craned at an awkward angle, as if they were about to fall into the field of melancholy and scrawny sheep below. The glass had been broken where one of Jesus' feet should have been, and because there was no one in Porter who knew the old craft, they had simply replaced it with black glass. It looked infinite and empty there, like a jagged piece of night.

I glanced down at my wrist in my lap, rolled back the bandage. The blisters were healing, most of them dried now, the skin brown and hard. I thought, *It was an accident, it won't happen again. I'm done with all that.* I wrapped the bandage back around my wrist.

Music chased the devil away, Luther said, and seeing my father at the organ, I believed it. Just as his rage came from nowhere, so did this music he called down out of the air to make him believe in a hidden world, where God's face, turned away from us, would one day turn back.

The rafters lunged above me, the church suddenly huge and hollow, floating. I wanted it to take me somewhere safe. The match heads in my pocket felt like seeds, and I thought about planting roses in the new place, wherever that was, not red ones, but yellow and pink roses, colors that didn't ignite the eye but blended easily into skin.

I got up, with the imprint of hard wood on my thighs, and walked up the side aisle. I ran my finger over the tracery in the window, the black outlines like soot. They were two hundred years old, brought over from Germany, and the glass looked watery, as if it would break easily. Up close the details were different: I saw Hanna's face hidden in the turn of a path, a disciple's cupped hand was an eye, the drape in Jesus' robe a gathering flame he was trying to let go of.

▲   ▲   ▲

A fire is only energy before it gets too pure, muscle behind the clear skin of air. The rules of science and safety can only pretend to fathom this, only hint at a way to bend it under control. Silent, the warmth slowly emerges, and the worms in the soil, if it's damp, thread away from the first blaze reflected in birds' eyes. The edge won't devour its middle, but teases it out and up until the flames streak blue. Only the core might eat its own flames, gobble its own like a path leading along a tame snake, then coiling up itself into a serpent about to strike.

▲   ▲   ▲

Upstairs a television chattered. I was in the back room facing the clean towels and sheets folded on the shelf, stacking the little pink soaps in a box. Part of me was keeping an eye on the door, but it was early and there were no reservations. All day I'd lain in bed reading and nibbling on crackers. Now I watched my hands line up the pink soaps in their yellow wrappers into even lines and uniform rectangles, the waxy residue on my fingertips like the oily moisture from the insides of roses. It was odd that the soaps' artificial rose smell, nothing like real roses, would remind me so much of them: brocaded on the bush, red, or yellow, none of them perfect, a few of them eaten by mites. Just as I finished the box, suddenly I was crying.

I went into the bathroom and shut the door. A hiccup stabbed at my chest. I looked at the metal stall and the chrome bulge of the soap dispenser over the rust-stained sink. I hadn't been thinking of Hanna or my grandfather. I hadn't been guarding against grief, only mindlessly stacking soaps. As I gasped between sobs, the sick sweet smell of the bathroom cleaner made me gag, and I had to go back out behind the desk.

I tried to look at the grain of paint in the wall, tried to hum the tune of that song about woodpeckers and moles. I didn't know exactly what had made me cry: Hanna's disappearance and my grandfather's locked-up life, the fear that I would be caught, and my mother's hold on me, tangled in a mess I hadn't meant to coax up. I'd only been stacking soaps.

I heard someone come in, but didn't turn around and hoped they'd go away and come back later. Keys jangled, and then a hand touched my arm. Paul. "What's wrong?" His voice sounded as if he were talking through a cloth.

I held my hands over my face in a ridiculous mask. Whose tears were these? I had to say one true thing so they'd stop. "My aunt died."

He put his hand gently on my back. "I'm so sorry. Today?"

I choked on this, shaking my head. "Weeks ago, no, months—"

My voice sounded like a metal lump dredged up with mud from a drainpipe. He put his arm around me, and my shoulders shook against him. I wasn't going to say any more.

Having him there made me panicked. The tears would subside and my breaths gain gravity, but only if I didn't try to speak.

He didn't say anything else, though when I drew back my fingers, I saw his lips move, as if he were struggling for the right words in Polish, then translating them in his head.

▲   ▲   ▲

Paul had gone to boys' schools and said he'd been painfully shy until he left Poland. "I used to be at my desk studying or taking a test, and I'd hear girls walking back from their classes, laughing and talking, and I would listen and watch them in their plaid skirts, but they might as well have been on the other side of the earth, because I couldn't say a word to them." He claimed to have had his first conversation with a girl his own age on the plane to Chicago, but that was hard for me to believe. "She was from Peoria, Illinois," he said, pronouncing the *s*. "And as soon as we landed she ran away from me into the arms of this guy who must have been her boyfriend. I didn't have any fashions on her, but I didn't want to cause trouble either, so I didn't wave good-bye."

"Designs, you mean," I said.

He'd brought me chocolate the night I told him about Hanna, about the time she'd come home and collapsed on my grandparents' couch, how everyone gathered around her and stared reverently as if she'd been destined to lie there asleep for the rest of her life. Calling her name, I finally woke her, and she groggily sat up, eyes glinting in the pepper of her mascara. One by one, my grandparents and parents left the room. "It was like they preferred her dead, or asleep anyway," I said.

He was standing under the chandelier reaching up to twirl it in his fingers, and the light scattered against the walls. "She was a runaway?"

"No, not exactly. She just made the family so nervous, she finally decided it would be better to leave."

He stopped twirling the chandelier and pulled at a strand of glass teardrops. "What made them nervous?"

"I don't know," I said. I'd seen her room, touched her things, and still had to guess. "She was . . . eccentric. Once she drove my grandfather's Plymouth into a ditch, and instead of calling anyone, she walked the rest of the way through the snow. She was wearing stockings, high heels, and an evening dress because she was going to a dance, but she just let the police find the car. My grandparents thought she had been kidnapped, when all the time she was dancing in the high-school gym." He looked away from the chandelier and smiled at me. He liked her. I told him about the time she cut off all the heads of my grandfather's roses and floated them like red lily pads in the neighborhood swimming pool, about the night when she went to the high school and wrote bawdy limericks in toothpaste on the windows of her classrooms, and about the Christmas Eve she'd wrapped blinking colored lights around her waist and figured out a way to keep them flashing with a battery as she went to the midnight service. No one had told me these stories—I'd made them up.

Paul laughed. "Maybe you take after her. Are you up to those kind of pranks?"

Pranks. If only I could have thought of the fires that way.

▲   ▲   ▲

I was so trembly during the day it was hard to eat, but at night when I was alone after work, I was starving. I ate whatever I could find in my tiny rental refrigerator, or else went down the hall to the vending machines for potato chips, peanut butter crackers, candy. It wasn't much, but I felt fat afterward.

Sometimes I'd undress and look in the mirror to see if it had made any difference. My stomach would curve out more than I liked, but the scars always looked the same. I'd turn around, following the currents that whipped over my buttocks up onto my back and ended in a watery, pale ripple. I'd lift my flawless right breast and stare at the scarred skin beneath it, red thorns, a cup with teeth, forked tongues. On my stomach, a horsehead with a thick mane. On my left breast, a swiveling rope, a serpent's tail. Just under my collar bone, two shiny ovals like an opened locket. No one is more vain than a woman who has been burned. In certain moods I could lose whole hours like this, looking with a different gaze at each scar, this one ugly, this one barely noticeable, this one a tattoo, this one a smear of lipstick, this one drips of honey.

Sometimes I'd step back in the dimness, let my eyes blur, and see myself naked without them, the outline of my breasts and hips, the flat spread of my shoulders, the length of my thighs— she was the shadow of a woman I might have been. I'd step closer, spread my dark hair around my shoulders and under my breasts. If I stood exactly in that pose, the locks of hair lying exactly right, most of the scars were hidden, but I would have had to paste my hair down to my skin to keep them that way.

I persuaded myself out of these trances by singing my favorite song and naming to myself the last ten new words I'd learned: *incommodious, erethism.* Or I told myself it was useless to think about my body—it was alive and breathing. I had all my limbs, my eyes, and ears, and teeth. To feel sorry for yourself was the ugliest thing in the world, and it was a kind of ungratefulness my father would not have forgiven.

XII

░▓▒░▓▒░▓▒░▓▒░▓▒░▓▒░▓▒░▓▒░▓▒░▓▒░▓▒░

That night Paul came around to the side of the desk, unlocked the gate and slipped behind it. "Do you know why we have two percent of copper and zinc in our bodies?"

I shook my head.

"Billions of years ago a star exploded, and those bits of the star got in whatever live material made us. Isn't that amazing?" He was moving his hands a lot, as if trying to swat something away so he could think. "We're made of stardust!"

Sometimes his enthusiasm embarrassed me.

"It sounds like a Frank Sinatra song."

Paul came closer, laughing. "I keep thinking I'll be able to see it. Look how shiny your hair is." He lifted a strand from my shoulder and rubbed it between his fingers like a watchband or a bracelet. I heard the far-off whistle of the train. Something pounded in the base of my throat. "Sorry," he said, pulling away his hand. "I just wanted to touch it." He cocked his head. "Guess I'll have another round."

He was taking a physics class at the college, and he liked to come into the lobby on his break and complain about the professor, who talked like a machine and put most of the students to sleep, then expected them to pass his trick exams, but Paul was

177

still always excited about what he'd learned. He smiled the whole time he explained the Uncertainty Principle to me. If you took a very small object, as small as an atom or an electron, and shone a light wave onto it, the photon bounced back to your eye, so you could see where the object was when the light hit it. But the photon also kicked the object away as soon as the light hit it. "So you can know where the object was," Paul said, "but not where it is."

"Like trying to know a person," I muttered.

"What was that?"

"Nothing."

He found a poetry in the way things functioned—he liked bridges, for example. I'd never thought of them as anything other than a way to get across water.

"Some of them are very delicately calibrated to bend a certain amount with the wind, so the whole structure doesn't collapse, but has just enough give. It must be calculated," he said. "And some lift up at a certain time, but only at an exact angle. It's the old ones that just sit there, but they are beautiful, too, because their stiffness makes them fragile."

"You should see the Golden Gate Bridge," I said.

"Oh, I have. It was the first place I went when I got here. It was a long train ride from Chicago all the way to California, and I had to sleep that night in the train station with the bums, but it was worth it."

When he talked this way, his face seemed to grow, in the lifts and turns of the folds in his skin around his mouth. "There was a bridge in Toruń that my mother and I had to cross every week when I went with her to the market. It was old, but very beautiful stone, and she would let me sit on the edge and look down at the river. The only reason it survived the war was because it was off the track, a road nobody ever took."

"How old?"

"From the Middle Ages, I think. It was mended, but the stone was original. During the war my grandmother tried to jump off it, she said, but she decided not to because the water looked too hard and cold." It would have been easy to say that, of course, she'd never really meant to jump, but the line suicides crossed seemed exactly that faint to me now: The water looked too hard and cold that day.

Later, I'd left the gate unlatched and didn't hear him come back from his round. He tapped my shoulder, and I flinched, holding my chest. He wasn't laughing the way he usually did when he startled me. His knuckles knocked against the desktop, and he bent down to look into my face as if he were searching for something on my cheek, then kissed me between my ear and my throat.

"I think I've seen all the rooms but yours."

I couldn't have lifted my arm, and my voice flitted higher. "It's like all the other ones."

"No it's not."

When we went upstairs, something bright turned in my stomach as I unlocked the door. Inside, I went straight to the bathroom to fix my hair and pour a little bourbon into two plastic cups.

I came back, and we sat on the knobby chenille bedspread. He seemed larger and louder than he had downstairs, trying to repress the smile on his purplish lips, a scent like soap and lemons in his clothes. He glanced at my suitcases. "You haven't unpacked?"

"I just don't have anywhere to put them," I said. My sweaters were strewn on the dresser, and above it, the square mirror hung like an empty television screen waiting for something to happen. My books lay towered under the painting of the dog standing taut and noble with its ears pricked and mouth parted, listening to some high-pitched whistle. I didn't know if Paul remembered what I'd told him about my scars and, if he did, whether he imagined them as slighter than they were, the vain exaggeration of a girl trying to seem tragic. I hated that idea, and knew I wouldn't attempt to fool him. I turned off all the lights, except the tidy lamp on the bureau, and made a joke about a sloppy fat man who'd followed Paul on one of his rounds to see for himself that the hotel was safe. "Good thing he checked, right?" We laughed, and his elbow knocked against my book on the nightstand. My bosom and thighs were warmly expanding, and we were kissing again, his hand squeezing my shoulder. I wanted to talk more until I could figure out what to do. I pulled away. "I have to tell you—"

He looked down at my lap and put his hand on my arm and turned it so the blistered spot faced the light. "What happened here?"

It wasn't me, I thought, *please, not me.* I shrugged and tried to smile. "Just the iron."

He put his other hand on my knee. "You have a scar here?"

I nodded. He moved his hand farther up my leg, to where the zipper began on my skirt. He spread his other hand against my stomach. "There, too," I said. He nodded and murmured something. The light seemed to flutter. He kissed me again, pulled me back into his arms. His voice was hoarse and shaky. "Will you show me?"

The light spun and needled against the wall. I gulped down the last of my bourbon and the rest in his glass, too. I was afraid, but if I didn't do this now I'd never be able to. I'd let him see them, and then that would be it. It would be over with. If he left, I would still be okay. It wouldn't kill me.

I stood up, slipped off my stockings, and my hand shook so much it took a while to find the catch to the zipper of my skirt. It swerved as I pulled it, and when I lost my grip, the skirt fell to the floor. That was enough. I could leave my sweater on. He leaned over and traced his finger along the border of a scar on my thigh, which in the dimness looked almost natural, like a mass of freckles or the spotted colors on an animal's fur. He inhaled a breath. "You're lucky it didn't—" Then he started to say something else, but swallowed. With his head lowered, his forehead and cheeks looked extremely wide, and I noticed how clear and pale the flesh on his face was, his mouth full and open. He looked up and stared at my sweater, a pale-blue one that I thought made my neck look long and my shoulders regal. I wasn't going to take it off. He reached up and flipped the ribbed band at my waist. "Come on," he said gently, and he seemed vulnerable in his largeness, as if his body were too much for him to carry around and he badly needed my help.

Do it fast, I told myself, quickly pulling it up over my head, and the scars burst red from my torso. Sitting beside him on the bed, as casually as I could, I unhooked my bra and shrugged it off, his shirt grazing my bare arm. I was breathing so hard my chest hurt. My body felt monstrously large, and the scars stung and rippled, the horsehead like a bad smear of blood, the pink thorns above it like claws. There were furred orangish flecks under my right breast, the rope looped on the left, but around the nipples the skin was perfect and white, like stone or velvet.

He closed his eyes, then opened them again. "So these are them," he said, stroking the marks whipping up the small of my back. He drew in closer, but I couldn't read his face. *Not pity,* I said to myself. *Curiosity is better than pity.*

His kiss was tense. I was sure he was going to leave, and I pulled back.

"You're not used to it," he said, coaxing me down to the bed so we were facing one another. His eyes were huge and dark, the lashes long and curved. "Don't be afraid."

He kissed my ear, and the stubble of his beard rubbed against my cheek, his hands puttered around my waist, then up to the first curve of my breasts. I kept thinking he would leave.

When he took off his shirt, his white skin sloped above me, his chest flecked with a few black hairs. I watched the arch of his neck, the pulse and swallow there in the paleness. The lamp on the bureau glittered. He stared down at me as if he were memorizing, going over a formula in his head that he would later recite. I kept waiting for the numbness, for that creeping sense of dislocation, like losing your hand in the dark, but it never came. The gold-white light behind his shoulder flickered, dangerous and lush.

Afterward, lying back beside him, I noticed the walls tilted at the sloped ceiling, and I felt lightheaded and dizzy. When I glanced back at his face, he grimaced and turned on his stomach. "Look," he said, moving the lamp closer.

Between his shoulder blades clung thin streaks of red. The scars briared down to the small of his back, not raised, but dark and definite, almost purple, from a belt or a stick. "It's where my uncle hit me." His hands pressed flat into the mattress, the tops of his fingers whitened. I sat up and ran the side of my thumb along one of the scars, then up over the curve of his shoulder. "He was a bastard, but I didn't tell anyone. He was paying for my school." He turned over and sat up. "We're the same enough, aren't we?"

That night I didn't sleep much, an unsteady shimmering every time I opened my eyes. Very early in the morning, when the light was still tentative and faint, I woke up, startled to see his face. I reached to smooth my hair, wipe the crust from my eyes. He cupped his hand next to my ear and combed his fingers down the length of my hair.

▲   ▲   ▲

I became strangely confident. A couple of times I wore shorter sleeves or shorter skirts to work. When I'd notice a guest stare a second too long at a scar, I'd look into their eyes and straighten my shoulders, and they'd gaze back at my face as if they hadn't seen anything much. It was easier than I thought.

"You should come back with me to Poland sometime," Paul said one night, in his basement room. He lived in his cousin's house, and there were maps pinned to all the walls, a little shaky card table desk where he worked, and a mattress on the floor.

"I'd like that," I said. *Only if you throw out all the matches,* I told myself. *Give that up or you'll ruin it.* I sat down cross-legged on his mattress and opened up the physics book he was reading to a bright diagram of circles and arrows. "Where would we stay?"

"With my mother in Kruszwica. I'll take you to see Lake Goplo and the Mouse Tower—a part of this old castle that I like, where this evil king lived with his syphilis. And there's the salt-springs spa."

He was good-natured in that way of people who appreciate absurdity and don't let it upset them much. He made me laugh with his impressions of the whiny woman who never had enough towels and the stiff, lantern-jawed man who kept insisting we were late with his wake-up calls. But when he was really angry, his humor had an edge. After the person left, he would pull out his mock sword and pretend to chop off their head or plunge it into their heart and say sarcastically, "There!"

As Jo put it, we became a couple, and a few weeks after this we were at the Big Wheel after midnight, drinking coffee. I thought the waitresses looked prettier than the last time I remembered, their eyes more luminous, their reluctant smiles less crooked. He was eating almost-burnt hash browns. I'd already asked him about his parents, and he'd told me that his mother worked in a textile factory and his father, who had been an engineer, had died. We had that in common, too, though Paul hardly remembered his father.

He was telling me that night about the uncle who had beaten

him, his mother's older brother, a foreman at the textile factory where she worked. "What's the phrase you have? The chewing image?"

I started to laugh. "The spitting image."

"That, I'm told I'm that for my father, and I think my uncle was jealous of his success, so he tried to beat it out of me."

The waitress brought us more coffee, and Paul poured cream into his cup. "Didn't your aunt try to stop him?" I asked.

He shook his head. "Couldn't." He wasn't secretive, but remarkably terse and straightforward when he talked about them—he didn't like to linger or tell any long stories. It was as if he'd drawn precise lines around them—a diagram like the ones in his books—and he had a formula for each person. I knew they had to be more complicated than he made them out to be, but still admired the confidence behind what he said. "She didn't do anything without his say in it," he said.

"I'm surprised you didn't run away."

He looked at me fiercely, and his hand clenched the end of his fork. "I loved school. He was paying, and I wasn't going to let him take that away."

I nodded and looked over at the pie under the glass dome on the counter. He took a large bite of hash browns, obviously eager to change the subject. "When are you going to take me to see these dunes?" The sand dunes on this side of Lake Michigan were the closest thing to a tourist attraction in our part of Indiana, but his cousin hadn't taken him there yet.

"As soon as it's warm enough," I said. "You'll see how tall they are. Mountains of sand. It takes an hour to climb one."

He grinned and pointed at a framed picture against the paneling. "Look at that." It was a painting of the dunes, the pine trees like spiked, twisted fingers, and a giant gull glided in a grape-colored sky, almost colliding with the sparkled sandy point. "It looks like Mars," he said. I was bringing the coffee to my mouth and laughed so hard I spilled it all over the table.

▲   ▲   ▲

One day he took me to a barn that belonged to someone his cousin knew. There were milk cows in the stalls and a pony tied to a post munched on grass. Hay on the floor, a grassy smell like pond water kept too long in a bucket. He was sure the owners would be gone for the next two days. "That's why they've got all the animals in here," he said. "You have to trust me."

We climbed a rickety wooden ladder up to the hayloft, where a fat cat sneered and slinked back against the wall. "Careful," he said, holding out his hand to help me up. There was a round window the size of a cake plate, nothing in it but green. We'd had to walk through the fields to get there, and our clothes were stained as if we'd been rolling in green paint.

He was making jokes and teasing me. He tied my hands to the window and blindfolded me with his shirt. I could see the red material pressed up against my eyelids and felt him unbutton my blouse, pull off my jeans. I could have kicked, but didn't, the silky-sharp hay pricking against my bare skin. "Now you're the only one in the dark," he said. "Next time it will be me." There was a recklessness in letting him see, letting him touch. My blood rolled fast as I waited for his hands, guessed wrong, and guessed again. The cow grunted, spilled something in its stall.

I heard a zipper, the wadding of material, and the plod of it hitting the floor. I felt his soft skin, then his breath and tongue just under my arm.

▲   ▲   ▲

Despite the chilly weather, we had a picnic late one night on the grounds behind the hotel. We spread a blanket on the grass between the two trees and sat in our coats facing the rows of windows in the back.

He poured some wine into curvy juice glasses from the cafeteria. "If I were to break in right now," he said, "I'd climb up that back fire escape and pull myself over that railing." He pointed to the third floor, "And I'd pry open that window. It's cracked a little."

"What would you steal?" I warmed my hands under my arms, pressed them against the wool of my coat.

He shrugged. "That would be the harder part. You'd have to be good enough to sneak into the rooms, find the purses and wallets, and leave before anyone noticed." He glanced over at me. "I'm probably too big and clumsy to make a good thief. You'd be better at it." Hanna was a thief, my mother had told me once, a shoplifter. *She took what she wanted, whether she needed it or not,* my mother said. Once she'd stolen a handsaw from the hardware store, just because she knew she could. She brought it home, hid it under the bed, showed my mother, and then forgot about it until Christmas, when she gave it to my grandfather as a present.

A light went off in one of the rooms. "There goes another one," I said, toasting it with my glass of wine. "Good night." I pointed to the two corner rooms, whose lights were still on. "Those are the insomniacs," I said. "I could tell. When they checked in, there was something weird in their eyes."

"Maybe they were sties," he said, smiling slyly.

"I can spot a person who can't sleep, you know," I said. "You're definitely not one of them."

His bottom lip pouted as he considered this, and he shook his head. "I can sleep on trains, buses, all the way through thunderstorms." For some reason this annoyed me.

"They always look like they have something that smells bad

they need to throw away, or something that's chasing them." We were eating torn bread and thick, peppery sausage. "The only time I can't sleep is when I'm worried."

"It must happen a lot, then. You worry too much."

I rummaged for a napkin. "It runs in my family." It was dark, but I could see my breath.

"Not true." His accent sounded strangely tart and slick. "It runs in your head. If you put your mind to it, you can relax." *Believe it and it might be* was one of Paul's philosophies. I didn't believe you could think your way into happiness any more than you could think your way into being rich and Parisian, but it fascinated me that he could: It seemed both childish and mature. I looked away into the trees, to the edge of the corner store, where a painted sign said SEAVER'S DRUGS. "It's because of that accident. I'm so used to people worrying I'll get hurt again, I've turned into a worrier myself."

He shook his head. "You worry because it's an excuse to hide," he said softly, wrapping the rest of his sandwich in a napkin. His legs looked especially long laid out there on the blanket and crossed at the ankles. "The way you hide scars."

I'd thought that I'd lost that habit, at least around him. "In a strange way," he said, sipping wine, "they tell the story you don't always want told. I know that."

Talking about this made me feel ugly. "I don't worry about them. They're just there." I flung my arm up awkwardly.

"You don't talk about it, but I can tell by the way you move. Like now," he said, putting his hand under my coat to stroke the small of my back. "Look at the way you're holding your arm, with your other hand covering it like that."

I shook my head and reached for the wine. I didn't see why he was going on about this. "I'm trying to stay warm." It was different since I'd met him. There were still matches in the hotel desk, but I didn't want them or even dream anymore of watching things burn. "I was thinking we should go to Chicago sometime on our day off, take the train in," I said, leaning over to kiss him, even though I was angry. I shoved him back on the blanket, put my hand through the opening in his coat, and pressed against his chest. I couldn't see his eyes in the dark. He'd made me seem like a coward, and I wanted him to know it wasn't true. I could take him to my old apartment building and point to the burned place in the ground where the shack had stood, go with him to the Housemans' and show him how I had started that fire, then take him to the ruins of the Barr house, where I'd burned myself. "I did these things," I might say. Then again, another, weaker part of me longed to pretend none of it had ever happened.

▲　　▲　　▲

I had just turned on the temperamental NO VACANCY sign in the window, and Paul walked into the lobby, at the end of his midnight round, his face flushed and his eyes bright. "Your mother's so skinny. Is she sick?"

I went back around behind the desk and pulled the guest book into the drawer. "How did you know that was her?"

He stood just outside the desk's gate and pushed it open to come behind the desk and stand beside me. I thought he'd seen her when she brought me a loaf of raisin bread, but I hadn't introduced them. "It was her then. She has your mouth."

I picked up a rag and began to dust out the key boxes. Paul opened a drawer, took out a flask he kept there, and poured us each a plastic cup of bourbon. "That was her sister, not your father's, right?"

"That's right." I slid the rag into a back corner. "But she hadn't seen her in seven years." The last part came out impulsively, and I wanted to take it back.

His own family was so far away, it was easier to act as if mine were just as distant. He wrote lots of letters to Poland, even to the uncle—Paul said it proved to himself that he had forgiven him but also left him the means to remind him of what he'd done, if he ever needed to. "Why not?" he said.

"I don't know. I told you. She just left." I stopped dusting and took a sip from the cup. The bourbon tasted like gasoline.

"Because?"

Whenever Paul and I slept together, I felt sapped and fragile, dried up and sensitive to wind like a twig, something that would light and burn too easily, and I felt that way now, too. I sat down in my wheeled chair and rolled myself back to the wall. "It was the best thing for everyone." My face pocked with the first sting of alcohol. I was afraid for him to know any more. I saw the way the muscles in his face would go limp, and I'd have to repeat what I'd said because he wouldn't believe it at first, and I imagined his affection for me draining through the sieve of what I'd said.

He heaved himself up to sit on the desk. "To leave your family? But you pay a price for that." He finished the bourbon in his cup and poured himself a half inch more. He could drink a lot more than I could before he ever acted drunk. "Or somebody does."

Thinking of my grandfather, I gulped down the bourbon, and it scalded my throat. "Ever since her father died, my mother won't eat. She says she's eating, but she's not. A couple of months ago, she even fainted and broke her ankle." *That should be enough*, I thought.

His forehead knotted into two clumps. "How long ago did he die? You should take her to the doctor." His question felt like an invasion, and I pulled my jacket closed in the front.

"She's not sick." Somehow I had assumed he understood how much I had to protect, and now his reckless questions sounded disingenuous and cruel.

I let out a long sigh, stalling for time. "She's angry, but she doesn't want anyone to see it, and it's coming out anyway." *Like some perversely reversed hidden pregnancy.*

"But why is she angry?"

I pushed the back of the chair into the wall, felt the metal scrape against the wood molding. He was pressing me too hard, but something in me wanted to give in. "My grandfather took some arsenic."

His head punched back, and his eyes widened. The chandelier lights twinkled over the dirty walls. It was different from when I told Jo because there was more at stake, but also stranger because he seemed to be pulling it out of me, this huge splinter no one else had noticed. "Look, they didn't even tell me Hanna was dead. I had to find out for myself. After he died, I went on a pointless search for her."

He looked confused. "But how could they keep those things secret?"

I got up and went to the end of the desk to pour myself more bourbon, resenting him. "Believe me, they've had lots of practice." As I drank, his eyes steadied on me. My mouth felt coated and aged. I had to get away. "So have I. Don't think you know everything about me." I could tell by his anxious eyes how baffled he was by my anger. He was waiting for the smile or the joke that would bridge us back to making fun of Mr. Linden or planning our day off.

"Wait." He pulled my arm and turned me around. His accent got more distinct, even though his voice trembled. "Whatever else, you don't have to say now."

"And what if I won't ever?"

"Then—" He didn't finish, but loosened his grip. He leaned back against the desk and slumped over his folded arms. I went up the stairs and looked down at the curve of his back, the line of his pale neck just above his blue collar, where I'd held my hand the night before.

▲   ▲   ▲

The next day at work, I saw Paul talking to the girl who worked as a housekeeper on the weekends, and the way he'd bounced up on his toes and smoothed the back of his hair when he said something about the third floor made me jealous. After a moment, shaking the pink rabbit's foot on her keychain, she left, and Paul came over to the desk.

I said I was sorry, that I didn't know what had come over me.

"It's all right," he said, a little too quickly, grinning. We went into the cafeteria. "You hungry?" He opened the large refrigerator. There were pies, blocks of cheese, and slabs of meat on the metal shelves. I wasn't.

He let go of it and let the door suck closed. "Come over here." He pulled my hand. A pot clanged to the floor, and it felt as if things would go on banging and crashing, but they didn't. There was a large burlap sack leaned against the wall, and he dragged another one over beside it. "Sit down."

He crouched so his head was even with mine. He smelled like grapefruits and salt. "Wait right there," he said. I slid my shoes against the grainy floor, closed my eyes. He stopped in front of me. His breath swayed in the air between us, and he jangled the keys in his pockets. Then he was beside me, unbuttoning my blouse, leaning us back into the sacks, so we made a hollow in them. There were rapid footsteps on the staircase, grand ballroom music from the radio in the lobby.

My body disappeared, then swelled again in the dark. The flour rose up in a fine powder around us. I was thinking how I wanted to make him shudder. I wanted him to lose his sense of balance somehow, to break his poise, that polite formality. And then something bulged in my throat. I pulled away, and he leaned toward me. "What's wrong?"

I sobbed into my hands. He touched my shoulder. When I looked up, the dark air muddied, and the lines of his face wobbled.

"Do you want to tell me why your grandfather did it?"

"No," I said. I might have let myself speculate about what had finally made him give up, if in that floury dark my voice hadn't sounded so fake and posed, if the fires hadn't flickered inside me, waiting to be found out.

▲   ▲   ▲

The moon bounced ahead of us as we walked fast down Maple Street, daffodils and tulips nosing their way out of the furred darkness. It was finally getting warmer, and we wore light jackets, no boots or gloves. We'd been silent for a few minutes, just walking, when Paul said, "When am I going to meet your mother?"

We passed a mailbox with an eager-looking plastic Easter bunny perched on top of it. "Why do you want to?"

He shrugged as we moved under a tree dotted with buds whose branches arched over the street. "I would have thought you'd want that."

Feeling very thirsty, I touched my throat and swallowed. "There are other things I want to do more—go to Paris, see that gangster movie in Merrilville."

He didn't laugh, his chin sharp against the dark. "Hasn't she asked about me?"

"No." I tried to grab his hand, but he floundered away. "We don't talk about that sort of thing."

It was windy, and he turned up the collar of his bomber jacket. "I want to meet her."

We turned onto Locust. I thought of my mother wringing her hands in her lap, her knuckles rubbed red. "But why?" I tried to make him laugh again. "Do you think you need to ask her permission?"

I had to skip to catch up with him, and when he stopped walking and threw up his arms, I almost tripped. "What do you think she's going to do, for God's sake?" For some reason, I'd thought I'd hidden this fear from him: that her knowing about us would make it too real, jinx our chances somehow.

"Let's just wait, all right?"

We started walking again, slowly. "Why? What are you ashamed of?" His fine hair blew back in a sheaf.

"Nothing—I just don't want her to think we're serious."

We stood at the corner, in a wash of streetlight. He pushed his hands into his jacket pockets. "Aren't we?"

I swallowed air to stop the flutter in my throat. I still didn't quite believe that he wouldn't one day get up from the bed where we lay and leave through the dark, as if he'd never known me. "Are we?" I said. "I still want to go somewhere though, leave."

He looked down at the toes of his boots. "You've been saying that since we met—I know. But it hasn't stopped me from falling for you." He smiled with one side of his mouth. The skin on his neck was red where the leather collar had rubbed against it.

It was hard for me to stand still there, the street seeming to swell up in a rich glittering black. I had to limit this, keep the street flattened somehow beneath us. "I'm just the first American," I said, squeezing his elbow through his jacket.

He looked down at me with his mouth open, as if he'd noticed something about my face for the first time, then kissed me on the forehead and said, "You're a strange one, anyway."

Holding hands, we walked past the corner to Oak Street, past trees with tiny green flowers and a yard with a languorous sprinkler moving like a large, glass-feathered fan. "Soon it'll be warm enough for the dunes," I said.

We passed a big white house with a blue door, where one of my teachers had lived before she moved to La Porte. Paul kicked a bottle cap down the street, a delicate scrape and ping.

We were in front of the playground. I closed my eyes. I was happy, and in the next second terrified. My knees buckled. Paul grabbed me around the waist. "Are you sick?" Even with my eyes closed, I still saw: The canvas straps of the swings drooped from the chains. The wire hurricane fence that checkered the grass. The picnic table squatted under the big tree.

"Let's just go to your room, okay?" We kept walking, and I didn't look back.

▲   ▲   ▲

At work Paul found me staring into the wood paneling, trying not to see distorted faces in the grain of it, trying to see countries, animals, vegetables.

"What are you doing?" he said.

"Nothing."

"What's wrong?"

"Nothing."

"Was it what I said the other night? I always do things too hasty." Whenever he was embarrassed, his English turned stilted.

"It's not that."

He took my silence as a cut. "Let me know when you'll be talking to me again, okay?"

I was too frozen to say anything else, and he slammed the lobby door when he went out to check the grounds. I heard his boots crunching in the gravel and stared down at the fibers in the red carpet, at the tongues and black laces crisscrossing my shoes.

I'd tried to drink enough bourbon to put me to sleep, but it only prickled in my skin and made me restless. I felt the insomnia coming, but methodically put on my nightgown, brushed my teeth, pinned back my hair, and lay down under the covers. As soon as I closed my eyes, I saw it again.

I'd put that day in a box and buried it, grateful to forget what it had felt like not to be a girl but a tree standing beside a girl, or a pole or a swing. Paul had pushed back the soil and dug it up.

On Oak Street, walking home, the blond-haired girl skipping toward me. Kristina. She went to the other school. I was eleven, and I knew her from Marietta's block.

There were two other girls with her, one with raggedly cut dark hair and a smudge on her cheek, and a plump girl, whose belly showed under her sweater, and two boys also, one with a buzz cut and a yo-yo that he spun around his hand, and another with large freckles the color of pennies. "Where are you going?" said Kristina. As they got closer, they walked toward me as if they'd been looking for me all afternoon.

"Home."

"Not yet," Kristina said, catching the eyes of the boy and girl on either side of her. They stood in front of me on the sidewalk, grinning. The girl with the ragged hair fanned out her skirt a little, and the boy with the yo-yo suddenly swung his head back behind him as if he'd heard someone calling him. The plump girl tugged her sweater down over her stomach, where her pants were fastened with a safety pin. "We want to see your scars," she said.

All the organs inside me turned silver and began to chime frantically. "I'm in a hurry, please," I said. You could hear the chiming in my voice, and why the *please*?

"But we want to see," said the plump girl. She was tall, too, and her arms were as big as my legs. She grabbed me and pressed her sharp fingernails through my blouse.

The boy with the buzz cut gripped my other arm, and they dragged me through the gate into the playground. In those days no one but my parents and the doctor had ever seen the scars. I shouted and tried to dig in my heels, but they scraped and stuttered along the sidewalk as they pulled me. When we stopped at the merry-go-round, I was out of breath, and they stood in a circle around me.

"How come we've never seen you at school?" The dark-haired girl, whose hair looked chopped by a knife, actually sounded friendly. I thought they would let me go.

"That's because I go to Grace."

"Not next year, though. Next year you'll have to go to junior high," said the boy with the buzz cut. "They put your head in the toilet if they don't like you."

A few of them giggled, and I thought they would let me go. Kristina edged herself in front of the other girl. "Is it true that your mother burned you?"

"No," I said, and turned a little in the circle and tried to read their expressions, but all of their eyes were moving, not looking at my face. I thought if they saw how afraid I was they would let me go, but they were different from the kids at Grace, louder and less fearful.

"Let's just look," said the plump girl, stepping close, so my eyes reached her armpit. Someone pulled back my arms so tightly my shoulder sockets hurt. Kristina pulled up my dress and held the hem around my ears, so I could just see the top half of her face, but I looked up at the sky, egg blue, framed by trees.

"Ew," said the dark girl, rubbing her rough hand on my torso. "It looks like when you burn the milk."

"Don't touch it," said the plump girl.

"I dare you to touch it," said one of the boys. Someone pulled off my underwear, lifted my feet through the holes, and threw it into the grass. The wind blew against my skin, and my feet were sweating so much in my shoes that my socks felt burning and wet. I almost fell over when I tried to kick, because someone had grabbed my ankles, too. I pushed my eyes up at the sky, thinking of the hymn my father played that sounded like the army marching, with the words about shields and swords.

Someone knelt down, and I could feel hot breath on my thigh, a clammy finger poking there. "It's melted," he said, laughing. A stick rubbed up along the scars.

"Monster legs," said one of the girls, giggling. I caught Kristina's gaze just above the green hem of my dress, but she quickly looked away. "Hurry up," she said. "My arms are tired."

Make them stop, I thought. The boy stuck the stick up into me, and I screamed. The pain shot up my spine. *Stop.* He twisted it once, and I felt something run down my leg.

"You're peeing," said one of the boys. He yanked out the stick, and the nub scraped hard. A piece of bark stayed in me. Pain darted between my thighs and up my back, but I gathered it up and pushed it *over there;* in the sunlight on their faces I barely saw through the weave of my dress. I watched the sunlight beat against them, twist their cheeks and dissolve their eyes and rub off their mouths. Something liquid trickled down my leg again.

"You're not going to tell anyone you showed us your scars, are you," said the freckled boy. "Because we could tell them all about it."

"Stand there," said the plump girl. "Just stand there until we say when." I caught Kristina's eye again, but she didn't look away, and her mouth curved in apology. I could see the rest of them only through the cotton of my dress, but I heard their shoes beat against the hard mud when they ran. Then Kristina dropped the hem of my dress, and I watched the S of her thin, pale-blue back as she scurried through the trees. Up the street, a door slammed.

I smoothed down the pleats of my dress. Stood there. I couldn't move. I was that tree there. That swing. The mesh of the fence. I was definitely not a girl. A pain flew into me like a bat with sharp claws, but I looked at the sky, and it went away. I wasn't a girl, but jaunty green grass, a four-leaf clover, and I stood there until it began to get dark.

It was painful when I walked, the splayed steps I took so small it took me a long time to walk three blocks home. When I came inside the door, my mother stood in the entryway. "Where were you?" Her mouth opened and shut and trembled when she saw me. There was a little dried blood still on my leg that I'd thought I'd wiped off.

"Some kids—" was all I could say, and it came out in a squeak.

"What did they do?" She put her hands on my shoulders and bent down. She had a panicked look, but I couldn't reassure her. "What did they do? Tell me."

My knees went limp, but I didn't want to fall down, so I leaned into her. She smelled of coffee. She led me gingerly into the living room. "You're not yourself, I can tell. Why don't you lie down and tell me about it?" But I didn't want to lie down, because they'd taken my underwear. I shook my head.

My father came in, and my mother said, "Some kids did something to her."

"Not from Grace?"

I shook my head. "She looks hurt," he said. "Are you cut? Did they hit you? Do you want to see the doctor?"

"No," I said in a voice so minuscule I was surprised he heard it. They knew how I hated going to the doctor, and what could he do now? "It's okay," I said.

"Did they tease you?" asked my father.

I looked down at the ripples of woven rags in our carpet, feeling more and more like a girl, and it was excruciating. "Yes."

He went on quickly. "Just ignore them. They're ignorant. It's the worst thing you can do to a person, pretend that they don't exist. Anyone who teases you deserves that."

"It's okay," I said. The panic flew off their faces.

"Do you want me to talk to them?"

"No." I was terrified that they would confess, and everyone would know what had happened. About the stick. I only wanted to hide in my room. "I want to go upstairs, okay?" I'd thrown the flaring sunlight into their faces, and I was exhausted and sore.

"If you're sure you're all right," said my mother, smoothing my hair.

When I went up to my room, I thought if only I had gone to the other school, I would have known how to stop a thing like that from happening. My parents had been wrong to try to protect me, and I wasn't going to get caught like that ever again. I could never tell them what had been done to me. Impossible. The house would split open and crash in on us, and none of us would ever be able to speak again.

▲   ▲   ▲

A year later when I got my period, it took me two days to work up the courage to say to my mother in the kitchen while she was busy chopping celery, "I'm bleeding . . . you know."

She pressed once more into the celery and ran her gaze from my feet to my head and said, "Well!" I hated her then for being someone I couldn't tell and knew it was only the beginning of a long string of secrets I'd have to protect her from.

Later, she put a box of sanitary napkins on my bed next to a book with a pink cover and gilt-edged pages. On the inside of the front cover Hanna's name was written in a rounder script than she used now, and there was a silver chocolate wrapper tucked inside to mark the place, with the initials H.K. and R.S. scratched into it. The book kept saying I was a woman now, but I felt like a freak.

When my mother called me down to dinner, I paused twice dizzily on the stairs, and when I got to the dining-room table my mother said, "Ella isn't feeling well." The bowls and plates were laid out in the center of the table like a small city, the silverware evenly lined up, and I thought of the way I learned the positions when I was first old enough to set the table: The knife was the father, the spoon the mother, the fork the wild-haired son.

XIII

▬▬▬▬▬▬▬▬▬▬▬▬▬▬▬▬▬▬▬▬▬▬▬▬▬▬▬▬▬▬

What is fire made of? Not dust, breath, the devil, despondency, stars, typhoons, or rank plasma, not eglantine, lip fern, kelp, narcissus, or pepper, not from the bellies of reptiles or pig snouts, not from sluts, tomcats, or seductions, inflammation or soreness, thirst, or spasm, not moon blindness or binoculars, not hydrophobia, parousiamania, ignorance, spit, or bells, not prophecy, luck, gorgeous breasts, mirrors, Sanskrit, baptism, aphasia, trickery, or hope, or cicatrix.

▲   ▲   ▲

For the spring, Marietta told me, she'd put special seeds in her bird feeder to attract the bird she was looking for—a kind of lark—and spent most of her time sitting on the little stone wall she'd built around it. Even when she was inside the house, she could watch from the hole she'd scraped in the purple paint on the window in the kitchen.

"Kingfishers are like milkmen," she said that cold spring afternoon. "They come regularly, and they like being efficient."

"I haven't seen too many robins yet," she said. "You know, they only come around if it's an early Easter."

"Easter's late this year," I said.

"That's what I mean. The robins know it."

I'd brought her a bouquet of the first blossoms I'd picked from the hotel's rosebushes and wrapped in a wet paper towel. I put it on the table near her hand, and she looked down at the pink roses, frowning. "Still seeing the same old jays I saw before."

"Mother says hello."

She nodded, staring at the roses. She was wearing orange lipstick that made her complexion chalky and gray. "There's a kind of bird called a yellow sword. That's really the one I want to spot sometime before I die." She gazed into the flowers as if she were trying to see something between the petals, the stems.

"You should do something with your feather collection," I said. "I bet there's a museum that would want it."

"Oh, I couldn't part with them," she said. "They're all I have to show for myself. This is the season for them, though," she said. "When all the birds cross paths, and you can get feathers you've never seen before."

I laid my hand on her arm. Before she went off with her birds again, I would make her tell me. "What's wrong?"

She wrapped her fingers around the throat of a blossom. "What's wrong is I haven't seen any new birds yet."

"Grandma, tell me," I said, rubbing the papery skin near her elbow.

"Roses." Her fingernails around the stem were yellow and ridged, clipped unusually short, and she trembled. She was giving up. A ring of sunlight through the hole in the paint hung on the Formica expectantly. She stared at the roses as if they might bite her.

"I shouldn't have picked them, I know, but there were so many on the bushes I didn't think it would matter," I said.

"Roses," she said in a disgusted voice.

"I thought you liked them."

"Like them? I couldn't ever get him away from them." They suddenly looked pink and grotesque, like bellies stripped from mice or a bouquet of ears.

"He was pruning the bushes that night. Said he couldn't understand why they hadn't bloomed more. And he wouldn't come in for dinner. He kept looking for that blackspot." She slid her eyes away from the flowers. Red tears streaked through her pale powdered cheeks. She got up and paced the room, put her shaky hand over her mouth. She knocked a bowl from the counter, and it crashed on the floor, blueberries bouncing under the table. She swayed near the wall, and the spice rack fell, a plate shattered. She hugged the sides of her torso, trying to hold her body together in one piece.

The room was uncomfortably hot, and I began to perspire under my blouse. "He wouldn't," I said.

Marietta stood up, went over to the sink, and rested against it, her hunched back shaking. Something crackled in her throat. She turned quickly and glared. Her grief clawed out at me. "Don't make me talk about that."

"It wasn't your fault," I said, walking toward her.

She leaned back away from me.

"When Hanna died, you didn't know what he was going to do."

She gasped and covered her face, took one step onto the broken glass and crockery, her shoulders heaving and the broken sun from the window playing on her hair. When she pulled her hands away finally, it looked as if she was smiling hard, but with her lips pressed together tightly, her chin trembling. I put my hand on her bony shoulder. Something shattered in her throat again, and she said in a quavery high voice, "I can't help it." She sobbed as if there wasn't any oxygen, rubbing her arms up and down her side. Slowly, she crouched over the broken pottery all around her feet, began to pick at the sharpest pieces, and scratched them in loops in the pink linoleum floor. Her fingers were bleeding.

I bent down, looking at the blue flecks scattered among the broken pieces and blood on the floor. "He loved roses," she said, fondly now. "He loved those *damn* roses."

▲   ▲   ▲

On my night off I took my mother to Strongbow's Inn. There was a turkey farm behind the restaurant, and if you sat near the back, you could look out the window and watch them gobbling and jerking in the distance. I knew I could get her to eat if people were watching.

We passed through the bar, where a collection of model airplanes hung from the ceiling around an upside-down plastic Christmas tree, and we went into the brown-and-gold dining room with studded chairs that were meant to look medieval. People tried not to stare at her skeletal frame, or that bare place on her scalp where her hair had fallen out.

A plump waitress with a waxy face came to our table, and my mother frowned when I ordered bourbon, but then her gaze smeared over the paneled wall.

She opened her menu. "I usually get Turkey Divine," she said.

The waitress came back with my bourbon and took our orders.

My mother looked frail when she asked the waitress a question about the side dishes. The waitress smiled at her sweetly, scratching on her pad and trying not to stare.

"Mother," I said, after the basket of rolls came, "I went to see Aunt Emily a couple of months ago. She said something about Hanna and some people down at Lake Eliza."

She stuffed half a roll into her mouth and started chewing, lowering her eyes.

"Hmm," she said, still chewing. I waited for her to finish, but instead of replying, she took another bite.

"What was she talking about?"

She finished chewing and looked at me, a mournful slackness around her eyes and cheeks. She didn't move for a second or two. "They were some people she got mixed up with."

"Mixed up with?"

She shrugged. "What's the point in talking about any of that? It was a long time ago." I had to stop myself from agreeing with her. What did it matter, now that Hanna was dead? She had helped me to envision another life outside Porter, but in order to have that life, I had to understand why my wait for her return had been futile. My mother's hand shook as she reached for the water glass. I drank half my glass of bourbon in one swallow.

Martin Luther said that our only hope was to wait for grace to descend on us, to ask for it and wait. I was good at waiting, but tired of it. I told my mother I needed to hear what happened.

Her face blanched. She played with the napkin in her lap.

The waitress brought our food. My mother pulled her plate close to her, cut her meat, and took a bite. For the first time in months, she looked hungry. I was so relieved to see her eating, I didn't say anything more for a while, and we ate without talking. I gratefully watched her mouth chew and listened to the sound of my own hollow swallows.

Then she blurted out, "She got into some trouble down at Lake Eliza. That was what started it."

The waitress balanced a huge tray above her head, piled with platters of turkey, the bones elbowing up over carrot medallions and potatoes. When my mother wiped her mouth and paused, I asked her what kind of trouble. She began eating again rapidly, pushing a forkful of mashed potatoes into her mouth. "What kind of trouble?" I asked again.

She swallowed the last bit of mashed potatoes and looked frantically around the table, her hands worrying her silverware. It was as if she'd suddenly felt that she was starving and wanted to make up for all the food she hadn't eaten. She took another bite of a roll, her eyes wide and red.

"I know she's dead," I said flatly. "I saw her room." She gagged, and her eyes got bright and round, glossy. She leaned over, her lips parted. The clattering of plates and chattering around us seemed to recede into the distance. She opened her mouth, her lower lip trembling, a gargle in her throat. Her head swerved away as if she'd been slapped. I heard her choke before she vomited on the floor beside her chair. People turned away from their tables to look at us and the sullen pink-and-yellow puddle at her feet. Wiping her mouth on her napkin, she rushed off with her arm crooked over her face.

The waitress came quickly with a bucket and a mop. "Poor thing," she said, mopping. She paused, looked at me sympathetically. "Is it cancer?"

▲   ▲   ▲

In the car on the way home, I asked her again. Between sobs, she began to talk, and I pulled over onto a dirt road in the fields. The cornstalks rustled beside us like torn green silk.

"I don't know," she choked out. "All I know is what they told me." She wiped the flats of her hands up and down her face as if her tears were a kind of salve. "She was baby-sitting. Some big house on the lake."

The wind ruffled the corn leaves and the airy yellow crowns at the tops of the stalks. The sky looked very small, cupping us there in my car. Our bodies seemed to have grown huge and smelled strongly of hair and skin.

Her voice wavered. "The family had a baby and a much older

boy, a stepbrother who came home with two of his friends. They
were on the basketball team." She pounded her fist in her lap and
said this almost dismissively: "They had their way with Hanna.
They said she asked them to." She looked at me, her eyes wide.
"They said she took off all her clothes and stood on the balcony
calling them." Then she turned sharply away, pressed herself
against the car door, so I could barely hear her. "She lost it. Didn't
remember a thing." After a moment, she turned back to me. Her
face looked beaten, her cheeks puffy and bruised, her eyes swollen
in their hollow sockets. "My father called her a whore and then
broke down crying. It was the only time I saw him do that. And
she just kept saying to him, I remember, 'Why do you believe
them?' And she stuffed some things in a brown bag and left. It
was awful."

"So there wasn't any baby?"

"A baby?" She stared at me, confused. "Oh no, thank God there
wasn't any baby."

I looked out at the stars, all those constant lights, imagined
switching them off, one by one. My scars bore into me, pressed
against my bones. I wanted to spit. I wanted to get out of the car
and lie down in the corn, leave her there alone. That was it? That
was the reason my grandfather wouldn't look at her?

"When I first heard the rumors going around the high school,
even before this, I didn't deny them. Can you believe that? I was
so jealous of my own sister. A girl I knew said that she'd heard
about Hanna in a car with a boy, and I just nodded. After she
went to Emily's and came back, and everyone was asking me
about it, I didn't deny it. I didn't say anything. And when I got
her alone, she wouldn't say what happened either." The corners
of her mouth turned down sharply.

I started up the engine.

"It was such a long time ago, and then it just worked out that she would live far from home. I missed her, but she seemed to want it that way. We never talked about it. Ever." My mother rolled a ball of Kleenex against her eyes. "She had this secret life." Driving back onto the road, I glanced over at her profile; her hands grabbed at the dashboard, groping for some solace.

"Mother," I said, my eyes aching, "what about *your* secret life. Why won't you eat anything?"

I stopped for the light at the intersection and turned to her. She looked into her lap. "I haven't been hungry." Her chin trembled as she unrolled the tissue and smoothed it.

"That's not it," I said.

"No." She looked away. "It's just—I can't."

"Since he died?"

She grimaced and nodded.

"You have to eat," I said.

She squeezed back tears. "And the way you were looking for her, I was sure you were going to leave, too."

The light was changing, and I waited a second more anyway, but then a car pulled up behind me, and I had to drive on.

She grabbed my arm. "You understand, my father loved Hanna, and he couldn't even see her."

"I know," I said, turning onto Maple Street. "He couldn't forgive himself."

"No, he couldn't. For letting it happen to her."

XIV

I'd brought Paul a postcard of the Golden Gate Bridge from my collection. He held it in his palm and stared for a long time. "The blue's too blue to be real," he said. "Looks like they touched it up." He turned it over to the yellowed side and read the scrawl of the stranger. He rubbed the picture side against his pant leg as if to polish it, get rid of fingerprints. "Thanks." He smiled but wouldn't look at me. "Better check those locks," he said, moving toward the door.

I opened the side gate to the desk and sat down, swiveled in my chair a little. I checked in an old man who wore a work suit with a red carnation in the pocket, and he winked at me when I gave him his key. I couldn't wait for Paul to come back after his next round, and I was too restless to relax. I wanted to tell him about all that had just happened, but he didn't show any interest in talking. I went into the bathroom and combed my hair, put on some lipstick, powdered my nose. It seemed to me that my eyes were getting smaller, narrower, but I didn't know why.

I went back to the desk and sat down, looked at the book. There were no other reservations, and Jo wouldn't be in that night—I'd called her to tell her everything Marietta and my mother had told me, and she'd said, "Aren't you glad you did that?"

"Yes," I'd said. "Definitely." But it had left me exhausted and disappointed that it had taken me so long to find out the little I knew. I also felt as if the floor might give way at any moment and fall into another layer of secrets, and I was worried about my mother and what she might do.

Finally Paul came back. He sat in the chair with his glass of milk, but he was still quiet and nervous, jiggling his knee. The NO in the NO VACANCY sign was blinking unevenly, so I went over and unplugged it. "Have to get that fixed," I said.

"Yes, and the walls upstairs in the hallway need repainting, too."

I didn't know what was wrong and hoped I hadn't hurt him the other night. I wanted to tell him I was ready to tell him more. I wanted to drape my arms around him, or go over to him and sit on his lap. He kept anxiously glancing out the window.

"We don't have any more reservations. It's going to be slow," I said, hoping he'd take the hint. I put my legs up on the desk and crossed them, so my skirt fell back above my knee.

He was lingering longer than he usually did. He lit a cigarette and smoked it quickly. He sat back in his chair, his knees spread, jiggling his leg, and rubbing the vinyl of the arm rest. Once he asked how many guests there were that night, but when I told him he just nodded, not saying anything more. The whole evening passed this way, with these awkward silences and formal exchanges. After work, he looked very tired, but he ran out the door without kissing me good night.

I began to worry I'd already told him too much about myself, but he'd pushed me to, hadn't he? I hadn't wanted to. There was a reason people kept things secret—a person had only this thin skin between himself and everything else in the world, and people needed more protection than that.

The next day before work I washed my hair, and it was warm enough to put on a loose gauzy dress Paul had once said he liked. All night only two people checked in, and I tried to read, despite the awkward silences between Paul and me. His cheeks looked heavy and white, and some chalky dust had settled around the hems of his pants.

At midnight I closed the guest book and locked the money bag in the drawer. Paul stalked into the lobby and collapsed in the chair, staring at his feet. "You ever go to that bar, the Paradise?"

The blood vessels embered under my skin. I grabbed a strand of hair, surprised at its softness and rubbed it between my fingers. "Sometimes, why?"

He didn't look up at me, but his eyes were anxious. "I went there with my cousin the other night." The black-and-white pictures of Mr. Linden behind the glass made him look young and larval, his goofy smile stretching his face. Upstairs, someone played a hiccuping song on the radio.

I wound the silky hair in a coil around my finger and noticed its gloss. *Come over and touch my hair,* I thought.

Paul stood up and started pacing the lobby, from the trophy case to the painting of the clown. "Someone was here looking for you the other night." His voice sounded testing, precarious, as if it might fall from a high ledge. "He was disappointed that you weren't here. It seemed like he knew you pretty well."

The folds in the heavy gold curtains were uneven and creased— why had I never noticed that before? The embers under my skin pricked out and turned to ash. I wasn't going to be able to lie to him, but I still hoped this might pass. "Really? Who was he?"

The soles of Paul's boots squeaked on the carpet, but in the room overhead the hard footsteps of a giant pounded. I would sit silently for as long as I could stand it, and maybe it would pass—it would turn out to be some friend of my mother's who'd wanted to invite me to a church function, someone from the college looking for a donation.

"He didn't say. He was here on some banking business." He kicked the wall, and the trophies in the case wobbled. "He looked forty at least. Who was he, Ella?"

I was shaking and trying to swallow the rotten piece in my throat, but at the same instant laughter welled up in me, like the time I was running to cross the street and fell, and a car stopped just inches from my body. I'd stood up, brushed myself off, smiled and waved at the driver, and up came this painful, retching laughter from deep in my stomach. I'd almost been killed, and I couldn't stop laughing. Now I had to pull my lips around the words and focus on the breaths I took. "I did some things— I never told anyone—" I stared at the closed door, willing it to open. The lock looked broken, as if we'd never be able to get it open again. I almost got up to try the knob. "It was before you. I didn't know how to—"

He lunged across the desk and grabbed my shoulders, shook me so my head jerked back and forth. "Stupid girl." His voice cracked, and he shook me again, but not as hard, then stopped and looked at me with red, watery eyes. "How could you?"

I couldn't stop feeling all those men's hands on me. They were all touching me now at the same time, rolling each scar in their fingers like ropes. "What did you expect?"

He pulled back, rubbing his elbow and saying something in Polish. He shook his head. He picked up his leather jacket from the coat hook and left.

▲   ▲   ▲

Sometimes the singing of spiders pushes back the fresh air, muddying it with orange light, and one or two crawl down to the

*center of it, their thready legs lengthening in tendrils. I want them
to father me away, carry my slight bones out of here. But they live
only a little while. In the end they just leave their smoke webbed in
the air.*

▲   ▲   ▲

It was an unseasonably warm spring night. I drove to Lake Eliza,
parked near a house in the woods, and walked up the dirt drive
toward the lake. Except for my footsteps grinding the gravel, it
was very still, the woods not quite real, like dark-green felt spiked
with the smell of bark and pine. The water slapped at the shore,
and silver flecked the lake's surface.

I took off my shoes and socks, let my feet sink to my ankles in
cold, wet sand. On the other shore, a thin light wavered, but it
was too late for anybody to be out on the water, and all the boats
were docked. I took off my blouse and skirt, draped them carefully
over a tree branch, slipped off my bra and underwear. Laying the
glowing pale nylon over my clothes, I could just see the outline
of my hip, the arch of my shoulder, but if I let my eyes go out of
focus, even these were gone.

There was sand between my toes, a breeze across my breasts
and sweeping my shoulders. I touched the silky place behind my
knees, and the faint hairs above there on my thighs. I strummed
at my rib cage, then traced the handle of my collarbone. I felt the
weave of the scars on my stomach, then went lower, following
skin the texture of a wet rock, and reached around to my back,
the fleeced shoulder blades. It was a relief somehow to feel the
scars again.

When I started to think of Paul, I walked to the water and
waded in, sank my toes into the grainy mud at the bottom of the
lake, water lapping around my knees. It was a small, placid lake
that smelled like cut grass. I couldn't swim, but I wouldn't go in

too deep. I kicked the surface and watching it ripple, suddenly saw Hanna on the balcony of that house supposedly near there, singing to herself. From the Hanna I'd called up when she died, I had to strip years and makeup and guile. Her hair then was a natural light brown, her skin an even, very pale olive color, and her pink lips curved into a smirk.

She liked one of them, I imagined, the half brother of the baby boy she was watching, and she was hoping he'd come back early from basketball practice. It was hot that day. The baby had been lethargic. From the balcony of the big house she could see across the lake, people swimming and paddling in boats. Her dress and the damp nylon slip beneath it clung to her skin. In the next room the baby slept, his tiny hands balled up next to his ears. The light breeze coming up from the lake had the same cadence as his breath.

The air smelled of something moist and green, and it must have made her aware of the sweep of her cheek and something sweet under her tongue. She took off her stockings and shoes, dangled her feet through the bars in the balcony, and felt the wind sneak up under her skirt. Except for the people across the lake, no one was around. No one was ever around when she baby-sat, and the solitude gave her a dreamy feeling, as if she weren't quite even there herself.

She took off her dress and sat cooling herself in her slip, wispy perspiration stains clouded in her lap and between her breasts. Across the lake, she watched the children splash in the sparkling water. The heat crowded her, gloved each of her movements. There was no one around. Unharnessing the straps of the slip, she pulled it down to her waist, felt the breeze luxuriant on her neck.

She stood up and put her hands on the balcony's railing, examining her body. Except for her belly and hips, she was very thin and too pale. Her skin was the color of a sheet bleaching on a line, and it never tanned, but only *oranged.* A faint blue line threaded between the top of her pelvis and her navel. Two small moles on her shoulders. Her feet were tiny, with thin heels and pink toes, pretty, she thought. She was looking down and caught herself off balance, her ankles tangled. For a moment she imagined falling into the water and then wished she had, it was so hot. She closed her eyes, swung her hair over her face, let the perspiration at the back of her neck cool in the wind.

Someday she'd have a house like this, with so many rooms you always forgot about one of them, and when you went into it, it surprised you—not like the crowded, dark rooms at home. When she tossed back her hair, it was a second or two before she could see in the light knifing off the lake.

There they were, walking up the drive, the stepson and two of his friends. She grabbed her dress from the balcony railing and, quickly stepping back, pulled it on over her head. She heard a motorboat zip across the lake's surface, which seemed to be sealing something.

She thought that when she went downstairs, pretending to be calm, she'd be able to tell whether or not they'd seen her, but she couldn't. Their faces were as polite and opaque as they'd been at school. The stepson's legs were deeply tanned, and he had a scab just above his knee where it looked as if he'd scraped against a dock or the rim of a boat. He was just her age, or maybe younger, and he had a sly, toothy smile. He asked about the baby. "Asleep," she said.

"Good." He went straight to a cabinet, unlocked it with a small key, and brought out a big bottle of liquor. He poured a glass for her first, then smaller ones for the others. It was the first time she'd tasted any liquor that wasn't Communion wine, and it chafed her throat, but she pretended to like it as much as he did. The year before, they'd been in an English class together, and he'd

ignored her except for the one time she asked to borrow a pencil
and he'd squinted at her as if seeing her for the first time before
he reached into his satchel. She was flattered at the way he looked
at her now, how while the others were talking about a basketball
game, he gazed at her and said he liked her long hair.

After she'd sipped through two glasses, he asked her to go upstairs with him to take a look at his brother, but when they got
to the top of the staircase, he put his hands on her hips and swung
her toward another room instead, where there was a prim bed
and a rocking chair. He pounced on the blue-ribbed bedspread.
"Come here," he said, grinning.

The liquor had furred over her shyness. She sat down beside
him, and he put his hand on her knee. "Has he cried much?"

"No," she said, shaking her head.

"Neither would I, if you were looking down at me all afternoon," he said. She liked the plumpness of his lips. "Let me see
what it's like," he said. He lay back, made a baby face by widening
his eyes innocently and rounding his mouth, and put his arms
around her neck, so her face hung above him. He kissed her, and
she couldn't help thinking how he was thinner than she was, his
bones pressing into her hips in a way she liked. He was talking in
a slow, breathy voice, stroking her hair, the tip of her nose. It had
been a long time since anyone had touched her. "You must be
hot in those sleeves," he whispered, slowly unzipping her dress.
She was embarrassed by the wet stains under her arms. She
shrugged out of the sleeves and pulled up the straps of the slip so
it wasn't so revealing and tried to smile. "I've always liked you,"
he said. She got scared when she felt his hand travel up from her
knee, and she pushed it down again. His eyes went rheumy, but
his mouth was hard now, decisive. He put his hand back where
it had been. She couldn't decide if she liked this or not. She wanted
to stop and think a minute, before she worried about where it

would go next, but she felt his fingers caterpillar up her thigh. The wind blew into the curtain, and she thought she could hear the baby crying.

"I'd better get up," she murmured, lifting her head.

"What for?" he said.

She lunged her torso off the bed, and the door pushed open. Hanna could never remember exactly what happened then. The friends stomped inside, their eyes pointed as nails. "Wait," one of them said, unbuttoning his pants. He was quick and agitated, like an old threshing machine, and the white gluey stuff went all over her leg. She closed her eyes, thought about jumping out the window. She tried to stand up, but someone was holding back her arms.

The other one stared at her breasts the whole time, not looking at her face until the end, when he pushed his pink rubbery thing near her mouth but missed, and she felt it graze her ear. When the stepson came back, he went quickly inside of her, his breath rushed and desperate, as if he were running away. Then they hurried out, tittering nervously. She heard the front door slam and a little later the nasal cackle of a boat starting up.

I watched the reflections of trees calmly stretch over the water's nervous surface and a light dangling in the water. My arms prickled with goose bumps. There was hardly any moon, just a sliver, like the lip of a glass. She had stood there, almost naked on the balcony, and how could she ever explain that? A girl didn't just take off her dress anywhere unless she wanted to do something. She didn't know whom to blame, those boys or herself, for forgetting where she was. It finally didn't seem to matter. Everyone knew. They believed what they wanted to believe. The truth about what happened would have collapsed the houses where they lived and the town's hopes for the next year's basketball team. It was as dangerous as the truth about me. Not even Paul, who said he loved me, could stand to hear it. I'd let myself trust him more than I should have—he'd only helped me put off what I really had to do if I was ever going to leave. Between us, I realized, was only another lie.

I wanted to scream at Hanna: She shouldn't have run away but instead smeared the shame back into their faces and let the light burn them. And for the way I'd tried to lose my body, as if fooling all those men could make it perfect, I raged at myself. What if it had been? How different would I be? As I went up to the tree where I'd hung my clothes, a pipe reached up from the pit of my stomach, writhed around my neck. I got dressed quickly and crouched there in the bushes to try to stop shaking. A light went on in the window of a nearby house, and I heard the scrappy whine of an animal and a toppling of tin near the garbage cans.

▲   ▲   ▲

When Marietta got another note from the landlady asking again for someone to come get "the personal effects" of Hanna, she pretended it was the first notice. She made an announcement to Pastor Beck and the ladies at church that they would hold a memorial service. The body, of course, had already been buried in some city cemetery, the arrangements made by Hanna's friends. It was strange to hear my mother and Marietta speak so calmly about her.

"She's been gone a long time," I said. "Shouldn't we just visit the grave site?"

Marietta was almost cheerful. "Henry would have wanted it."

The service was arranged for Friday afternoon. My mother ordered flowers, and Marietta planned the hymns. She said she didn't want any of them to be sad, only Easter hymns. She said, "I couldn't make it through if we sang anything gloomy."

▲   ▲   ▲

What fire shines on, it colors; what it cooks is easier to swallow.
An arsonist comes from a family of savers, with full attics
and basements, crowded rooms where nothing is ever lost, and the
only way to lose something is to burn it. Potential arsonists become
opium addicts or movie stars or exiles, but she had no other op-
tions—and this distraction made her faceless and ugly, not just cu-
rious, but desperate to see wounds radiantly, though she was secretive
herself, no more than a black arm.

▲   ▲   ▲

In my dream, Paul and I were swimming in Lake Eliza, the moon
swirling with smoke, the stars sparking in the dark water. He
kicked up a white spray and paddled away from me. I arched my
back in the water, which was the temperature of sweat, and
floated, looking down at my body, the scars washed in the gray
moonlight, my ears humming underwater. The water pooled in
the little triangle between my thighs. I closed my eyes, then felt
him swim under me, his hand in the small of my back, his finger
plucking at the strap of my bathing suit. I looked up again. He
came up from the water, pulling my legs down from the surface.
When he kissed me, I wrapped them around his waist. My skin
burned wherever I touched him. I saw the skin on his neck turned
red in the shape of my hand, and the few hairs on his chest were
singed.

▲   ▲   ▲

It rained the night I got drunk at the Paradise. The bartender
wouldn't look at me, even when he pushed my drink across
the bar. He probably felt guilty for spreading the rumors. Who
knew how many men he'd told? I drank, watching the jukebox's

pink and green lights dribbling on the floor, and I was so wobbly when I finally stood, I had to steady myself on the stool before I walked out.

I went back to my room at the hotel and poured another bourbon. I paced the room, trying hard not to cry, paced and kicked the walls. Someone upstairs was playing an aria, and it flew like a moth around the ceiling. I took off my dress and rubbed my arms the way Paul had liked to, warming me with the friction under his fingertips. As I walked away from the window, I saw *The Poetry of the Universe* on the nightstand. I opened it and read the inscription again: "To Ella—with best wishes for your late night reading. Your friend, Paul." It seemed cold and insincere in a way it hadn't when he'd given it to me, and I'd been so happy that he could teach me something and wanted to. Under my chest, there was a hollowing, an emptying-out that slowly grew—one by one the muscles there were disappearing, next the bones, then the organs. It was a slow rip I could almost hear.

I dropped the book on the floor, rushed to the bureau, opened the drawer, and took out the Zippo lighter. Sitting on the floor, I had to shake it and flip the wheel a few times before I could even get a flame the size of an eyelash.

I pressed the corner of a page to its flicker. A knock, then the door opened. Jo ran over, tripping on my knee. "No, don't," she said, blowing on the flame. I stared at the ragged blackening pages as they shrank back. She ran to the bathroom and came back with a wet towel and slapped at the fire. "My God," she said. "Smells like a bar in here."

The flame went out in a second, and I was disappointed that the book was only half ruined, just a few pages gone and an ashy cover.

She sat down cross-legged beside me. "Ella," she said, "you've got to get a hold of yourself." She opened the book jacket and quickly read Paul's note. "Oh," she said, sighing. "I thought you were just drunk."

She was blinking a lot. "He'll be sorry, you know," she said. "When he realizes what a good thing he let go of." I knew she didn't mean it, but I nodded and tried to smile. "You can't go starting fires. There'll be others. It's just that—" She stammered, patting my back as if to make sure to keep something inside me. She picked up a shirt from the floor and wrapped it around my shoulders. "He was starting to get on my nerves a little anyway, if you want to know the truth."

There was nothing to say, and she knew it, but she went on talking in the kindest voice. "Got any more bourbon?" she said, pulling me up. "I'm going to spend the night here, okay? There's a good movie on."

My scars pulled and twisted away from me, but I didn't want to let them go.

▲   ▲   ▲

I understood my aunt Emily and why she'd had to break all those windows. I only wished now they'd never caught her, and she'd moved on to breaking windows in another state, having boosted her energy with a penchant for cocaine, living the high life on her husband's retirement money.

I thought about Hanna at Emily's house and wondered what they did all day. I imagined Emily's friends from the Queens of the Golden Mask, coming by with rum cake and cherry pie, a Parcheesi board and cards, spongy pink curlers and rosy lotions, and, for anyone tempted to philosophy, the longest knitting needles and balls of mohair yarn. The one who still had her dark hair would bring a bottle of sherry on Saturday night, and they'd all giggle as they drank their glasses down. Emily would make a lot of jokes about broken windows, and the women would gaze at her admiringly, fiddling with their girdles. Hanna would try to be one of them, try to forget, but then she'd glance down at her breasts, at the swell of her calf, and she'd see, no matter how much she wished for it, that she wasn't yet an old woman.

XV

When the Holy Spirit visited the apostles, and their tongues were
flames, did the voice leave ash in their mouths? Did it scar
their lips?

▲   ▲   ▲

When I closed my eyes, white sheets twirled through the dark
of my eyelids. *Arsonist.* I didn't know if I could ever stop.
If I did, it seemed I'd only spend the rest of my life walking
through a deep, lightless sleep. At the women's prison in Gary,
the inmates spent long tedious days making license plates or
Christmas ornaments, took showers in an open cement room, and
lived in cells no bigger than pantries. Once, I'd ridden on a bus
past the state home for mental illness in Indianapolis: tall, frilled
gates, a wide green lawn still and quiet as a faked heaven. I prayed
that night, not knowing what to ask. *Don't let me get caught. Don't
let me want to do it.*

I hadn't slept more than an hour at a time for days, even with
all the bourbon before bed. There was a bottle on the nightstand
and another smaller one in my purse. It warmed me, calmed me
down until the real drunkenness flickered, and then I got angry,
nodding my head and stamping my feet, kicking the walls. I clung

to the little control I had; there were matches in a drawer I didn't touch, more downstairs in the desk, a lighter in one of the key boxes, turpentine and gasoline in the cluttered trunk of my car. All the things worrying me were written down in ink on a list I kept between the pages of a book I was reading—*Paul, Mother, Marietta*—and put away in the top drawer of the bureau behind the pert knob.

I was in the bathroom, brushing my teeth. My face was very red, my cheeks so dry they stung, and the blue veins in my hand rooted brightly under my skin. I felt someone watching me from behind the shower curtain. I could see just the outline of her, a pale silk gown, long, curly red hair. She'd come to reassure me. She'd come to warn me that I had to leave. She had Hanna's ironic smile, my mother's pensive gaze, Jo's white skin. The muscles in my face relaxed. When I drew back the curtain, there was just the cracked, mildewed tile, pink soap worn to a blunt charm in the dish, but I felt sleep gathering in me, and I knew what I'd seen.

Later that night I woke up calm, almost rested, and saw her standing next to the bed, smoking. Her white gown was like the one Marietta had worn in the picture, but slit up the sides, and cut low in the front in the style of a cocktail dress. Her hair and mouth glistened in the light of the cigarette tip, but she kept her head inclined back, so I couldn't see her eyes. "You'll get out of here," she said. "But I don't know how yet." I fell asleep again and dreamed of women in white gowns running through the halls of the hotel, breaking windows and locks. It was very beautiful, how they turned into a flock of birds in that first coughing ascent into flight, and then their wings blazed orange and yellow in the clouds.

▲   ▲   ▲

The next afternoon I finally got out of bed. Shaky, I ate a sandwich, showered, and went down to work with a flask of bourbon in my purse. By the time Paul came, I was almost drunk again, and while he walked his rounds, we tried not to look at one another. Each time he rushed through the lobby, my heart fisted and beat against my chest. There was a party across the street near the courthouse. Streamers of little plastic arrows and bunches of balloons resembling huge fake fruit hung from the trees. The light was dusty and intense, like old silver that needed polishing, and the crowd milled around speakers blaring polkas and hokeypokeys. I remembered now what it was—Jo had mentioned it—the Spring Fling for the Shriners. They were drinking beer from dirty-looking plastic cups, and somewhere in the back near the jail a roasting pig was turning on a spit.

I went away from the window and sat at the desk, staring down at the leather blotter and my hands. They were chapped, the cuticles torn into gauzy strands. The burn on my wrist had healed into a purplish and dotted scar, like the design on certain duck eggs.

I went into my purse, unscrewed the little brown bottle, bent so my chest touched my legs and no one would see. I took another long swallow, the bourbon snickering in my teeth as I screwed the cap back on. Tomorrow I'd pack the two blue suitcases, leave a day before the memorial service, before the lies strung out in the martial, dutiful prayers.

I didn't have much money, but I could go up through Michigan to Canada, Montreal, or Vancouver, and write for what my grandfather had left me. I would eat in cheap restaurants and live in a rooming house, blend into my surroundings like a happy green leaf. Then I thought of my mother, and my plans withered.

The new seams in the dress she'd sewn for me were stiff and precise, and the gray fabric didn't wrinkle, even in my lap. When she'd come to the hotel to give it to me, the people in the lobby turned and stared at her tiny shins and spindled arms. "I hope it fits," she said. "I guessed at the hem."

A man called down to ask for more soaps. "I like the smell of them," he said. "You don't mind, do you?" I didn't, because there weren't any other tasks left to distract me. I took a small stack up to his room, knocked on the door, and left them dominoed there on the floor. A woman came out of a room in a towel, said "Oh," and went back inside, closing the door. On my way down the hall, I heard a little girl screeching in one of the rooms, "More ice!"

I held on to the banister to keep my balance walking down the stairs. When I glanced down into the lobby, the chandelier's glass drops seemed to scatter like unstrung beads, and I knew that fuzzy brown line of drunkenness was behind me.

With his new haircut that made his chin look long, Paul passed me in the lobby without turning his head, without a word, but his lower lip quivered. We didn't know what to say to one another anymore, each of us trapped in our own furious skins.

When I got behind the gate and sat down, the phone rang. I stared at the black receiver in its notched cradle, the numbered, smiling face. I watched it and counted, two, three, four. What felt like marbles sputtered and clacked in my stomach. *Wait,* I said to myself. *Just wait and it will pass.* I rifled through the drawers in the desk—pencils, pens, a box of crayons, ancient yellow peppermints, sticky in their wrappers, a tampon, a glove, a box of tissues, two quarters and a penny, some browned old stationery that said *The Linden Hotel* in script and under these two sheets, a book of matches that said *The Linden Hotel* in matching gold script. The matches sang into my palm.

Standing up, I walked over to where the gas line made a seam in the old paint. It took five tries before the match would light. I held it in my fingertips, a tiny bit of hope.

I didn't intend to hurt or frighten anyone. I wasn't even thinking of watching the building burn—I was just clinging to this
nameless hope, watching it, thinking it was all I had, when I let
the match half fall from my fingers onto the base of the gasline.
The force pushed me back, and I fell into arms, stepped on a foot.

Paul's. "What are you doing?" He ran for the fire extinguisher
behind the desk. The flame shot up toward the ceiling: a perfect
yellow column, almost like part of the wall. I suddenly wanted it
to be that and wished it wouldn't take up any more space than
just a beautiful gold pillar. But it came billowing at me.

Paul sprayed the extinguisher up and down the flame, and a
puny hissing sound sputtered from the tube as the white clouds
moved against the flames. The fire shrank back, injured, the wall
browned there in a shape like a tree. Paul took a step behind
him, looked urgently up and down the wall for sparks, spotted
one near the ceiling, and sprayed a gray funnel toward it until it
went out.

He dropped the extinguisher and turned to me. "Are you all
right?"

"Fine," I said, steeling myself.

He put the back of his hand to my forehead as if checking for
a fever. "What—were you trying to light a cigarette?" He knew I
didn't smoke.

"No," I said, biting my lip.

"Had the lights gone out?"

I shook my head.

"Then how did it—?"

I squeezed my arms just above the elbows. I was very hot, but
not sweating. He shook his head and tripped as he stepped back.
"What's wrong with you?" I was shivering. My knees locked in
and out like cardboard knees.

"I dropped it," I said, though I knew it didn't explain anything.

"No you didn't." He took another step away, his eyes saying, *I thought I knew you.* His mouth opened. He knew now.

"Shit, what are you doing?"

He grabbed both of my shoulders and looked into my face. I didn't have an answer for him, but I couldn't let him hold me either. I had to move. In my head, I was already someplace farther away than India, flying in an airplane, jumping out into the atmosphere.

A man in a brown suit scurried crookedly down the stairs, shouted, "What in God's name . . . ?"

I pulled back from Paul's grasp and started for the door. "It was an accident," he said to the guest. "Don't worry, it's out." I heard him call my name when I was already outside, hidden in the thorn-leaved bushes. He followed me through the door, but couldn't find me.

The Spring Fling was over; people gathered around their cars, laughing, holding bright balloons and ribbons, pies, and stuffed animals. As I slid along the square-cut hedges, the sharp leaves pricked my dress. At the corner of the building I touched the parchment-colored brick. A hotel the color of old paper, old skin. I saw how quickly it would burn. Voices and footsteps tapped down the sidewalk behind me. My hands and face felt very hot from all the bourbon.

As I ran out from the hedges, the sidewalk pinched up, split, and flattened again. I was running toward the darker part of the sky. I was running for the wall in the air I would shatter. In the corner of my eye, things blurred into flame as I ran past them— the Big Wheel Restaurant, Bell's Hardware, the white house, Herstein's department store, all lit up and blazing, these fires taller than the trees, galloping in my vision as I ran.

At the end of Pine Street I was out of breath, and my feet and shins had begun to sting. By the time I got to my mother's house, the stinging had risen up to my thighs. I looked down at my leg and almost fell. At first I thought it was the dress's lining, but then I knew better. A tiny blue flame had split the skin just above my knee. It was shaking and transparent, but spreading up toward my hip.

With my heels on the curb, I rubbed at my leg and studied the house. A shutter had fallen from one of its hinges, the first floor squat because it had been sinking. In the window of her room upstairs, a light shone, the lamp by the bed. I ran up the walk, pushed open the door, and slammed it so hard the walls rattled and pressed farther into the foundation. The floor beneath me shifted. "Mother?" I shouted up through the ceiling.

On the coffee table, a half-knitted scarf circled a coffee mug. Her worn yellow slippers sat catty-corner under the couch. I went into the kitchen, turned on the light, and the heavy black squares of the windows crushed into the walls. There was a spoon on the floor, a napkin with crumbs on the counter. I opened the oven, turned the gas all the way up and threw a match into the crusted black hole. At the door again, I heard it bloom.

There were two fewer stairs because of the sinking. The hallway tilted toward the slab of light at her bedroom door. When I pushed it open, I saw her lying back on the pillows, a book in her lap, a glass of water in her hand. She stirred slightly, fumbled with the pink wool blanket, then bolted up. "What's happened?" She sighed, staring at the torn collar of my dress.

"Get up, okay? The house is burning." Flames nibbled the seam between the wall and floor. An orange vine wound its way up a crack, blossomed into roses. The sharp hot petals opened, red, blue, yellow.

I pulled at her arm. The petals of the roses were peeling back to black pistiled centers. I could hardly take my eyes off them.

They multiplied and bunched together in bursts. I slid her legs off the bed, put her arm around my shoulder, and dragged her up. She felt about as heavy as two winter coats.

Outside her bedroom door, the hallway was in a haze. She coughed as I took the steps and pulled her weight onto my shoulder. She unhinged the photographs on the wall and pressed them against her, and the frames' corners poked against my ribs. I couldn't see through the smoke at the bottom of the stairs, but found my way by habit into the living room. Squinting and coughing, I guided her past the couch, around the easy chair, and scraped my shin on the coffee table. Small flames pranced toward the doorway. My mother was weeping in my arms, her legs limp, and I dragged her along beside me. When we got to the entryway, fire swept up the living room rug behind us.

The handle of the front door was too hot to touch; wrapping my hand with the material of my skirt, I rattled the knob, but the wind from the fire had locked it shut. I sidled with my mother over to the front picture window, hiding her face with my elbow, and kicked at the glass until it shattered, and then I kicked at the sharp rays to make the space bigger. Forming a harness with my hands to lift her foot, I helped her through onto the porch. Stepping through the jagged space after her, I cut my arm just above the elbow on a spike of glass. We ran and stumbled down through the yard and fell into the weeds near the mailbox. When my mother saw the blood staining my dress, she took off her sweater and tamped it against my arm. "Hold it there," she said, coughing from the smoke.

From the outside, it looked as if the house had been lit by a mass of lamps. There was watery movement in the windows, a faint shiver in the white wood walls. That furious orange light on everything: the practice organ, my girlhood bed, the sewing machine, all the mended furniture. Flames shot out of the first-floor windows, and coming out of my drunkenness, I panicked. I hadn't remembered to grab my father's music books, my mother's wedding dress, the brass bookends of rearing horses.

My mother held my arm just above the elbow, her fingertips pinching the tendons. Flames trickled through striped seams in the wood. She squeezed shut her eyes. "How did you know?"

My heart beat fast. "I had to get you out of there," I mumbled.

She opened her eyes, pushed her lips out as if about to speak, swept a strand of hair away from her face.

Shifting my legs in the dry weeds, I tore at the frayed hem of my dress, checked the cut just over my elbow, where blood had dried into the weave of my mother's sweater. "It started in the oven." We'd lost everything, and I so wanted her to see how the fire wept and breathed. I wanted her to look at it. "I dropped a match."

"Don't." She jolted up. Her face slipped in a wave of darkness and heat, and when she hit me, the star of her open hand exploded on my cheek. "Oh God." She turned and grabbed the post of the mailbox. The fire popped and crackled.

Talk fast, I told myself. "After Dad died, you never wanted me to leave the house, but don't you see that didn't change anything? We were still alone. Together or not, we were still alone. I started with matches then because I had to do something." A shutter creaked and toppled into the bushes. "I tried to stop, but I just kept doing it, and no one suspected because I was already burned and so quiet. . . . You never knew, did you?" The fire hooked around in the back of the house over the bedroom where my father had lain with blood on his mouth and we hadn't said he was dying. He just died. "Because I was a nice girl."

My mother groaned and pressed her cheek against the wood

post. The flames turned quick and violent and covered the house. "I'm sorry," I said. I'd destroyed her walls, all her rooms, and they'd fortressed her.

"I didn't want to—" But I couldn't finish. The fire reddened our hands and faces—we were too close to it.

Her voice seared through me. "You didn't have to. Don't tell me that. You didn't have to do it." Her mouth gaped open. "I didn't raise you for—" Her limp, open hand flung out at the fire.

The flames clacked like wood planks, and I had to shout over them. "Send me away, then."

She clattered the pictures of me together and pressed them to her breast. "No." It was so hot it was hard to breathe. Her cheeks glittered. "You're my daughter," she said incredulously, as if there had been another one she was only now betraying.

The air just at the edge of the fire turned liquid, blurring the sky above it. "We're too close," I said, taking her arm and pulling her to her feet. We hurried across the yard to the opposite side of the street. Smoke flew over us like wispy crows.

The crowd grew to about a hundred tense faces, luminous and grateful-looking.

At the corner, the fire truck screeched and slanted to a stop, and the firemen, beetled in their hats and coats, unwound their gray hoses and strung them toward the house. Someone must have pointed us out, because one of them, a young man with a small, tan face, came over to us. He threw a blanket over our shoulders, asked us if we were okay, and said, "Any idea how this one took?"

His flashlight spiraled over the crowd, and I spotted Paul, craning his neck, pushing past shoulders, his frantic gaze leaping from person to person.

My mother stood up straighter. "I thought I'd smelled gas coming from the oven." Another lie, but what if she had told the truth?

The fireman said, "We'll do our best," nodding at us apologetically, and went back to stand at the wheel of the truck.

The fire reflected in my mother's stunned eyes. We watched until the flames died down, and the fragile charred boards leaned together, cinders flying off.

XVI

On the other side of fire: ashy daylight and myself alone. My new apartment, bright with window light and bare, had a view of the lake. When I looked out my window on a sunny day, the water appeared ruffled and silver as a party dress; under clouds, opaque and cragged as rock.

They called Chicago the Windy City, and I blew through it, high and low. One minute I floated through chromy streets, seeing my reflection waltz through store windows, and the next, as I watched a man with no soles on his shoes pick through garbage with a stick, this fear hit me that no one would know if I was dead.

I told myself my mother had lived for years with an absence. So had I. We knew what to do.

Lying awake in my grandfather's bed the night before I left, my neck stiff on the tamped down pillow, I'd listened to my grandmother's voice amplified by the linoleum but still indecipherable and heard my mother's sobs, which I pictured in the dark as small, wounded animals that needed care but wouldn't be touched. I didn't expect her to forgive me.

All night I lay with my eyes open to my mother's weeping, and when the curtain sheers in the window began to lighten, I got out of bed and walked to the train station and stood on the platform for an hour before the commuters arrived, their suits and newspapers smelling of cigarette smoke, their talk clipped by yawns and coughs, until the first train finally pulled in.

Watching the passing tracks and rails from the window once I was gone, it seemed it had always been just a matter of boarding a train, buying a ticket. Whenever I saw again the orange-and-yellow streamers of that fire, it pained me to think of my mother homeless and angry. Each time she lied about the cause of the fire, she'd think about what I'd done, remember how I came into her room and told her her house was burning, and she wouldn't know yet how I'd freed her.

The first few days I would think often of Hanna and wonder where she had eaten her first city meal, and if she had found her way easily among the crisscrossed streets, or got flustered by the thunder of the el train overhead, and if she had felt that same heady lack of direction that I did, blowing through the city. Quickly, though, thoughts of her submerged in the frenetic surf of the streets, and when I did think of her, her life seemed incomplete, a sentence broken off by a burst of anger, and I no longer wanted it for myself.

The life I had would be small and collapsible, travel-sized, so that it could be left at any moment—I decided not to open a bank account or buy any furniture and scarcely ate, not liking to walk and catch the train on a full stomach. The hunger helped fuel the buzz, this electricity radiating in my fingers and toes and the top of my head, so that a movement as simple as crossing a street or buying a pack of mints could feel deliberate and ecstatic.

I found an apartment and a waitressing job at a café. The days passed quickly, and so much happened in each one that I didn't want to lose or forget, so I made lists at night of what I'd seen and done. At the café, I tried to settle into the comfortable anonymity I'd felt at the hotel, but it didn't work. Too many of the customers asked me my name or wanted to talk, and the other waitresses invited me to crowded parties. I didn't mind, though— it gave me a wild courage. Flirting with a blue-eyed man, I told him I'd once had a penchant for setting fires, laughing so he wouldn't believe me. When a girl I worked with was complaining about her boyfriend, I blurted out that I was scarred, but knew how to hide it when I undressed.

I bought a radio, and sometimes after waitressing I'd open the windows, take off my food-stained shirt and dance alone, casting shadows along the empty walls of my apartment. I cut off six inches of my hair, so it swung over my shoulders, and after a long night of fat tips took all the money to Marshall Field's and bought a blue silk dress, which I wore walking in the city on my days off, the scars flashing when the hem flared in the wind. Trying on the dress at the store, I'd thought of Jo and wondered if she was married by then. She would be furious with me, but I wasn't ready to call her yet.

Once in a while at work, I'd see a head shaped like Paul's, or someone walking with his bendy stride—my chest would clench, and I'd have to put down the tray of clattering plates and cups on the nearest table. If he had really walked into the restaurant, though, I wasn't sure I'd have wanted to see him. All that time in Porter came to feel like a long, scaled, heavy tail behind me that I wanted to lop off.

But one night in a fit of loneliness I wrote him a short note: It took three hours and seven pieces of torn-up notebook paper to say this much: *I'm waitressing in Chicago now. There are two things I should have told you before I left: (1) About that banker, I never let any of the men but you see me. I was nothing to them, nor they to me. (2) I'd been setting fires like the ones you saw for years (please don't tell anyone). If not knowing these things hurt you, I'm sorry.*

A couple of weeks later, I found a manila envelope from Paul in the mail. He'd written my name in giant block letters, as if he were afraid no one would see it otherwise. Inside the envelope there was a clipping from *The Vidette Messenger*: a grainy picture of the Linden Hotel and a short article saying it had been broken into by at least one thief, maybe two. One woman's jewelry had been stolen, a pearl necklace and a diamond ring, and oddly, a salesman's suitcase filled with screw and bolt samples. They'd broken into the front desk to get the money box, too. "The security guard on duty that night went outside to check on a loud noise he'd heard near the Dumpster. When he came back inside," the reporter wrote, "the front desk had been pried open with what looked like an ax." Paul had enclosed a note on the Linden Hotel notepad paper: *They need me more than ever around here. Since you left, they haven't found another full-time night clerk and I'm working double duty. It's quiet at night here alone. They're saying it was an accident. It wouldn't hurt anything if you came back.* Reading the note, I heard his accent, tinny and small in my head, saw his bruise-colored eyes and acrobatic hands and hoped there might be a time when I could see him again.

I usually slept soundly during those months, exhausted from all the walking and waitressing, and comforted by my reams of lists. Sometimes I would dream that Paul, Jo, or my mother had died, and I could touch the loss of them like a ragged hole blown out of a wall, the bricks and wires and pipes cutting my hand. If I leaned through the hole to see the body though, the wall gave way, and I was falling past an endless series of balconies and windows and confetti. Only later, clearing a table, or washing clothes at a crowded Laundromat, would I remember the dream, when I was too busy to stop and take in what it meant.

It wasn't until the end of the summer that the attacks of vertigo began, and I'd forget what street I was on or where I'd meant to be going in the first place, or suddenly feel sure a skyscraper was about to topple over but didn't know where to run. It was the opposite of the claustrophobia before I set a fire, more like the dissolute trance I felt afterward, watching the smoke.

Once I got lost on the South Side, and a hulking drunk man in a fishing hat, holding his hand like a gun, tried to mug me. Another time, in the midst of the Saturday rush, I fainted into a crowd of shoppers on Michigan Avenue, and when a nice woman splashed cola on my face and I finally came to, there were footprints on my skirt and legs.

In October, with the yellow leaves shimmering in the trees, and the days suddenly shorter, I finally went back. After my being so long in the city, Porter looked miniature and still, like a community of dollhouses with people and cars that moved in dreamy slow motion. Except for that, little had changed. My impatience for it depressed me. Walking down Lincoln, I saw a house built as an octagon, an actual eight-cornered roof, in one yard milk cartons someone had exquisitely cut into lanterns and strung from the trees, and a tiny angular woman wearing a purple velvet hat the size of a sombrero. My eye flew to each of these sights, for my mother's sake.

I stood in the wind, knocking at Marietta's lavender door. When she answered, she smiled vaguely and gazed just past my face into the street. "How'd you get here?"

"The train."

"Oh." She still wasn't quite looking at me, as if, since I'd left, something had happened to her eyes. When I asked if my mother was there, I heard Erma's voice in the living room and a shuffle of cards. "Oh, no, honey." She hadn't often called me that before, and this *honey* had a coy stickiness. "She moved to one of those apartments on Union Street." She could have been talking to the testy man who ran the dry cleaner's or the retarded girl who sometimes helped her mother at the fabric store. "I've got Erma and some friends here, playing pinochle, but you run over there. Five-E." She looked at me straight then, with dry, blank eyes, as if to tell me I wasn't going to get any more tears out of her. "You've been hard on your mother. She doesn't deserve it." Her green eyes looked the color of moss. "I told her you'd be back."

Walking those few blocks to Union Street, past houses with V's of red corn husks on their doors and pillows of turned leaves next to the walkways, I counted the months since I'd left, six. The hum of Chicago and the customers' orders and figuring up their checks and their myriad voices and faces had filled up my head, so I'd been able to put away my exile as if it were a book I might or might not read. Now the closer I came to my mother, the more real it was: mica sparking in the sidewalk, the collar of weeds around the post of the mailbox, my own worn leather shoes and my legs, hardened from the waitressing. My chest felt tight. Thinking of the difficulty of my return, my reasoning splintered and ran off in a hundred designs, and I had no idea what I would say. I didn't expect her to forgive me, but hoped the vertigo attacks might subside at least, if I showed her my face.

The apartment building had been built to look like a colonial house: tall, fluted white columns, a heavy flint roof like a giant arrow tip, black shutters nailed permanently open. Knocking at Five-E, I heard the train in the distance, its horn a nervy question. A girl around my age came out of the next apartment holding a carton of milk and an armful of books.

I heard my mother's footsteps stutter, saw the white curtains swing back, then the door opened wide. Her expression was disarrayed and inward, as if she'd been sewing. She slapped her hand against her chest. "My God, I thought we'd lost you." Her shoulders collapsed, and she bent over, gasping.

Her hair had grayed. "I've been in Chicago."

"You didn't call. . . ." She huffed and grabbed my arm, pulled me inside with one hand and slammed the door with the other.

The apartment was clean, but crowded and mismatched. There was a square blue chair, a rectangular yellow couch, a perfectly circular red table. My mother looked out of place and anxious against that furniture, as if she were in a bus terminal or an airport. She wore a red sweater, and the weight she'd gained back was visible, her breasts full again, her arms rounded. A thick lock of gray hair fell out of a pin and hung on her forehead, where the lines had deepened into a large equal sign. A certain tightness had left her face, and the softness in her cheeks made her lips part youthfully.

"Why would you do that to me?" Her voice was louder and sharper than I ever remembered hearing it. Vibrating with its force, she stood in front of me, holding out her arm in a curved gesture like a teapot handle, but I could tell she was too furious to touch me yet.

"What else could I do?" I said. Now I felt fatigued from the miles of walking in the city and wanted to collapse on that ugly yellow couch, but my mother didn't move.

"After all that happened, you really thought you could just leave?" She flung up her hand. "Look at Hanna. Where did leaving get her?"

When she folded her arms, their shape on her chest reminded me of a soldier's breastplate, and she looked larger and more muscular than before. Was it possible she'd grown taller in my absence? Her eyes scowled at me. It was hard for me to look at them.

"I came back," I said feebly, but she knew I wouldn't stay. I wanted to go over and embrace her, but didn't move, holding the back of a wooden chair with its nautical ropy spokes.

She paced the small area over the flat red carpeting between the easy chair and the edge of the open kitchen. Her anger slit us apart, and the separation felt almost surgical, as if she'd finally got rid of some web of mucus and cartilage between us, and it was such a relief.

"Don't think I bought any of this ugly furniture. It came with the apartment." The shapes were primitive, the fabric cheap, but the vivid shades countered the dimness of a room with a single back window.

"It's colorful," I said.

She shook her head and made a clicking sound with her tongue. She held out her open palm. "I loved that house. My kitchen, my sewing room. Your father taught you to read in that house. Every day he practiced his music there. Before—"

Over the couch I noticed a photograph she must have taken of my father and me barefoot in the sand at the dunes, his hand resting on my shoulder, my scars carefully hidden from the sun inside long sleeves and blue jeans. My father smiled widely so his underbite showed, and his shoulders were freckled and narrow. I guessed that she had found it somewhere at Marietta's house and put it in a frame.

My head filled with a watery pressure. The silence was painful. I wanted to crawl into it, let the sharp glass edges cut me, endure the torture of being exposed to her.

"Before the fire." My mother cleared her throat nervously. "I was going to have the whole outside painted. I was going to gather up the last pieces of your father's music and send it to someone who would appreciate it." She watched her foot take a small step.

To think I had betrayed my father's music, the notes he'd drawn, counted, the turmoil in his head marked down in that wordless translation—this hurt me more than anything we'd lost.

Even in his illness, it was the one thing for which he'd had enough strength. Taking another small step, my mother swayed forward. But I'd saved her, hadn't I?

"I lost everything in that house," she said.

"Mother, you made yourself so weak you could hardly leave your room." She stared at me. "You looked like you were dying."

She choked. Her hand wavered as she brought it up to cover her eyes. When I'd practically carried her out of the house, she'd felt like a girl in my arms.

"And it wasn't the only fire I set," I said, lifting my chin, shocked at how boastful it sounded. She must have known to put the Houseman fire with this one.

She wept into her hand. "Yes." *Fire moved as soon as you looked, multiplied, and split off in pieces, the desire dissolved just as secretly as it had once come and burned through.* Her head dipped heavily as she took another wavering step. "Since your father died, I've been afraid you'd do something————" Her mouth bunched in a frown.

The fire had to hurt her, or it would have never brought her out. I wanted her to forgive me, but not if it meant denying what I'd done.

She sniffed and fought back more tears. "You changed your hair. I clung to the back of the chair, felt a sting in my knuckles. "I always thought your long hair was so pretty." She wiped her eyes. I needed her to keep looking at me.

"My scars aren't so pitiful, Mother."

She lifted her wet face and fiercely lowered her voice. "I never said anthing about that." I'd blamed her for this, though, for guarding the scene. Wishing so fervently that the memory fragments would vanish, she'd grown them large and distroted instead.

"You can't use my scars as an excuse. You have to face this, Mother" I said.

"Face what?"

"The fires."

She went over to the couch, leaned against its arm, and bowed her head. "You tripped on a rake," she said. "I just looked away for a second that day, and you were gone."

I took a few steps closer to her. "I always knew it was an accident." The words felt foreign and carved by my lips and tongue and teeth. How could they have taken so many years to be forged into syllables, the simplest sounds for what had happened to us?

She looked at me and nodded. Something unclasped painfully in my chest. A breeze thrummed in the loose windowpanes, and the curtain pull beat against the wall. When I hugged her, it was surprising to feel the mass of her body, the brush of her hair against my cheek, and just then that room seemed more distant and strange than any place I'd ever thought of traveling to. I noticed a fuchsia silk scarf on the back of a chair and the orange curled gourds she'd arranged thoughtfully on the coffee table.

The last train was coming soon, but there would be another one in the morning. I was tired and hungry, and it occurred to me that the yellow couch might make a good enough bed, that maybe we could go out somewhere for dinner. It was almost five o'clock, but it still startled me how quickly it got dark, and the bright pieces of furniture floated up in that watery dim like rough maps of lost countries.